The Ares File

by

Andrew French

The Ares File

To Mel

Best Wishes

For all of my children, who never stop making me proud.

Chapter One

Fiona Mabbitt was usually a heavy sleeper and quite accustomed to being in the house on her own at night. After all she had been an army officer's wife all her married life and had long since accepted that she would sometimes have to spend long periods apart from her husband. Now, with her sixtieth birthday approaching in two weeks, she had quietly hoped that Charles would consider the possibility of retirement. She knew better than to voice such hopes however. Her husband, the Colonel, was as passionate and devoted to his work now as he was as an eager second lieutenant forty years ago.

Fiona stirred and, pulling her pillow into a more comfortable position, she settled again without opening her eyes. The door to the study downstairs creaked momentarily. "How many times had she asked Charles to oil those hinges?" she thought as she drifted back to sleep. The creak came again. She opened her eyes and listened, silence. Leaning over she switched on the bedside lamp and looked at the clock, three fifteen. She decided it must be Sebastian, their long haired white Persian, prowling around as he tended to do, until she saw him curled up asleep on the oak chest at the foot of the bed. Anyway, the door to Charles' study was always kept shut.

Slipping on a dressing gown and sliding her feet into her slippers, Fiona quietly opened the bedroom door and stepped out onto the landing. The house was Tudor grade two listed, built around 1540, and she was familiar with all its ageing timbers' creaks and groans. The house was in complete darkness except for the light now flooding from the bedroom partially illuminating the top of the staircase. Putting her hand to the panelled wall she flicked on the light. The large bronze chandelier lit the stairs and the hallway. To the left of the bottom of the stairs she could see the study door ajar. Pulling the ties of her dressing gown tighter around her small waist, she began to descend the polished oak staircase. Far from a meek woman, she had spent too much

1

of her life around fighting men for that, she crossed the hallway to investigate without the slightest hint of fear. As she passed the front door she noticed the lights on the alarm system control panel were out. Certain that she had set the alarm before retiring as she always did without fail, her pace slowed. She rubbed her arms as an uncomfortable prickling sensation made her feel less confident. Nevertheless undeterred she squared her shoulders and slowly pushed open the study door. The familiar creak that had woken her came again.

Almost half of the study was obscured by the large door as her slim elegant figure hesitated in the doorway. What she could see of the room was eerily lit by the full moon shining through the small leaded panes of the casement windows. Nothing appeared to be out of place. As Fiona stepped into the study she felt something soft touch her leg causing her to cry out. She caught sight of a bushy white tail disappearing under the desk. "Sebastian!" she scolded, more cross with herself that she had screamed like some silly girl. Switching on the light she turned back into the room. Instantly a gloved hand covered her mouth and with one swift professional movement twisted her head, breaking her neck.

Sebastian watched from beneath the desk as Fiona's lifeless body dropped to the floor. The intruder crossed to a painting of The Charge of the Light Brigade on the panelled wall behind him. Hinged on its right edge, he pulled the picture open revealing a large steel safe. He pressed a thumb sized quantity of plastic explosive onto the door and pushed in a detonator. Without making a sound he moved effortlessly behind the desk, crouched down and covered his ears. Seconds later the safe door exploded hanging open by a single charred hinge. As the smoke cleared he emptied the contents into a large black rucksack examining it all carefully as he did so. Jewellery boxes, assorted personal documents and half a dozen buff coloured files. Flicking through the folders he smiled as he read the title on the cover of the third one "Operation Ares". With the safe empty he slung the rucksack onto his shoulder and casually stepping over Fiona's body, walked from the house into the night.

Thomas Fisher could not have envisaged the murder of Fiona Mabbitt when four weeks earlier he instigated the sequence of events that culminated in her death. It was mid July 1984 and the seemingly endless weeks of deep snow of the cold wet winter were now just a distant memory, replaced by the warm humid days of summer in New Hampshire. Following the murder of his former employer, Donald Boyle, in a Londonderry pub four years earlier, Fisher had become a very wealthy man. With Boyle having no next of kin, Fisher had taken advantage of an obscure legal loophole and, as his lawyer and personal secretary, taken control of his vast oil empire. Selling it to one of the oil conglomerates, whose suited executives fought like pack dogs to acquire it, he liquidated all of Boyle's assets. From the Montana ranch and the beach house estate in Malibu to the private executive jet, Fisher systematically sold everything. It wasn't long before there was not a single trace of Donald Boyle or his multi million dollar empire. All that remained were a few archived newspaper and magazine articles and interviews regarding his outspoken sympathies for the IRA's cause in Northern Ireland. Fisher was confident that they too would be forgotten with time. By Thanksgiving in 1980 he had moved to a magnificent country house estate twenty miles west of Concord near the Green Mountain National Forest.

The next few years were spent distancing himself as much as possible from his former life working for Donald Boyle. He would often lay awake at night sweating with shame and anger as he painfully remembered the toadying subjugated gopher he had been forced to become for so long. He hated himself for having sold so much of his professional integrity and personal values for nothing more than a fat salary.

Fisher was now a successful lawyer with a flourishing private practice in the New Hampshire state capital, Concord. He had married well. In 1983, in a whirlwind three month romance, he met and married Grace

Spinale, the only daughter of the eminent Appellate court judge, Douglas Spinale. Popular at both the tennis club and on the polo field, Fisher, with Grace on his arm, was a regular at the very finest and most exclusive social functions. With his tremendous wealth, successful career and beautiful trophy wife, life was good for Thomas Fisher.

It was following a conversation with his father-in-law at a dinner party one evening that Fisher decided to embark on a course from which he could never turn back. The resulting death of an innocent woman thousands of miles away in rural England would only be the beginning.

There were six at dinner that evening. The food had been simply exquisite and the mood convivial. Thomas Fisher circled the table with another bottle of Bollinger, refilling the glasses of his guests while his butler offered the open solid gold cigar box to the men. With his thick sausage-like fingers Joe Espinosa, the state Chief of Police took one of Cuba's finest and, holding it under his nose, savoured the aroma. "One thing I always say about you, Tom," he said as Fisher refreshed his glass, "you know how to throw one hell of a dinner party, don't I, Martha?"

"Yes, Joe, that's what you always say." The plump woman with enormous bubble permed blonde hair to his left replied, giggling hysterically as she took a long sip from her umpteenth glass of champagne.

After the butler clipped the cigar he patiently held the lighter to its end while the big police chief took several long draws before nodding that it was lit. Fisher patted him on the shoulder. "Well you know, Joe, I always say we owe it to ourselves to live a little. Or better still, live a lot!" There was spontaneous laughter from around the table, not least from Martha Espinosa who by this stage would have laughed at just about anything.

With all the glasses filled and the cigars lit Thomas Fisher resumed his seat as Douglas Spinale rose from his. "I would like to propose a toast."

"Are we having some more pâté?" Martha interrupted, giggling uncontrollably until her husband's stern rebuke to get a hold of herself resulted in her laugh petering out into an embarrassed silence.

Spinale spoke again. "I would like to propose a toast to Tom and our lovely daughter, Grace, for a most splendid evening." The champagne flutes chinked to admiring comments and gushing words of thanks.

Fisher looked around the table contentedly puffing on his cigar. To his left sat Martha and Joe Espinosa. Neither of them had any of the social refinements usually associated with such a high ranking public figure. New Hampshire was a world away from the New York back streets they had both grown up in. Far from being embarrassed by it, Joe was proud of his humble beginnings and referred to it constantly.

Sitting opposite them and in complete contrast to Martha and Joe were Douglas and Amanda Spinale. Douglas Spinale was a flog 'em and hang 'em judge of the old school. A crusty old misogynist who at sixty five was so set in his ways he couldn't conceive of anyone's opinions other than his own to be worth consideration. Amanda on the other hand was a kind and gentle woman with a dry sense of humour. She worked tirelessly on the charity circuit raising money for both domestic and overseas causes.

Fisher looked at Grace sitting opposite him at the other end of the table. From the moment he had seen her he knew she was the one. He always described her as the most beautiful girl he had ever seen. Grace was indeed stunningly beautiful. Her shoulder length blonde hair was tonight tucked behind one ear, held in place by a diamond encrusted silver comb. She had an innocence about her and a laugh that lit up the room. As she listened attentively to Joe she noticed Fisher looking at her and she smiled adoringly at him. Yes, Fisher thought, life was good.

After a few moments Fisher asked if anyone would care for a cognac. Douglas Spinale suggested that they have it in Fisher's study as there was a matter he thought the three men might discuss. Intrigued as to what it might be, Fisher kissed Grace lightly on the cheek as the three excused themselves and proceeded to the study.

A few minutes later Spinale eased himself into a high backed leather armchair and swirled his brandy in the crystal balloon in his hand. Espinosa sat opposite puffing on his cigar as he stretched his short fat legs in front of him. Fisher leant against the front edge of his panelled desk between them and waited for one of his guests to begin. Spinale looked sideways at Espinosa before turning to Fisher. "Have you ever considered running for public office, Tom?" Fisher raised his eyebrows as he considered the question.

"Can't say that I have. Why do you ask?"

"You have become a prominent figure here in New Hampshire. Respected, intelligent, charismatic, well connected not to mention about as financially secure as a body can be."

"With a lot of influential friends," added Espinosa winking.

"Bob Jackson's six year term is up later this year and we think that you should stand as a candidate to replace him," Spinale said staring into his swirling cognac. Fisher took a swallow of his as he paced slowly around the desk finally standing behind its chair.

"You're suggesting that I run for the Senate?" he said at last looking incredulously at his father-in-law.

"You would have a great deal of support, Tom and with your credentials you would be a great state Senator. Think of it, as one of the hundred in the higher legislative chamber you could make a real name for yourself. Who knows, in time you may even want to run for the Presidency."

"The Presidency! Now let's not get ahead of ourselves here." Fisher replied.

"I want the best for you and Grace, Tom. You're a good man. This country needs good men like you to lead it. To stand up for the rights of this great nation of ours and lead by example."

"I'm a plain speaking man, Tom," Espinosa interjected. "Just a beat cop from New York's Lower East Side. Me and Martha, we've come from nothing. Hell, my mom took in washing just to put food on the table we were so poor. I feel I can speak for the common man when I say that America needs a champion, so that future generations don't have to grow up in the same poverty that I did."

"Just look at you, Tom" Spinale continued gruffly "You're everything this country stands for. You're honest, hard working and most of all trustworthy. The American people want that in their leader. Some of these goddamn politicians have such a murky past I'm amazed they have the brass neck to be as so goddamn righteous as they are."

Fisher smiled, embarrassed at the tidal wave of compliments from the two men. It was true he hadn't considered running for public office let alone the senate although the thought of it certainly appealed. At thirty-five he was the right age and he certainly had the money to fund an election campaign. Spinale and Espinosa glanced at each other as they watched Fisher thoughtfully pace slowly behind his desk. He ran a manicured hand through his fine black hair. At six feet two he cut an impressive figure in his tailored dinner suit. His clean cut all American features would undoubtedly come across well on a televised campaign.

Before Fisher could speak the study door opened and Grace stood in the doorway.

"Sorry to interrupt, Tom." she said, smiling and turned to Espinosa hesitantly. "Joe, I think you had better come back to the dining room." Espinosa took the cigar from his mouth and leant forward.

"Is there a problem?"

"It's Martha."

"I know, it's late and she wants to go home." he looked at his watch "Well I suppose it …"

"No, not exactly, Joe. She's passed out under the table and we can't get her out." Espinosa, with a combination of anger and acute embarrassment, apologised profusely to Fisher as they both managed to man handle the semi conscious Martha out of the house and into the car. As he watched the Cadillac drive down the gravel drive towards the electric wrought iron gates, Grace and her parents joined him at the foot of the steps. Spinale shook Fisher's hand saying.

7

"Thanks once again, Tom, for a great evening and give that matter some thought." Assuring the judge that he would, Fisher kissed Amanda goodnight and they all walked to the car. As they were about to drive away Spinale wound down the window smiling. "After all, it's not as if you've got any skeletons hidden anywhere is it?" He laughed as the car pulled away. Grace took Fisher's arm and squeezed it.

"What did Daddy want to talk to you about?" Without looking away from the disappearing car's tail lights Fisher replied, "He wants me to run for the Senate."

"My God, Tom!" Grace said excitedly "Will you do it?" As the car vanished through the gates he replied distantly "I don't know, I'd like to but..."

"But what? There's nothing stopping you. Oh, Tom this is so exciting." Fisher smiled weakly as they walked back up the steps into the house. He didn't share his wife's excitement at the prospect of running for state Senator. It wasn't that he didn't want it, he did. In fact the more he thought about it the more he wanted it. As they stood in the hallway Grace put her arms around Fisher's neck "Let's go to bed," she said, kissing him.

"I'll be up in a few minutes," he replied. Telling him not to be long, Grace went up to bed leaving Fisher making his way to his study. He slumped into his chair having poured himself another very large brandy. As he took a drink his mind was catapulted back to that Londonderry pub four years earlier. Donald Boyle, the evil odious man he had successfully managed to expunge from his memory, was back. He could hear his voice; smell the foul stench of his body odour. He felt sick. That same sick feeling in the pit of his stomach he had endured for so long all those years ago.

Fisher knew that this was his chance to rise to the very top. He was intoxicated by the possibility of becoming Senator Thomas Fisher and who knows, dare he even consider the possibility, President Fisher? But none of that was possible while there was the slightest chance that his secret would be discovered. It would come out - it was inevitable. There would be someone somewhere that would bring it out of the shadows into the light and then that would be the end. He took another long drink draining his glass. No, he wanted this, he deserved it and nothing was going to stop him. All he had to do was to make sure that his secret was kept safe and that there was nobody left to reveal it.

Chapter Two

Steve Bannon hated getting up in the morning. Right from being a small child he had always left it until the last possible minute to get out of bed. Today was no different. He had finally returned to his apartment in Concord a little after four that morning having attended a charity dinner. He peered blearily at his watch and, in a flurry of bedclothes and profanity, leapt out of bed and into the shower.

Bannon was a confirmed bachelor. He lived alone and liked it that way. At a little under six feet tall he was clean shaven, his pale skin heavily freckled and his head covered with thick, closely cropped, curly red hair. With a stocky physique and sparkling green eyes, Bannon wasn't short of female companionship. It was always on his terms however and he ensured that it never involved any kind of commitment. At the age of thirty five he ran a successful consultancy firm with offices up and down the eastern seaboard specialising in the strategic analysis of business, industrial and economic intelligence.

Having studied law at Harvard he had been approached, shortly before graduating with honours in 1974, by the CIA with their usual "Would you like an opportunity to serve your country" line. He decided that he did and spent the next six years as an Operational Officer in the Clandestine Service posted to Central America, specifically Nicaragua. There he had a front row seat during the ousting of President Anastasio Somoza Debayle by the Sandinista movement in July 1979. Then followed two years as a Collection Management Officer based at CIA headquarters at Langley, Virginia. Identifying and establishing intelligence collection requirements, Bannon validated and evaluated information and developed his natural ability for strategic analysis.

Feeling stifled and disillusioned working for the government, Bannon decided to take his skills and contacts to the private sector, so in 1982 moved to New Hampshire to indulge his passion for skiing and water sports. It was then that he re-established his friendship with his classmate from

Harvard, Thomas Fisher, having lost contact with him eight years before.

Fifteen minutes later, as he threw on his suit jacket and was heading for the door, the phone rang. He answered it as he fumbled in his pockets for his keys.

"Tom!" he said cheerfully, instantly recognising the voice. He listened as Fisher asked if they could meet as he had something really important to talk to him about in confidence. Bannon apologised saying that he was already late for a meeting but he could do later in the week. Once Fisher impressed upon him the urgency of the matter and that it really couldn't wait, Bannon agreed to meet him for lunch at Gregoire's in Concord. In his study at home Fisher replaced the receiver, relieved that his friend had agreed to meet with him. He knew that if anyone could help him, Steve Bannon could. He opened a desk drawer and took out a small white business card bearing the logo of the Central Intelligence Agency and the name Brad Mason. That was the place to start.

Gregoire's was a small French bistro tucked away off North Main Street. With just a dozen tables and three Michelin stars it had a very select clientele and a long waiting list. This however wasn't an obstacle to Thomas Fisher when he rang to make a lunchtime reservation for two later that morning. As a personal friend of the owner, Gregoire Choulat, Fisher was assured of a table whenever he wanted one.

"*But of course, Mon ami*" Gregoire flamboyantly exclaimed having been called to the phone by his *Maître de.* "*You are always welcome here. I have some magnificent lobster today and the wild sea bass with truffle sauce is just superb.*" Confirming that he would arrive at one, Fisher washed and changed and drove his gleaming red Ferrari the twenty or so miles into the state capital.

It was just after one fifteen when Steve Bannon entered the restaurant. Fisher, who had arrived twenty minutes earlier, stood as his guest was shown to the table. Shaking Bannon warmly by the hand, Fisher thanked him for coming at such short notice. Two large whiskies already sat on the table and they both took a drink. As the two men sat an uneasy silence hung in the air until Bannon, not renowned for his patience, decided to press the matter.

"So, what's the problem, Tom?" Fisher's weak smile disappeared and his expression became serious. "How long have we been friends, Steve?" Fisher asked.

"Fifteen years, with a few gaps here and there."

"Have you ever done anything in your past that you wouldn't want anyone to find out about? Something you needed to go away, forever?"

"Hell, Tom I worked for the CIA." He paused and looked into Fisher's eyes. "What is this?" He had seen enough scared men's eyes from his time running agents in Nicaragua to recognise it now.

"I need your help, Steve. I've been asked to run for the Senate."

"Great so what's the problem?"

"The problem is something that happened four years ago while I was working for a man called Donald Boyle."

"Boyle? The oil guy that was murdered? I didn't know you worked for him. England wasn't it?"

"Northern Ireland. I was his lawyer." He leant forward and lowered his voice to barely a whisper. "The thing is…" Fisher was interrupted as the waiter came to take their order. Frustrated at the interruption Fisher sat back in his chair as Bannon, wanting him to continue, asked the waiter to give them a few minutes. As the waiter walked away Fisher leant forward once again. "The thing is, Donald Boyle was murdered while he was delivering half a million dollars in cash to fund an IRA terrorist cell." Bannon's eyes widened.

"And you knew about this?" Bannon asked. Fisher looked him earnestly his face ashen.

"I was there." Bannon mouthed the word "shit" incredulously as Fisher continued. "If Boyle hadn't been shot when he was it would have been my job to remain in Londonderry with these terrorists to report back to him what they were doing with his money. He got a real kick out of seeing people suffer, me in particular."

"And you were there when Boyle was killed?"

"No, not exactly. We were in this pub called The Anchor owned by the IRA cell leader, Liam Donnelly. Boyle followed this French student, a guy about twenty, into the rest room. He had this thing for young men and the sick bastard liked to play very rough. That was something else he got a kick out of." Merely recounting the events after so long of trying to forget them appeared to be physically draining Fisher in front of Bannon's eyes. Fisher loosened his silk tie a little and continued. "This French guy turned out to be some kind of hit man. He shot him through the head right there in the toilet. When I saw Boyle there later, I tell you Steve, I'd never seen so much blood."

"Go on," Bannon urged, lighting a cigarette.

"I was outside the rest room arguing with Marcus Hook, Boyle's bodyguard, when the French guy came out of the rest room. Before I knew what was happening he had killed Hook and he was about to kill me too." Fisher took a large swallow of his whiskey, draining the glass.

"But?"

"He was standing over me pointing his gun at my head. I had Hook's blood all over me. I pleaded with him, begged him not to kill me. That was when I gave him the money to let me live."

"Jesus H Christ, Tom, and I thought that I'd had a colourful past," said Bannon seeing his friend in a completely new light. "And you think that if you run for Senator all this is going to come out and bite you in the ass?" Fisher nodded. Bannon thought carefully for a moment "Look Tom I don't see why it should; nobody's going to believe the word of some terrorist hit man. The fact you've managed to keep it secret for so long means that I'd have thought you're pretty much in the clear."

"The trouble is I'm not convinced that it was a terrorist hit man." He pulled the business card from his pocket and put it on the table. "I found this amongst Boyle's things when I got back to his ranch." Bannon looked down at the card with its familiar logo and his reassuring expression changed to one of concern.

"Would Boyle have had any dealings with the CIA?" Bannon asked.

"Not willingly. He had no reason to want to. Do you know this guy Mason?"

"Yeah, I was with him at Langley for a while. He's a good guy, straight talking, been with the agency for years." Bannon replied. Fisher hesitated for a moment then said, "Steve I hate to ask you this but..."

"But you would like me to have a quiet talk to him and see what he knows, right?" Bannon interrupted. Fisher smiled, "Something like that."

"I'll make a call. If the agency was involved in this guy's death I'll find out. I've still got a few favours I can call in." Bannon's tone became brighter. "But it's gonna cost you, starting with the most expensive thing on the menu 'cos I'm starving," he said laughing as he picked up the menu.

"Thanks, I appreciate this," Fisher said earnestly and gestured to the waiter they were ready to order. Bannon slipped Mason's card into his pocket.

"Forget it, what are friends for?"

Fisher had been quiet at dinner that evening. Despite Grace's best efforts to engage him in conversation her husband had been remote and distant. Finally she implored him to tell her what was wrong, concerned at his uncharacteristic behaviour. Apologising for the gloom of his mood he took her hand and assured her that there was nothing wrong and that he simply had a difficult case at work. Grace sat quietly for a moment then said, "Tom, when I was having lunch at the tennis club today I was telling Charlotte about you running for the senate."

"Grace, I told you I..." exasperated Fisher.

"Oh I know you wanted to keep it quiet, Tom but I just couldn't help it. While I was telling her who should be at the next table but Fiona Fontaine from The Union Leader."

"The journalist," he said quietly.

"Yes," she continued excitedly. "Well, she overheard the conversation and said that she wanted to do a feature on you. Isn't that just great?" Her brilliant white smile vanished in an instant as Fisher exploded with rage.

"For God's sake, Grace I told you I wanted to keep this quiet for the time being but no, you have to go telling the foremost journalist in the entire goddamn state!" he threw his napkin down and ran his fingers through his hair.

"I only did it because I was so proud of you!" she said running out of the room with tears welling in her eyes. Fisher slammed his fist down on the table with anger and frustration as Bannon appeared in the doorway, the butler at his shoulder. On seeing him Fisher crossed the room eagerly. "Did you speak to Mason?"

"Is there somewhere we can speak privately?" Bannon replied gravely. Fisher showed him into the study and poured them both a large whiskey. Sitting opposite each other in the armchairs Fisher took a large drink. "Well?"

"Okay, Tom it's like this. The agency weren't behind Donald Boyle's murder, the British were. More specifically a secret army intelligence unit usually tasked with gathering information on IRA activities in Northern Ireland."

"So what's the CIA's involvement?" Fisher asked.

"That's where it gets complicated. One of this secret unit's officers went rogue; collaborated with the terrorist leader, your guy Liam Donnelly, in exchange for half of Boyle's money. This officer convinced MI5's Head of Northern Ireland section to ask the CIA to coerce Boyle into passing information about Donnelly's activities."

"So that was why that bastard Boyle wanted me to stay in Londonderry. To feed him information for the CIA," he said angrily.

"Exactly; it would have been only a matter of time before Donnelly realised what you were doing and had you killed. The British did you a favour, Tom." Bannon took a drink as Fisher considered what he had been told.

"How many know of my involvement?" he asked finally.

"For political expediency the operation to kill Boyle was a black op, completely off book, so fortunately there aren't many in the loop. Brad Mason is pretty much the only one left at the agency that had anything to do with it, leaving only a handful from the British army unit. According to

Mason it's run by a Colonel by the name of Charles Mabbitt. He's got to know him pretty well over the past four years. Mabbitt's been in the intelligence game a long time, very hands on and plays his cards very close to his chest. He'll have made sure that there won't be any official army records, just too sensitive, so any records of the operation will most likely be kept at his home." As Bannon spoke Fisher rose from his chair and poured another drink, listening attentively.

"I need to see those records," Fisher said handing Bannon another whiskey.

"Tom, are you sure you want to do this? It may be better just to leave well alone."

"And have it hanging over me for the rest of my life waiting for the day that it all comes out? It would finish me, Steve. I've already got a journalist sniffing around and this is only the beginning. Once I officially announce that I'm going to stand who knows who'll start digging? No, I need this whole affair to go away. Grace's father is talking about the Presidency for Christ sake."

"The Presidency?"

"Yes," Fisher leant forward and grabbed Bannon's arm, "and I'll need good friends around me, people I trust like you, Steve. Think of it for a moment, I'm offering you a seat at the table. I just need you to help me get those records." He stared intently at Bannon. "Will you do it?"

"Jesus, Tom. What are you going to do if you get hold of them?" Bannon asked looking down at Fisher's hand gripped tightly on his arm.

"I don't know yet, I haven't thought that far." Fisher took his hand away. Bannon took a drink. The two men sat in silence for a while then Bannon spoke first.

"There is somebody I can send."

"There is?"

"A guy works out of my New York head office, ex navy SEAL. He's done some black bag work for the CIA and he's the one I give my more sensitive contracts to. If anyone can get Mabbitt's files, he can."

"Can you trust him?"

"Implicitly. I tracked him down and recruited him when he was down to his last dime in a Brooklyn bar. Trust me when I say he's as loyal as they come."

"He sounds perfect. When will you send him?"

"Just leave all of that to me. It's probably better that you don't know any of the details about this." The relief was visible on Fisher's face as Bannon got up to leave. Fisher shook his hand and thanked him. They walked through the hallway to the front door together. "Just one more thing, Tom," Bannon said. "There are going to be quite a few expenses if I do this for you, and I don't mean the price of a phone call to Brad Mason."

"I don't care how much it costs. Whatever it takes just get it done," Fisher replied. Bannon nodded thoughtfully and said that he would be in touch. As Fisher closed the door he turned and saw Grace looking at him from the landing at the top of the stairs.

"What are you up to, Tom?" she said suspiciously.

"Just work, nothing you need to worry about." He turned to go back to the study but Grace called after him.

"You would tell me if there was something wrong wouldn't you? I mean, we don't keep secrets from each other, do we?"

"There's nothing to tell." Then his voice softened. "I'm sorry about earlier - I guess I'm more nervous about running for Senator than I thought. I just want to make sure everything's right before I throw my hat into the ring."

"And that's what Steve Bannon is doing? Making sure everything's right."

"Yes," Fisher replied smiling. "Something like that."

Chapter Three

Colonel Charles Mabbitt stood in a classroom before half a dozen new recruits. The four men and two women had successfully completed the arduous recruit selection course and were being welcomed to the unit by their new commanding officer. It was a little before nine in the morning and they were assembled in Repton Manor, an imposing brick manor house situated in a remote part of Templar Barracks, the home of the army Intelligence Corps near Ashford, Kent. The two women were originally from the Intelligence Corps while the four men were a combination of SAS, Royal Marines and Paras. The Colonel looked at each one of the six in turn and smiled as he stroked his thin pencil moustache.

"You six are all that remain of the ninety that applied to join my merry little band. You are about to embark on a tour of duty the like of which you could never have imagined six months ago. Forget about what you have learnt in your previous formations. We tend to do things a little differently here. This is the Fourteenth Intelligence Company, more colloquially known as The Detachment or simply The Det. The primary role of this unit is to gather intelligence on terrorist activities both in Northern Ireland and, more recently, here on the mainland. The work we do is dangerous. You may have to endure long periods undercover, often with only yourself to rely on. Officially we don't exist. You can put away those smart uniforms of yours because you won't be needing them any more. This is a covert unit. Grow your hair, cultivate some facial hair if you wish, ladies excepted unless you want to of course; because I don't want you to look like soldiers any more. That way you might live a little longer. We are fighting an enemy with no honour that plays a very dirty game. But let me tell you, we play dirty too. There are no Marquis of Queensbury rules here, no niceties observed merely because we are part of Her Majesty's armed forces. Our job is to stop these people at all and any cost and I can assure you that, regrettably, occasionally that cost is great." The Colonel reflected momentarily on how many of his unit he had lost over the years as he looked at the six sitting stoically in their seats. He could remember them all, their names, their faces, feeling the loss of each one far more keenly than perhaps a commanding officer should.

As Mabbitt was about to continue the door to the classroom opened and a young woman in civilian dress entered and silently handed him a note. Reading it quickly he left the room accompanied by the messenger, telling the recruits that the remainder of his splendidly inspiring pep talk would have to wait.

"Have them escorted to my office in the admin building," Mabbitt ordered as he walked down the long hallway, out of Repton Manor and climbed into a Land Rover.

Ten minutes later a maroon coloured Ford Orion pulled into a parking space outside the administration building. An Intelligence Corps corporal in shirt sleeve order got out of the rear seat and replaced his cypress green beret. He showed the two civilians into the building where Mabbitt was waiting for them. The Colonel studied them as they approached him. If there was one constant in the universe, Mabbitt thought, it was the unmissable expression of suspicion on the face of a police detective. The older one of the two was in his mid forties and clearly the senior officer. The other looked about fifteen but was probably late twenties with no idea of how to tie a decent knot in his tie not to mention polish a pair of shoes. The senior one spoke first.

"Colonel Mabbitt?" he said taking a small warrant card from his pocket and offering it to the Colonel. "Detective Inspector Allen, Ashford CID, This is Sergeant Pearce." He nodded towards his colleague. Mabbitt confirmed with a simple yes as he glanced at the police identification.

"Is there somewhere we can talk privately, sir?" both the Inspector's tone and expression were grave. Mabbitt showed them to his office and invited them to take a seat. The Inspector cleared his throat.

"I'm afraid we have some rather bad news for you, sir." Mabbitt stiffened. "At approximately six thirty this morning we were called to your house near Biddenden. The milkman had discovered the front door open and went in to investigate." Mabbitt grew visibly concerned but said nothing. "It appears, sir, that at some point during the night somebody broke in."

"Fiona," Mabbitt whispered under his breath then spoke louder "My wife was alone in the house last night." Inspector Allen shuffled uneasily in his chair.

"Yes, sir, it appears that she disturbed the intruders. I'm afraid that there's no easy way to say this, Colonel. Your wife was found dead this morning." Mabbitt remained silent but swallowed hard. He had been surrounded by death his whole career - friends, colleagues, enemies - but this was different. The one person to whom he was closest had been suddenly and senselessly taken from him.

The Colonel's mind drifted for the next few minutes unable to take in what the Inspector was saying. It was only when he heard the word 'safe' that brought him sharply back, forcing him to focus. "What did you say?" Mabbitt asked quietly.

"The safe in your study had been blown and completely emptied. It would be helpful to know what was in it," Allen repeated patiently. Mabbitt looked at the Inspector as he considered the importance of the safe's contents, realising the purpose for the break in.

"Personal documents, title deeds to the house, will, that type of thing and all of my wife's jewellery," Mabbitt replied matter of factly. As the Sergeant noted it down he asked, "Was there anything of a sensitive nature, classified material that sort of thing in the safe?" Mabbitt raised an eyebrow.

"My dear Sergeant, I find that when one is engaged in my type of work it is advisable not to take material of any kind home."

"No, sir," Pearce said feeling uncomfortably stupid for even asking the question as Mabbitt stared at him with his pale grey eyes.

The two detectives finished asking their questions and, assuring Mabbitt that they would keep him informed of any developments, were shown out of the office and escorted off the camp thirty minutes later.

Mabbitt sat thoughtfully in his office when there was a quiet knock on the door and a friendly face appeared. Colonel James Denison was the Intelligence Corps commanding officer and the base commander. Although he was a similar age to Mabbitt his hair and thick moustache were still jet black giving him the appearance of someone much younger. He sat opposite his old friend.

"I'm sorry, Charles."

"That didn't take long," Mabbitt replied striking a match and lighting his pipe.

"Surprisingly there's one thing you can't keep for too long in this place and that's a secret," he smiled. "Is there anything I can do?" Mabbitt puffed on his pipe then blew a long plume of smoke into the air.

"Who's your best intelligence and security man?" he asked finally. Denison considered for a moment.

"It's a woman actually, veritable bloodhound. Staff Sergeant Cheryl Evans, a terrifying woman. She's about as subtle as a hod full of bricks but probably the best investigator in the corps."

"Would you have her mount an investigation and liaise with the local plods at the house?"

"Of course." Denison studied Mabbitt's face carefully. "Charles, why do I get the feeling that there's something you're not telling me?"

Mabbitt forced a smile. "Whoever it was after the safe took everything inside it."

"And not just the family silver?"

"In addition to the usual bits and pieces there were the files of all the unsanctioned covert operations my lot have carried out over the last ten years." Denison swore under his breath at his friend's revelation. He didn't condemn him, how could he? Denison was aware of the type of operations Mabbitt's unit carried out and that he sometimes had to operate under the official radar. The conventional intelligence work that he, himself was engaged in was hard enough. Denison could only imagine the political and operational tightrope Mabbitt had to walk and all the vagaries that accompanied it.

"How many?" Denison asked.

"Six."

"In a way I'm relieved. I thought it would be more."

"I do try and play nicely most of the time, James." Mabbitt said as he rose from his chair. "You'll set your bloodhound on as soon as you can?"

"She'll be at your house within the hour; I'll brief her personally." Denison reassured as he stood. "Are you going home?"

Mabbitt tapped out his pipe into the ashtray on the desk, his brow furrowed.

"No, I've got to go and identify Fiona's body." Denison couldn't find any words of consolation and simply patted him on the shoulder.

By eight o'clock that evening Charles Mabbitt was at home alone in his drawing room. The police scene of crime specialists had taken their photographs and dusted for fingerprints. Leaving their tell-tale white powdery residue on just about every surface, they had found nothing. Mabbitt sat in a big armchair and closed his eyes. As the polished mahogany Grandfather clock ticked inaudibly in the hallway the silence in the house was overwhelming. He felt old and tired out. He opened his eyes and looked over to a silver framed black and white wedding photograph of two young people starting their lives together such a very long time ago.

As the tears began to well in his eyes as he remembered their wedding day, Mabbitt was brought back to the present by the sound of the doorbell breaking the silence. Wiping his eyes with his handkerchief he opened the front door. James Denison stood before him dressed casually in a blue shirt and grey flannels.

"We need to talk," he said earnestly. Minutes later the two officers were sat together in the drawing room, Mabbitt having poured them both a large pure malt.

Denison came straight to the point. "I have Evans' preliminary report of the break in and she has some very disturbing findings. The electronic equipment that must have been used to by-pass the alarm system is state of the art. As in, government issue state of the art. The explosive used to blow the safe was a military grade shaped charge, simply not available to your average safe cracker." Denison paused hesitantly for a moment. "And there's one more thing, about Fiona's death."

"Yes?" Mabbitt said, appreciating that his friend was trying to spare his feelings but impatient to hear what he had to say. "What about Fiona's death?"

"The Home Office pathologist's post mortem report revealed that Fiona's neck was broken, very clean, very professional. Whoever it was that was in here last night knew exactly what he was doing." Mabbitt's eyes narrowed and his face became hard as he considered what Denison's bloodhound had discovered.

"The question is," Mabbitt said, "whose government would want those files? And more importantly, what are they going to do with them now that they have them?"

"I suppose the most likely suspects are your Irish friends. After all, they must know who you are."

"And they've brought someone in with this kind of expertise? Yes, I thought about that. The thing is, James I've got four of my people undercover at this very moment, one of them, in particular, with access to some high grade intelligence. Not to mention the dozen or so phone taps and surveillance operations I've got going on. If somebody in the province had brought in a specialist like this, we'd have got wind of it."

"Well, there's something in those files that somebody wants very badly," Denison said "So what will you do now?"

"I don't know yet," Mabbitt replied, deep in thought. "I want you to bury Evans' report for the time being. Don't share any of this with the local plods or I'll have Special Branch and MI5 beating a path to my door asking their singular brand of awkward questions."

Denison nodded and finished his drink saying that he had better be going. Mabbitt showed him to the door. "I am sorry about Fiona," Denison said.

"Thank you, James," Mabbitt replied. As Denison's car drove away Mabbitt returned to the drawing room and picked up his wedding photograph. He looked at Fiona's beautiful young face. His expression became cold and resolute. There would be plenty of time to grieve later. First, he had a job to do. He wouldn't rest until he had found his wife's murderer and those behind it. They would all pay dearly for what they had done.

As Charles Mabbitt sat alone in his drawing room a British Airways 747 was on final approach to New York's John F Kennedy international airport. The uniformed stewardess quietly walked along the aisle in the exclusive business class section and gently nudged the sleeping American. He was sound asleep with his mouth slightly open, his big hands resting on his stomach. The stewardess nudged him again and called his name, "Mister Grant." The American opened his eyes and stirred his muscular frame. He looked up at the stewardess focusing on her doll-like face and perfect smile. "We're coming in to land, Mister Grant. Would you please fasten your seat belt?" Grant moved his seat into the upright position and did as he was asked. He peered at his watch, eight-thirty, still on London time. He wound it back five hours as it was now the middle of the afternoon on the US eastern seaboard.

He had telephoned his boss from Heathrow and arranged to meet him at their New York office at five. He enjoyed his work and was very good at it. Grant had a unique talent to adapt to any situation and turn it to his advantage. His skill set was wide and extensive but very particular to his trade. His main character strength, as he saw it, was that he had no conscience. He reflected on his performance during his visit to England. Although his trip hadn't gone as smoothly as he had hoped, Grant was pleased with the outcome. It was unfortunate that the old woman had got in the way but she had been dealt with satisfactorily during an otherwise faultless mission.

As the aircraft began its descent Grant closed his eyes and smiled contentedly as he eased himself deeper into his comfortable seat. Above him, in the overhead locker, was his brown cowhide attaché case. A few hours earlier he had casually passed through airport security at Heathrow, his case having been x-rayed without raising the merest hint of suspicion. Why should it? The sharp suit, the well groomed appearance all suggested that he was nothing more than a businessman returning to New York. He had returned the hire car to the rental company leaving no trace of him ever having been in it. The car was, in fact, spotless except for a few splashes of mud on one side where he had briefly pulled off the main road. Just before dawn he had thrown a rucksack containing thousands of pounds worth of jewellery and a few old documents into the River Medway.

Twenty minutes later Grant had cleared customs and, with no luggage except for his attaché case, walked towards the long string of yellow cabs. Getting in he gave the cab driver the address of an office in Manhattan and sat with his case on the seat next to him. As Grant rested his hand on the soft brown cowhide, inside, sandwiched between assorted magazines and newspapers, were six buff coloured files.

Chapter Four

It was Monday July 23rd, three days after Grant had returned from England to New York. Steve Bannon had been waiting for him at the company offices of Bannon Strategic Solutions on Lexington Avenue on Manhattan's East Side. New York was hot in the summer and that day was no different. At almost ninety degrees the heat was oppressive as Grant got out of the cab and headed for the blissfully cool, almost chilled, air conditioned tower block.

Grant handed over the files and gave Bannon a detailed account of his trip to England. Bannon angrily demanded to know why he had found it necessary to kill the woman rather than to restrain her. Grant sat impassively, calmly reminding Bannon that he had ordered him under no circumstances to leave a trace of anything that could connect the burglary to him.

Once Grant had gone, Bannon took the files and caught an evening flight home to Concord. Taking only thirty minutes to fly the two hundred or so miles, Bannon was back in his apartment by nine thirty. He then spent the weekend going through the stolen Operation Ares file and by Sunday evening had produced a strategic analysis and risk assessment report.

Bannon had arranged for Fisher to come to his apartment at ten o'clock that morning. There they could speak openly without fear of being overheard or interrupted. Fisher arrived early, just after nine thirty; Bannon greeted him warmly and, having invited him inside, they sat opposite each other on large brown leather couches. Between them the two folders containing the stolen operation file and Bannon's report lay side by side on a glass topped coffee table. Fisher looked at the dog-eared file marked 'Operation Ares' and picked it up.

"My God, Steve you did it, you got the file." There was a broad grin on Fisher's face.

"Yes, but there was a slight complication," Bannon replied.

"What kind of complication?" Fisher's grin faded.

"Mabbitt's wife discovered my man at the house; he had to take care of her."

"He killed her? There was no need for that!" Fisher exclaimed.

"There was every need, Tom. If my man had been caught it would have led straight back to me," Bannon insisted, "and then to you. I couldn't allow that. Yes, her death is regrettable but necessary in the circumstances." Bannon calmed his voice again and continued. "I've carried out an analysis and threat assessment, the report is in here." He handed the other file to Fisher. "The page you'll be interested in is the conclusions and recommendations at the back." Fisher flicked through the report to the final page. Bannon watched him expectantly as Fisher silently read the four paragraphs. Fisher finished reading and closed the file.

"Are you sure that this is the only way?" Fisher asked quietly.

"I need this whole affair to go away. They were your words to me when you asked for my help. This is the only way to be absolutely certain," Bannon said, staring at Fisher intently.

"But to kill them all?"

"There's no other way. There are only six people left that know of your involvement with Boyle and Donnelly - all the rest were killed either during or shortly after the operation. With the remaining six dead and the file destroyed, this whole thing will be gone forever, like it never happened. That is what you want isn't it, Tom?"

Fisher threw the file down onto the table and picked up the much thicker Ares folder. He began pacing around the room, thumbing through it as he did so. He stopped suddenly as he reached the page containing the photograph of Michael Prentiss, Boyle's assassin. At seeing that face again and knowing his name Fisher's hands began to shake.

"Michael Prentiss," Fisher whispered as he was transported back to The Anchor pub in Londonderry four years earlier. Fisher relived the moments when the young man he now knew as Prentiss had emerged from the rest room having shot Boyle and killed Marcus Hook. He vividly remembered he and Hook arguing before seeing Prentiss shoot Boyle's bodyguard in front of him. The image of him cowering on the floor against the wall flashed through Fisher's mind. He recalled with intense clarity being spattered with Hook's blood, how he had pleaded for his life as Prentiss had stood over him pointing the gun at his head. As he remembered staring into Prentiss' eyes that night waiting for him to pull the trigger, he now looked into those same eyes in the photograph in front of him and shivered.

"Can you make it happen?" Fisher asked finally.

"Oh yes but it won't be easy and a clean slate comes at a price," Bannon said spreading his arms along the back of the couch.

"What do you mean?"

"We're friends, Tom but this goes way beyond doing a buddy a favour to get him out of a sticky situation. I want paying to take the risks I'm about to take."

"How much?"

"Ten million. I'll give you the details of a little account I've got in the Cayman Islands. When I've received confirmation the money is in, I'll move. The whole thing should be over in no more than four weeks, okay?" Bannon's voice had become colder, more business-like.

"Okay, I'll have the money transferred by the end of the day," Fisher replied responding in a similar tone. Bannon got to his feet.

"This is your last chance to change your mind, Tom. Once it starts, there's no going back." Fisher nodded thoughtfully then said icily, "Just do it."

Bannon flew down to New York the following morning having phoned Grant the previous evening to meet him in his office at ten. Punctually, on the dot of ten o'clock, Harry Grant casually walked into Bannon's office without knocking. Grant moved with the relaxed swagger of a man with supreme confidence. This self assuredness came from years of being neither frightened nor intimidated by anyone.

Casually dressed in blue jeans and a polo shirt, his large tanned biceps stretched the short sleeves as Grant nodded and sat down folding his arms. Bannon had long since learned to tolerate the man's arrogance, regarding it as an acceptable character trait rather than a lack of respect.

"I've got another job for you, Harry, but this one's a bit more complicated than usual, but a lot more lucrative."

"What sort of job?"

"I suppose you could call it information containment," Bannon replied, smiling as he handed Grant a sheet of paper. "I want you to neutralise the six names on that list."

"Why?" Grant asked dispassionately as he read the names.

"They have information that my client wouldn't want to become public knowledge."

"Who's the client?"

"That's unimportant," Bannon said abruptly. "What is important is that he is prepared to pay you one million dollars to do the job." Grant looked up from the list.

"Interesting," Grant said nodding slowly as Bannon sat behind his desk. "Any conditions or do I have a free hand?"

"No conditions. The detail I'll leave to you but it needs to be done quickly," Bannon insisted. Grant rubbed his smooth chin thoughtfully.

"Okay, let me have their profiles with photos, locations, etcetera ASAP so that I can draw up an equipment list for you."

"The first four names aren't a problem; I can let you have their files by tomorrow. The remaining two I don't have locations on yet. I've got a team here working on their whereabouts and I'll send you the information when I have it. In the meantime you can get started with the others beginning with the name at the top of the list," Bannon explained then added, "Anything else?"

"Just one thing and it's not negotiable," Grant said, folding the list and putting it into his back pocket. "I want half the money up front."

"I thought you'd say that, Harry," Bannon said with a wry smile "Which is why I had it transferred into your account an hour ago."

Three days later Harry Grant was in his apartment on the third floor of a graffiti covered four storey building off Eastern Parkway in the roughest part of Crown Heights in Brooklyn. The television was switched on for background noise as it always was when he was at home. The apartment was untidy and the furniture, tatty and threadbare. Ageing pizza boxes and Chinese take-away cartons, their contents congealing slowly, littered the small living room. Grant lay on the couch reading the first of the four files Steve Bannon had sent him. A Marlboro hung out of the corner of his mouth as he read the file carefully page by page. It was a comprehensive document. The minutia of a man's entire life from childhood to present day was there. Career, interests and hobbies together with his likes, dislikes, family and friends were all examined in the finest detail. He squinted as the smoke drifted up into his eye, stinging briefly before he stubbed out the cigarette into the overflowing ashtray on the floor next to him.

As he studied the black and white photograph of the file's subject he lit another Marlboro with his rather battered and over used Zippo lighter. This first one was going to be difficult. Brad Mason was a professional; highly trained and extremely cautious. Grant considered how and, more importantly, where he could make the hit. Mason worked at the CIA headquarters in Langley, Virginia so getting to him at work was completely impossible. His Washington DC apartment wasn't feasible either. With security in the lobby and surveillance cameras in the elevators and on every floor, getting into his home was problematic at best.

Grant closed the file and rubbed his eyes. He decided that there was no use over-complicating things and his best option was a hit in public, preferably in a crowded place. Grant suddenly opened his eyes as he remembered something about football. He flicked through the pages again until he found what he was looking for. Mason was a massive Redskins fan. He had travelled to Tampa, Florida in January of that year to watch them lose to the Los Angeles Raiders, thirty-eight to nine, in the Super Bowl.

As a plan began to form in Grant's mind he continued to read. Although the Redskins played in the Robert F Kennedy Memorial Stadium in DC during the season, their training camp was at Dickinson College, Carlisle in Pennsylvania. As Mason was a personal friend of the head coach he would drive the one hundred and twenty miles north once a month to watch them train. Grant smiled. That was it. According to the file Mason's next visit would be tomorrow, on Saturday July 28th. He let the file rest on his chest as he considered how best to exploit this window of opportunity. Grant took a long slow draw on his cigarette. There wasn't much time to plan but the timescale exhilarated rather than intimidated him. He closed his eyes again and began to think.

Brad Mason came out of the elevator into the secure parking lot beneath his apartment building. He was dressed for the hot summer weekend in an open necked pale blue short sleeved shirt, jeans and sneakers. He walked over to his parking bay where his white 1983 five litre Mustang GLX convertible was waiting for him. At six feet five and still retaining his college football physique, Mason eased himself into the white leather seat behind the wheel. The roof was already down when the twin tail pipes shuddered as the engine growled into life. Putting on his sunglasses, Mason drove out of the parking lot into the sunshine and headed north out of the capital.

As Mason headed north on Route Fifteen he glanced at the clock on the dash; eight twenty. He was looking forward to watching the Redskins train. It had been a long week and this would give him the opportunity to unwind a little. As a career intelligence officer with the CIA Mason had spent over twenty years with the agency. He had started as an Intelligence Officer in the covert action staff based in the US Embassy in Grosvenor Square, London. His career flourished in the clandestine service taking him all over the world. He loved the work and the life it gave him. He was totally devoted to the agency and now, at forty-eight, had recently been appointed Deputy Director of Operations at Langley.

The traffic was fairly light at that time on a Saturday morning and the white convertible was making good time. Almost subconsciously, Mason changed lanes periodically and varied his speed to ensure that there was nobody following him. Years in the job meant that such precautions came as second nature to him. Mason looked in the rear-view mirror and noted what was behind, nothing suspicious. Not that he was expecting anything. It had been years since anyone had tried to kill him, he thought to himself. Not since he was parachuted into the Russian Kola Peninsular in 1977 to snatch a defecting scientist. As Mason drove he remembered Demitri Gregorov, a mathematician in his early fifties, disillusioned by the Communist war machine and the complete absence of human rights. Gregorov was a thin wiry man, almost completely bald with a long hooked nose on which perched a small pair of steel framed spectacles.

The CIA wouldn't normally have contemplated lifting Gregorov from a location as remote as the secret installation at which he worked. Located twenty miles north east of Kostomuksha, it was a wild inhospitable landscape of harsh mountainous terrain and constant freezing winds. Gregorov, having passed information to the CIA for five years, had had enough and made it quite clear that they would get nothing more until he was safely in the west. It was decided, therefore, that the CIA had no alternative but to send a man in to get him out of Russia.

As Gregorov was permitted to walk around the inside of the perimeter fence, after all there wasn't anywhere for him to go, Mason met him just before dark at the north east corner. Timed to coincide with the roving security patrols to be at their furthest away, Mason cut the fence and the two men began their forty mile 'dash' to the border with Finland - no easy feat when trying to evade the Russian army with a man that has all the speed and stamina of a three legged tortoise who considered scratching his head exercise. Mason rubbed his shoulder as he remembered, following Gregorov's pathetic cries of "I can't go on", having to carry the spindly scientist most of the final ten miles to the border. Just before reaching it, and in a hail of gunfire, a Russian bullet caught him in the shoulder. Ignoring the pain Mason had continued until, as the Finnish army laid down covering fire, they staggered over the border to safety.

At nine forty-five Mason revved into the parking lot at Dickinson College and pulled up adjacent to the sports field. There were just a handful of cars already in the lot and Mason parked his gleaming Mustang away from them to avoid any accidental dents from carelessly opened doors. Mason sat in his car and stretched as he watched a dozen or so athletics students make their way to the locker rooms to change for a training session. As he did so he became vaguely aware of the black and white police motorcycle turn slowly off the main road and into the parking lot. He glanced across at it briefly as it crossed in front of him and pulled up alongside a few feet away. Mason removed the ignition key and began to open the door but stopped and looked over his shoulder over the passenger door. Standing next to the car was the police officer still wearing his helmet, his eyes hidden by dark sunglasses.

"Is there something wrong officer?" Mason asked. The officer stood expressionless as he stared down at Mason without replying. The hairs on the back of Mason's neck began to prickle. He didn't like this, it didn't feel right. He felt vulnerable sitting there and knew whatever happened he was better off out of the confines of his car. As he pulled the door lever to get out, the cop pulled a silenced .38 special from his holster and fired once. The bullet thudded into Mason's right temple killing him instantly. His large frame slumped over the door, his left arm hanging limply outside the car. As the athletics students, too far away to hear the muffled shot, continued to the locker rooms unaware of what had transpired, the cop got back on his motorcycle and, unnoticed, simply drove away.

As Harry Grant drove south to New York in his battered brown Oldsmobile he turned up the volume as the news report came on the radio. The sombre sounding news reader announced that "a man had been shot to death in his car at Dickinson College in Carlisle. There were no witnesses to the murder in this apparently motiveless crime. This is the second murder in the same day as the body of a motorcycle police officer was found under the off ramp of Highway Eighty-Three this morning. His motorcycle had been stolen and has yet to be recovered. Police believe the two murders are unrelated at this time."

Grant turned off the radio with a sigh and said to himself, "This is going to be easier than I thought."

Chapter Five

Charles Mabbitt stood by the grave in the tiny Biddenden churchyard and looked down at the silver name plate on the polished mahogany coffin. It had been ten days since his wife had been murdered. The coroner had opened and adjourned the inquest to allow Fiona Mabbitt's burial to take place. As he threw a single red rose down onto the coffin lid, surrounded by his weeping family and friends, Mabbitt's face remained characteristically stoic. He couldn't allow himself to weaken even a little or be anything other than totally resolute.

All his efforts to track down who had killed his wife and stolen the secret operation files had led to nothing. Despite numerous unofficial meetings and telephone calls with informants and members of the intelligence community, both in the UK and the Republic of Ireland, he didn't have a single lead.

As he sat alone in his drawing room once the last of the mourners had left, the frustration at his lack of progress burned like a flaming knot in his stomach. Then in a moment of inspiration his eyes widened. "Of course!" he said reaching for the telephone. As he dialled the last digit of the long international number he looked at his watch. Three minutes past four; that meant it was just after eleven in the morning over there. Mabbitt waited patiently as the phone rang a few times before being answered by a bright female voice. "Central Intelligence Agency how may I direct your call?" she said in a mature educated tone.

"Brad Mason, Deputy Director of Operations, please," Mabbitt said authoritatively. There was a pause as the voice hesitated then asked who was calling. Once Mabbitt gave his name and organization he was politely requested to hold. After what seemed an eternity but was in actuality two or three minutes, an unfamiliar male voice came on the line. Introducing himself as Greg Moore, Operations Director and Brad's boss, Mabbitt clearly detected a very dark tone in the man's voice.

Andrew French

"Colonel Mabbitt, I'm sorry to have to tell you that Brad was killed a couple of days ago." Mabbitt met the news with silence. He didn't know Mason very well but had worked with him on a number of occasions and found the man extremely likeable. "How?" Mabbitt asked finally.

"He was murdered, shot in his car while on a trip to Pennsylvania."

"Work related?" Mabbitt said simply, aware that he was speaking on an open line.

"We don't think so. He wasn't working the day he was murdered; he was just going to watch one of the Redskins pre-season training sessions. We've begun a full investigation but so far it seems to be completely motiveless."

Thanking Moore, Mabbitt asked to be kept informed of any developments in the investigation and hung up. "Coincidence?" he thought to himself. Mabbitt didn't believe in coincidences, he didn't like them. Something was happening here, something sinister and calculated; he could feel it. Without any idea of what it could be he was impotent as to his next move. He needed more pieces of the puzzle first.

Three hours earlier in their New Hampshire home Thomas Fisher was having breakfast with his wife, Grace. As he eagerly tucked into a plate of ham and eggs Grace sipped a cup of strong black coffee as she read the morning newspaper. Fisher was talking about a particularly difficult case he had at the moment. He had immersed himself in work, as a diversion to occupy his constantly troubled mind, since his meeting with Steve Bannon. Grace told him, from behind the paper, that she was sure that he would work it out as he always did. Her sentence trailed off as she read something that caught her eye. Putting down her cup she read the article intently.

"Is there something interesting in the paper honey?" Fisher asked. Grace finished reading and looked at her husband quizzically.

"It says here that a man was murdered in his car at the weekend. He was shot in the head." Fisher took a mouthful of coffee and dabbed his mouth with the napkin before replying.

"Probably one of those drive-by shootings. Apparently they're quite common on the west coast."

"But his name was Brad Mason," she persisted. "Isn't that the name you and Steve mentioned when he was here the other night?" Fisher stopped dabbing as she said the name.

"No darling, I think you're mistaken," he said smiling. When she insisted that she was certain that was the name she had heard, Fisher angrily cut her short causing her to visibly jump saying, "I said you made a mistake!" He threw down the napkin and got up from the table. Grace remained silent, startled and a little frightened at her husband's sudden and uncharacteristic outburst.

"I'm late for the office," he said irritably and marched out of the room leaving Grace worried and confused. She was becoming more and more concerned about his increasing and sudden mood swings. His behaviour over the past few weeks had become erratic and introverted, almost secretive. If this was the effect running for the senate was going to have, she thought to herself, then perhaps it wasn't such a good idea after all.

Broadway was bustling with foreign tourists the following day. They buzzed like bees around the quaint little shops and galleries. Nestling in the shadow of Fish Hill on the western Cotswold escarpment, the picture postcard English village in Worcestershire was often referred to as the 'Jewel of the Cotswolds'. Caroline Rawlins had fallen in love with the place when she visited it years ago while on leave from the army. She adored the peace and tranquillity as much as the warmth of the local people. It was then that she decided that this was where she would settle when she had completed her twenty-two years military service.

Two years ago, at the age of forty, she took off her Intelligence Corps sergeant's uniform for the last time and trained to be a teacher. She couldn't believe her luck when, soon after qualifying, a job came up teaching the five year olds in one of the three small Broadway primary schools.

Caroline now lived alone in a small stone cottage on the outskirts of the village. Despite having a number of dalliances over the years, she had never married nor wanted to. Her job as an intelligence communications specialist had taken her all over the world, often at very short notice. Like most intelligence professionals the work always came first. Personal considerations were confined very much to second place but she had been content with that.

It was four thirty in the afternoon as Caroline walked home down the High Street. Her lightweight cotton summer dress accentuated her slim figure. Her brown hair bounced loosely on her shoulders as she casually looked in the shop windows, waving to those she knew inside. Caroline was a woman who was content with life. With a full army pension, her salary and her savings, she lived very comfortably. She went skiing twice a year, a passion for which she had developed while on a NATO posting to Austria early in her career, in addition to having an annual beach holiday in the Bahamas.

In Caroline Rawlins' cottage a leather gloved hand ran a finger along the edge of the Victorian mantelpiece. The dark brown eyes examined the four delicate china figurines that were placed equidistantly along its length. The hand stopped in front of the large mirror that hung above the fireplace. Grant smiled at his reflection. He had let himself into the small sitting room from the garden through the French windows with the aid of a large rock.

He turned his attention to a framed photograph of a woman in her thirties wearing an Intelligence Corps uniform. Three silver medals hung from above her left breast pocket and there was just a glimpse of a pair of sergeant's stripes on the arms of her tunic. Grant picked up the photograph from the table and looked at the smiling face. He then sat down in one of the armchairs facing the door, crossing his legs, and rested the picture on his lap. As he continued to look at the photograph, Grant pulled a large automatic pistol from beneath his light grey windcheater. Taking a long black silencer from his pocket he slowly began to screw it onto the end of the barrel.

It wasn't long before he heard the key turn in the lock and the front door open. Caroline breezed into the sitting room stopping abruptly in the doorway as she saw the large muscular intruder pointing the gun at her.

"Hi there," Grant said warmly in his thick New York accent, his cold emotionless eyes staring intently. Caroline didn't reply as she quickly scanned the room to see if he was alone. Grant held up the photograph at arms length and looked first at the picture then back at Caroline. "You look much better out of uniform." He looked down at her tanned bare legs exposed from just above the knees. "You look as if you keep yourself pretty fit," Grant remarked admiringly as he mentally undressed her.

"What do you want?" Caroline asked coldly. She knew that this was no burglar or even rapist. They didn't come armed with a silenced Colt forty-five automatic pistol. She looked at the man sitting in front of her. Late thirties, closely cropped black hair, smooth square jaw and although he had a large frame she could tell that he was athletic and agile. Clearly ex-military she decided, but what was he doing here?

"Had a good day at school, teach? All the little brats behaved themselves, huh?" Grant asked cheerfully as he replaced the photograph on his lap. Caroline was contemplating how far she could get if she made a run for the door. She looked down at the gun. He held it steadily pointing at her abdomen with no sign of shaking, the hammer was cocked and the safety off. Concluding that she wouldn't even get out of the room she decided to stay put and see how it played out.

"You're an American. That's a New York accent unless I'm mistaken. You're a long way from home."

"I like to travel."

"Do you mind if I sit down?" Caroline said as she started to move into the room.

"Sure honey, take a load off. You've had a long day." Grant's smile remained as he watched the woman slowly sit on the sofa opposite him. They looked at each other. Grant was impressed at how little fear ex-Sergeant Rawlins showed.

"So, are you going to tell me what you are doing here?" she asked calmly with a hint of frustration.

"Do you like being a teacher? It must be strange after all those years snooping around, sticking your nose where it didn't belong, and keeping all those little secrets." He looked at the photograph, "and medals too. What were they for, sleeping with the commanding officer? Still if you've got it flaunt it that's what I say." Grant sneered and tossed the photograph onto the floor smashing the glass. "I remember my teacher, Miss Finkelstein. She was nothing like you though; she had legs like an ostrich. A more foul mixture of repression and hatred you'll never meet. She always looked as if she had a bad smell under her nose. We used to call her Miss Frankenstein. Jesus, she was some monster alright." Caroline could clearly hear the loathing in the man's tone of voice as Grant continued. "She had to flee from Germany to escape the death camps. As far as I was concerned the Nazis had the right idea. They would have done the world a favour getting rid of her. Do you know she made my life hell just because I couldn't do algebra? Algebra for Christ sake! I've never needed algebra in my entire fucking life." Grant spat the words out as he remembered being that small tormented child. "She said I was stupid, good for nothing and that I would never amount to nothing. Well, I showed her. I tracked her down years later. She still had that nasty disapproving look on her wrinkled up old face. So I stuck her head in the oven and did what the Nazis should've done years before and I gassed the bitch."

"And now you're going to kill me." She stated it as a fact rather than a question. Grant didn't reply. "But why? What have I done?"

"It's not what you've done, it's what you know. Somebody is prepared to pay a lot of money to stop you telling."

"What? What do I know?"

"Secrets or more specifically, a secret. I'm here to see that it stays just that."

"Don't you think there'll be questions asked? They're bound to investigate the murder of a former intelligence officer and when they do they'll dig up whatever it is you think I know."

"I'm sure they would if you were murdered, but you're going to have a terrible accident in that lovely fish pond I noticed as I came in." Grant's smile disappeared. Caroline shivered as she began to realise that this was not going to end well for her. Her only chance, albeit a slim one, was to fight. With her heart pounding she lunged at Grant in a futile act of desperation but he clipped the side of her head with his gun, knocking her to the floor. As she drifted in and out of consciousness she looked up, trying to focus as Grant picked her up and lifted her light frame onto his shoulder. Playfully he slapped her bottom as he carried her helpless out through the French windows and into the garden.

Fifteen minutes later Grant was making amusing conversation with a group of fellow American tourists as they stood together outside an antique shop in the High Street. As they laughed, one couple expounded the virtues of Stratford upon Avon insisting that Grant must visit before returning home to the states. As Grant reflected with them just how quiet and peaceful England was, in the fish pond of a small secluded garden a few minutes away the body of a school teacher lay floating face down.

Chapter Six

Doctor Simon Alexander lived on a quiet leafy road in one of the more select suburbs of Ashford. His detached house and finely manicured front lawn was set well back behind a high privet hedge. On the tarmac drive, in front of the garage, stood his brand new white Porsche 911 Carrera. It was eight thirty in the morning on Friday August 3rd and Doctor Alexander was half way out of the front door when his wife called to him from inside. She reminded him that they had been invited for dinner at the Mason's that evening and if he could break the habit of a lifetime and be home on time, she would be eternally grateful. Replying in his strong Glaswegian burr he promised that he wouldn't be late then closed the door.

Simon Alexander had graduated top of his year from Edinburgh Medical School. He then spent the next few years specialising in psychiatry before going into private practice. During this time Alexander had joined the Territorial Army as an Officer in The Royal Army Medical Corps. As a first Lieutenant his work had come to the attention of Colonel Mabbitt, who was seeking a psychiatrist for his unit. Alexander fitted the bill and was seconded to the Fourteenth Intelligence Company as the unit shrink. Simon Alexander now held the rank of Major but, like so many others in the unit, rarely wore his uniform when on duty and was simply referred to as "Doc". He successfully managed to balance his army commitments with his private psychiatry practice in London.

He stood in front of his gleaming white new Porsche. His wife was convinced that he was going through some kind of mid-life crisis buying such an extravagant car but he was delighted with it. He loved the way the 3200cc engine roared when he put his foot on the accelerator, which he did at every opportunity. "At least," he told her, "it's not a motorbike."

Even though it was early morning the sun was warm as he opened the door and sat inside. Throwing his briefcase onto the passenger seat, he put the key into the ignition and turned it. There was an almost inaudible click from somewhere under the dashboard as the car erupted into a fireball. As the car bomb exploded the blast sent shards of burning metal in all directions, shattering windows as acrid black smoke plumed high into the air.

Colonel Mabbitt sat in his office in Templar Barracks. He had just arranged to fly out to RAF Aldergrove, The Det's headquarters in Northern Ireland, later that morning. So absorbed was he in finding out who had killed his wife and stolen the files from his home, he had left operation control to his second in command. Mabbitt's best efforts, however, had led to nothing. He was certain that Brad Mason's death was linked somehow to that of his wife's but as yet couldn't determine how. He decided that, for the time being at least, he would return to work and wait to see what, rather than if, the next move would be.

Mabbitt looked at his watch, nine forty-five. He had ordered a Gazelle helicopter from his unit's 'Bat Flight' to depart at eleven. As he packed a couple of document files into his briefcase the office door opened and Colonel Denison came in. From the grim expression on Denison's face Mabbitt knew that something was wrong.

"I've just had a call from the local police at Ashford. Your Doctor Alexander had a bomb put in his car this morning," Denison said gravely.

"Dead?" Mabbitt asked.

"I'm afraid so. I've sent a Special Investigations team from the RMP along with some of my people to liaise with the local force. I don't suppose it'll be long before Special Branch turn up and take over."

"You think it's the boyos then?"

"Surely there can't be any doubt, can there? It's got Provos written all over it. Simon Alexander was an easy target and they exploited that fact."

"Maybe," Mabbitt said thoughtfully.

"I'll keep you informed, Charles. I'm told you're off to the province this morning?" Denison asked as he turned to leave.

"Yes. I think it's time to roll my sleeves up and get back to work. I don't want them thinking that I've retired to sit in the garden, do I?" Mabbitt's comment jogged Denison's memory.

"Oh I meant to tell you, I got a phone call yesterday regarding the sudden death down in Worcestershire of a former 'I' Corps sergeant. I don't know if you'll remember her, she did a spell with your lot in the late seventies, early eighties over at Aldergrove; Caroline Rawlins." As Denison said her name a tiny bell started ringing in the back of Mabbitt's mind.

"Sergeant Rawlins? She couldn't have been very old if I remember correctly. How did she die?"

"She drowned in her garden pond. Police initially suspected foul play as one of the windows to her house was broken but the post mortem confirmed accidental death by drowning. She must have tripped and banged the side of her head on the rocks surrounding the pond as she fell. Shame, she had become a primary school teacher on leaving the army, was only in her forties."

"Why were you notified, James?" Mabbitt queried.

"She was still on the reserve list. I've been asked to attend her funeral to represent the corps."

"I see," Mabbitt said distantly. Denison wished him a good flight and left the office. Mabbitt stroked his pencil moustache as he sat behind his desk deep in thought. Picking up a pen he wrote three names on a jotter; Brad Mason, Doctor Simon Alexander, Sergeant Caroline Rawlins. As he finished writing the last name he stared at the list. What was the connection between these three people? They had never met each other as far as he was aware. The only common denominator was himself. Sergeant Rawlins was only attached to the unit for two years or so around 1980. The little bell began to ring louder. Mabbitt wrote down the year and circled it round and round as he cast his mind back considering its relevance. That was the year he met Brad Mason for the first time. Then it hit him like a thunderbolt. "My God, of course, how could I have been so blind? Ares!"

he exclaimed. "It's Operation Ares!" He threw down the pen and reached for the telephone.

"This is Colonel Mabbitt; get me Major Dickinson at Aldergrove immediately." Mabbitt waited impatiently as the switchboard connected him with his second in command. "Nigel, is Richard Jordan still under in Liverpool?"

"Good morning, Sir. It's good..."

"Never mind all that is he still under?"

"Yes he is," Dickinson confirmed, surprised at the urgency in the Colonel's voice.

"Extract him," Mabbitt ordered.

"But Sir," Dickinson began.

"You heard me. I want him lifted immediately. I don't care how you do it but I want him standing in front of me here tomorrow morning at nine o'clock. Do I make myself clear?"

"Yes, Sir; quite clear. Does this mean that you won't now being flying over?"

Mabbitt barely registered Dickinson's question as he recalled the details of Operation Ares. After a few seconds, realising that there was a silence, Mabbitt replied, "No, Nigel. There's something I've got to do here that can't wait." He hung up the receiver before Dickinson could speak further. He lifted it again and spoke to Lieutenant Parkes who acted as his personal assistant. "I'll be out for the rest of the day and unable to be contacted. Any problems, refer them to Major Dickinson."

Mabbitt began to change out of his uniform and into a suit. It wouldn't pay to advertise who he was, not where he was going.

Toxteth had become the epitome of inner city poverty. With a long standing reputation for being one of the roughest parts of Liverpool, mugging and street crime were commonplace. Since the containerisation of the nearby docks, and the subsequent massive unemployment it caused, it was only a matter of time before Toxteth would inevitably descend into lawlessness.

In 1981, following increasing tension between the police and the local community, the arrest of a young black man, watched by an angry crowd, sparked a nine day riot, the ferocity of which had been hitherto unseen. This devastated the area and Toxteth as a community never recovered. Three years later the blocks of council flats, largely uninhabitable, still bore the scars of the petrol bombs and vandalism of those nine days of anarchy.

It was in one such run down block, just off Lodge Lane, a four man IRA bomb-making cell had lived in a small flat together for almost two months. Posing as Charlie Graham, a court marshalled British Army explosives expert, Richard Jordan had successfully infiltrated the cell six months earlier in Belfast. His cover, or 'legend', was as solid as it could possibly be. It had to be, his life depended on it. Richard Jordan had been a special operator with The 'Det' for ten years and this wasn't the first time he had spent a long period undercover. It was, however, one of the toughest assignments the RSM had ever had.

The IRA was always suspicious of former British army personnel offering to sell their services to a former enemy, it being such an obvious way to get an agent inside. Colonel Mabbitt, therefore, had to use a little more guile and subtlety to achieve his objective. He had to engineer a way for them to make the first approach. Following his court marshal, Richard Jordan, now known to the world as disgraced sergeant Charles Graham, moved to London and quickly became involved in petty crime. Mabbitt had meticulously planned the operation so that Graham would come to the IRA's attention without any possible suspicion that he was an agent.

Having been caught attempting an armed robbery on a Fulham building society, Charlie Graham was arrested, tried and imprisoned. Only a handful of people outside the unit knew his true identity and, with the co-operation of the Special Branch and the Prison Service, Graham was sent to Wormwood Scrubs prison. It was here that he first met Brendan Reece, it having been carefully arranged that he share a cell with the skinny Irishman who was finishing his three year sentence for plotting acts of terrorism.

During the next few weeks Jordan, as Graham, gradually got to know Reece. Initially hostile and distant, Jordan resisted Reece's overtures of conversation, playing the man with all the tactical skill the experienced intelligence officer had. Finally Jordan allowed himself to become friendly with the man who had planted a car bomb in an RUC officer's vehicle before fleeing to England.

At last, after lights out three days before his release, Reece made the offer Jordan had been waiting for. "What are you going to do when you get out, Charlie?" Reece asked from the top bunk.

"Dunno," replied Jordan. "Might see if I can get some mercenary work overseas. I hear good demolition men are always wanted."

"What regiment did you say you were in?"

"Royal Army Ordnance Corps."

"You were a corporal weren't you?"

"Corporal, my arse. I was a sergeant," Jordan replied knowing that he was being quizzed so that Reece could check him out with his army contacts later.

"I beg your pardon, Sergeant." Reece paused "Listen, I might have something for you should you be interested." Jordan smiled in the darkness before answering.

"Doing what?"

"Like you say, good demolition men are always wanted. When you get out in a couple of weeks, come and look me up in Belfast and we'll have a chat."

Two weeks later Jordan had made his way to a terraced house in east Belfast. As he banged on the front door he tried not to show any sign of the apprehension he felt. If his cover story hadn't stood up to the close scrutiny it would certainly have undergone during the past few days, the only thing he could expect now was a bullet in the head. As the door opened and Reece shook him warmly by the hand, Jordan knew he was in.

Graham and Reece had set up the bomb-making factory with two Provo heavies, Taylor and Sharpe; brainless muscle whose only function was to do as they were told. Once installed in the Toxteth flat, they began acquiring the components necessary to construct a variety of explosive devices. From nail bombs to incendiary devices, the four men sourced, built and stockpiled an arsenal of explosives ready for a concerted campaign of violence on the UK mainland. Prior to joining The Det, Jordan had served twelve years in the 22nd Special Air Service Regiment as an explosives specialist so his skill and proficiency was quite genuine.

It was three in the afternoon on Friday August 3rd and the sweltering heat did nothing to help the mood in the flat. Reece had been waiting for instructions from Belfast for almost a week and the boredom was fraying tempers and causing friction between the men. Taylor's disgusting habit of never changing his socks, tolerated in normal circumstances, made the close confines of the flat reek of sweaty feet to the growing irritation of the other three. Jordan sat in a chair next to an open window. The cool breeze felt good against his face. He wiped away the beads of perspiration from his brow. As he flicked the dead flies that lay on the sill out of the window, Jordan was feeling tired. While he had been undercover during the last few months he had decided that this was going to be his last operation. He was forty-five and had been doing this kind of work most of his military career. He had grown weary of pretending to be someone he wasn't, living in close proximity to people who he would much prefer to put a bullet in rather than have to be friendly with. Jordan now longed for a small remote farm in the Welsh mountains. Somewhere quiet and uncomplicated, where he wouldn't come home feeling dirty.

"How much longer are we going to have to wait? I'm tired of living in this shit hole," Jordan asked as he handed Reece a can of beer from a rusting fridge.

"Until we get our orders. Don't worry; you're getting paid well enough aren't you?"

"Not well enough to have to put up with the smell of his bloody feet." Jordan nodded towards Taylor as he took a long swig from his can. Before Taylor could grunt a response there was a loud bang as the front door crashed open, splintering the frame. A dozen armed figures, wearing helmets and body armour, poured into the small flat amid yells of, "Police, nobody move!" Both Taylor and Sharpe leapt to their feet reaching for the handguns that lay on the table close by but were mercilessly clubbed to the floor. As Reece and Jordan were ordered at gunpoint to get on the ground Jordan, overwhelmed with rage, turned on one of the police officers.

"What is this?!" he yelled.

"It's called a raid, you terrorist bastard!" the officer sneered and, with the butt of his handgun, struck Jordan above the left eye knocking him to the floor, unconscious.

Two hours later the phone rang on Major Dickinson's desk in his office at RAF Aldergrove. It was a call he had been expecting and he recognized the voice of Lieutenant Sheldon instantly. As Jordan's controller, it was Sheldon that Dickinson had phoned when Colonel Mabbitt had unexpectedly ordered Jordan's immediate extraction earlier that morning.

"We've got him, Sir," Sheldon said.

"Well done. Where are you now?"

"Clive Barracks, Tern Hill. I'll carry out his debrief and have him choppered down to Ashford later."

"How is he?"

"Nasty bump on his head. The local police got a bit carried away in all the excitement but he'll be alright." Sheldon hesitated for a moment then asked, "What do I tell him, Sir? He wants to know why he was lifted. To say he's a bit cross about it is putting it mildly. To be honest, Sir, I haven't heard language like it since my sister found out that her husband was seeing another man."

Dickinson replied to Sheldon's question abruptly. "Just tell him it's Colonel Mabbitt's orders and to report to him tomorrow at 0900 prompt. And while you're at it, send a message to Colonel Mabbitt's office that Richard Jordan has been extracted as ordered, right?" Dickinson replaced the receiver without waiting for a reply. He opened a file and, as he realised what Sheldon had said, looked at the telephone and muttered, "Another man?"

Chapter Seven

As the Merseyside Police Special Patrol Group were raiding the Toxteth flat, Colonel Mabbitt was driving through the winding Norfolk roads heading towards Cromer. The little seaside town, renowned for its freshly caught crabs, was heaving with holidaymakers.

Having negotiated the town's one way system, Mabbitt parked his dark blue Jaguar XJ6 in a small public car park opposite the double fronted detached building of Daniel Fearnley Funeral Directors. As he walked inside, Mabbitt was greeted by a middle-aged woman wearing a grey striped skirt, pristine white blouse and a genuinely warm smile. When asked if she could help him, Mabbitt replied that he was looking for Michael Prentiss. The woman looked at the immaculately dressed gentleman that spoke with a fine university accent and bore a striking resemblance to the actor David Niven, curious as to why such a man wanted to see a junior member of her staff.

"He's out interring some cremated remains at the moment and won't be back for an hour or so. Is there anything I can do to help you?"

Mabbitt smiled. "That's very kind of you, my dear but it's more of a personal matter. You see, Michael is my nephew. I thought I would just call in and surprise him as I was in the area."

"Oh, I see. Well, you are more than welcome to wait if you wish. We haven't met any of Michael's family and he never talks about them. To be honest my husband and I have sometimes wondered whether he actually has a family at all."

"Yes, Michael has always been what you might call a very private young man. I wonder, would it be possible for me to go to where he is at the moment only I am a little pressed for time and I would hate not to have seen him?"

"I don't see why not, there aren't any family present so he is on his own. He's at Beeston Regis church, just off the Sherringham road. Do you know the area?"

"Thank you, madam. Most helpful," Mabbitt said, his smile still fixed as he turned and walked back to his car looked on approvingly by Mrs Fearnley.

All Saints Church, Beeston Regis stood in one of the most spectacular settings in all of Norfolk, sprawled as it was on the cliff top looking out to sea. Not connected by any form of road, the church could only be approached by driving the five hundred yards over the grassy field toward the cliff edge.

Michael Prentiss dug the last spadeful of earth from the foot square hole in the cremated remains section of the churchyard. It was warm work on such a hot day and he loosened his black tie, undoing the top button on his white shirt. Prentiss had been working for Daniel Fearnley and his wife, Audrey, for almost three years. He'd had a difficult time following the Boyle assassination. Betrayed by his controller, brutally tortured and beaten by Liam Donnelly and seeing the girl he loved die in his arms had left him with deep psychological scars. He had become withdrawn, unable and unwilling to trust anyone. For a long time he had felt lost, empty, incapable of seeing or even wanting any kind of future.

It was a chance meeting with Daniel Fearnley in a seafront café whilst on a day trip to Cromer that changed Prentiss' life. As the Funeral Director chatted to the eighteen year old Prentiss, he saw something in him that he liked. Prentiss had an air about him, a calm intelligent maturity far beyond his years. Fearnley had seen enough death and bereavement in his twenty-five year career to know that this young man carried some kind of painful loss he still hadn't come to terms with. Needing a funeral assistant, Fearnley offered Prentiss a job and the use of the small flat above the funeral premises. Two weeks later, Prentiss had moved to the little Norfolk seaside town, been fitted with a black suit and begun his unexpected career in the funeral service.

Prentiss enjoyed the work. There were so many similarities to the life he had so badly wanted in the army before being recruited by Colonel Mabbitt for Operation

Ares. The constant requirement to look smart and the public ceremonial duties, together with the organisation, planning and teamwork of the funeral itself. Daniel and Audrey Fearnley became like second parents to him as they themselves had no children of their own. They never asked about his past or what pain he was hiding. The Fearnley's felt 'young Michael' as they called him would tell them when he was ready.

Prentiss had a natural aptitude for the job, becoming a popular figure in the small community. He was liked for his caring and understanding nature and respected for his professionalism.

As Prentiss picked up the small oak box that lay on the grass near the hole, he looked past the fifteenth century church and out to sea. Prentiss loved it here. The gentle warm sea breeze and blue cloudless sky made this the most perfect place on earth. As he placed the urn reverently into the freshly prepared grave he said quietly, "There you are Mister Tyler, rest in peace." It was then that Prentiss heard the faint sound of a car approaching behind him. Squinting in the bright sunshine, Prentiss looked over his shoulder and watched the Jaguar get closer on the uneven ground.

The car stopped a few feet away, next to Prentiss' polished black Granada estate. As Prentiss recognised the tall figure getting out and walking towards him, his mouth dried. He hadn't seen or heard from Colonel Mabbitt since he had returned from Northern Ireland almost four years ago. The Colonel had pleaded with him to join the Det but Prentiss had been adamant. He saw no future with Mabbitt and his secret unit. All he wanted was to forget the previous ten days had ever taken place and, as much as he liked the Colonel, remaining with him would never let him do that.

Colonel Mabbitt extended his hand as he reached Prentiss, his eyes twinkling as he said, "Michael, my dear boy. How are you?" Prentiss, despite everything, was pleased to see him and shook his hand.

"Hello, Colonel; you're looking well. Just passing, were you?"

"Well I thought I would come and see how you were doing, you know."

"Yes, of course you did." Prentiss smiled and regarded Mabbitt with suspicion.

"So, what's it like being an undertaker? Bit of a dead end job, I suppose?" Mabbitt quipped.

"Trust me, Colonel I've heard them all," Prentiss laughed picking up the spade and began filling in the cremated remains hole. Mabbitt looked around the churchyard and then out to sea.

"There is a quotation, I can't for the life of me remember who by, that says if you don't want to be found move to Norfolk?"

"Who said that I don't want to be found?" Prentiss replied without looking up.

"You're not running away, then?"

"Running from whom?"

"Yourself, perhaps?" Prentiss stopped shovelling and looked at Mabbitt earnestly.

"I don't get the nightmares any more, if that's what you mean. I like it here. I like who I am, who I've become. That's good enough for me." Prentiss returned to his work. "So, Colonel, why are you really here? I don't see you as one of the kiss me quick hat wearing bucket and spade brigade somehow."

"Quite right, Michael. Quite right. A serious situation is developing and, if I'm right, I believe you are in very great danger."

"Danger from who?"

"At the moment that's unclear. Nevertheless I assure you that the danger to you remains quite real. You remember Doctor Alexander?"

"How could I forget him? I got the distinct feeling that he was going to make it his life's mission to get me to bare my soul to him. Irritating bloody Scotsman." Prentiss replaced the sod of turf on the tiny grave and patted it flat.

"That irritating bloody Scotsman was blown up in his car this morning. He's the third person connected with Operation Ares to have been killed in the last few days.

There are only three other people left alive associated with it - you, me and Richard Jordan."

"I'm sorry about Doctor Alexander, I suppose he meant well."

"He did, but you are quite right, he was rather irritating."

"And you're sure that Ares is the only connection?"

"Absolutely certain." Mabbitt was unequivocal "I feel it would be much safer if you came back to Ashford with me, just for the time being." There was genuine concern on Mabbitt's face. He felt personally responsible for what had happened to the young man he had persuaded to assassinate Donald Boyle in a Londonderry pub years before.

"I appreciate the concern, Colonel but I can't just leave. I've got commitments here, Daniel and Audrey rely on me and I'm not about to let them down. I don't do that, remember?"

"Michael, I can't impress upon you enough just how dangerous this situation is for you. I can't protect you if you stay here," Mabbitt implored.

"I don't want your protection. I don't want to be drawn back into your world where everything is a matter of life or death, do or die. I barely got out with my sanity last time, let alone my life," Prentiss said, anger creeping into his voice. "I'll take my chances here. I can't go back to all that crap, not again!" Prentiss shook his head trying to regain his composure. "You just find whoever it is that's killing your people. After all, it's what you do, isn't it?"

"Is there nothing I can say to persuade you?" Mabbitt asked.

"It's been good to see you, Colonel. Give my regards to Richard when you see him." There was real warmth in his voice as Prentiss shook Mabbitt's hand.

"Be very vigilant, Michael. Whoever it is is very good. You must take care."

"You too. If what you say is right, it's only a matter of time before they'll be coming after you as well."

The following morning at nine o'clock precisely, Richard Jordan gave two hard raps on Colonel Mabbitt's office door. Barely waiting for Mabbitt to shout "come", Jordan marched in and stood to attention in front of his seated commanding officer. Dressed in combat fatigues and wearing a large dressing above his left eye, Jordan seethed silently. Mabbitt looked up at him.

"How's the head? You've been playing rough with the plods I understand."

"Regimental Sergeant Major Richard Jordan reporting as ordered, Sir," Jordan said, glaring. Mabbitt raised an eyebrow.

"Now, now Richard, don't be peevish. It really doesn't suit you."

"Request permission to speak freely, Colonel."

"Granted, not that you usually need my permission to say what's on your mind."

"Sir, up until now I have never questioned the sanity of any order I have been given in this unit, but who the bloody hell thought it was a good idea to pull me out of Liverpool now? One more week and we'd have had the targets for the IRA's bombing campaign over here. Six months of my bloody life, wasted, for nothing!"

"Richard, I gave you permission to speak freely but I'll thank you to adopt a more moderate tone when you are speaking to me," Mabbitt said testily. "It's unfortunate you had to be pulled out, I know you have given up a great deal for this operation. I can assure you that it wasn't a decision I took lightly. What you have achieved over the last six months is a credit to you. We have a bomb factory that they will never use and we'll sweat Reece and his two pet monkeys for what they know before we throw them back into prison." Mabbitt's voice softened. "Sit down, Richard, and I'll tell you why you are here."

Fifteen minutes later Mabbitt had told Jordan everything that had happened since the burglary at his home. Jordan had listened in silence as the Colonel went through the sequence of events concluding with his visit to Norfolk the previous day.

"First of all, Colonel," Jordan said "I'm sorry for your loss. Mrs Mabbitt was a fine woman. She'll be sadly missed."

Mabbitt nodded his appreciation. "What exactly was in the file?"

"Operation debrief reports, profiles and background information on Boyle and Donnelly and, of course, a summary of Michael's file."

"So two questions immediately spring to mind. Who? And why?" Jordan said thoughtfully.

"If we discover the why, we'll find the who."

"Before whoever it is adds our names to the hit list," Jordan replied. "But where do we start?" Mabbitt opened a drawer and took out a folder.

"I spent last night attempting to reproduce the Ares file. Unfortunately four years is a long time and my memory isn't all that it once was." He passed the file across the desk to Jordan. "Go through it, Richard and see if you can fill in the gaps from your perspective. Between us, with a little luck, we can hopefully find a motive for what is happening."

"How was Michael when you saw him?" Jordan asked as he took the folder.

"It's hard to tell. He's deep, that one; doesn't give much away. The death of that Irish girl who helped him during the operation has clearly had a lasting and profound effect on him. More so than the torture I suspect."

"I suppose that's the trouble with doing this job," Jordan said distantly "The longer you do it, the more of you it takes away." Before Mabbitt could ask Jordan if there was anything wrong, the telephone rang. Following a brief conversation with Lieutenant Parkes, Mabbitt put down the phone.

"There's been a message from Inspector Allen. Apparently he needs to see me urgently at the police station in Ashford. Some crucial information has come to light regarding the identity of the intruder."

"Do you want me to come with you, ride shotgun?" Jordan asked. Mabbitt took a Browning automatic pistol from his drawer and slipped it into a leather shoulder holster beneath his jacket.

"That's quite alright, Richard, You stay here and work on the file. I've got my own shotgun."

Ten minutes later, Mabbitt's XJ6 nosed through the security gates of Templar Barracks and out onto the road bound for Ashford. Varying his speed and watching for following cars, Mabbitt was consciously aware that outside the high level security of the Barracks he was far more vulnerable to attack. A couple of miles outside Ashford, Mabbitt slowed as he approached a line of six cars waiting at temporary traffic lights. The road had been undergoing resurfacing work for the past three days and was almost complete.

It was just before ten o'clock on Saturday morning and the traffic going into the town was beginning to build. Instinctively Mabbitt undid his seat belt so that, should it be necessary, access to his gun was unrestricted. As he waited for the lights to change he scanned his mirrors and each of the oncoming vehicles. He wound down his window. As the glass wasn't bullet-proof it wouldn't stop an assassin's bullet but it would stop him being able to return fire. The line of oncoming traffic stopped and the lights changed to green. Slowly the cars in front began to move. Mabbitt's Jaguar crept forward but had to stop as the lights frustratingly changed to red just as he reached them.

At Templar Barracks, Richard Jordan was working out of a small office in Repton Manor. He was reading through the file Mabbitt had prepared to reacquaint himself with the operation. As he read, the memory of him shooting Liam Donnelly returned as vividly as if it had happened yesterday. He sneered as he closed the file. Jordan wasn't a man who believed in dwelling in the past. He had always approached his work with the same professional detachment. Focus on the job in hand, get it done then move on. He sat back in his chair and put his hand up to the bandage above his eye and winced. "Bloody coppers," he muttered. A thought then occurred to him and, picking up the phone, he asked the switchboard to put him through to Ashford police station. A copy of the information concerning the identity of the burglar could prove very useful. Once connected, he asked to speak to Detective Inspector Allen. Seconds later

Jordan threw down the phone, snatched up a handgun from the desk and ran out of the Manor. Flagging down a Land Rover, he pulled the corporal out of the driving seat throwing him to the ground and sped off towards the main gate. With his headlights flashing and horn sounding he forced his way through the morning traffic praying that he wasn't too late. Colonel Mabbitt had no idea that he was being lured to his death. Inspector Allen wasn't on duty this weekend.

Mabbitt drummed his fingers impatiently on the steering wheel as he waited for the traffic lights to change to green. Finally the oncoming traffic stopped and the lights changed. Mabbitt pulled forward. A car horn repeatedly and urgently blaring some distance behind attracted his attention. He looked in his mirror, catching a glimpse of an army Land Rover, its lights on full, swerving violently to avoid the oncoming traffic. As Mabbitt's car drew level with the traffic lights, with his attention still drawn to his mirrors and the approaching Land Rover, the yellow generator powering the traffic lights exploded. The force of the blast lifted the Jaguar tossing it sideways through a low hedge. It rolled over and over down a short embankment finally coming to rest on its roof in a field fifteen feet from the road.

From a safe distance in a group of trees on the other side of the road Harry Grant, sitting astride a scramble bike, pushed the telescopic aerial back into the remote detonator unit and smiled. As he twisted the throttle and rode away unnoticed, Jordan reached the top of the embankment having abandoned the Land Rover and sprinted the last hundred yards. As he looked through the smoke at the tangled wreckage he could just make out Mabbitt's motionless arm hanging out of the open window.

Chapter Eight

It was early evening before Colonel Mabbitt was taken from the operating theatre to the intensive care unit at Ashford Hospital. It wasn't the numerous cuts and severe bruising but the fractured skull he had sustained that had kept the surgeons busy for most of the day. Richard Jordan looked at his commanding officer through the small window of the side ward. Mabbitt lay unconscious. The doctors had induced a coma to avoid the brain swelling, trying to avoid the possibility of brain damage. The only sound was the rhythmic beeping of the heart monitor and the steady breathing of the life support machine.

Jordan spoke to the two Military Policemen from Templar Barracks he had assigned to guard Mabbitt's room. "Nobody gets in to see the Colonel except for the authorised medical staff, understood?" The two men nodded. Jordan, satisfied for the moment that there was nothing more he could do sitting around the hospital, decided that it was time he paid Michael Prentiss a visit. As he turned to leave he saw two suited men walking towards him down the corridor. Both men had the supercilious sneer of one of the Metropolitan Police's elite specialist units as they simultaneously reached into their jacket pockets. "Richard Jordan?" one of them asked, producing a warrant card. "Yes, I'm Jordan."

"Detective Chief Inspector Gallagher, this is Detective Sergeant Lyle, Special Branch."

"I think I feel a song coming on." Jordan said sarcastically.

"Thank you Mister Jordan, we haven't heard that one before," Gallagher said with a forced smile. "Is there somewhere we can talk privately?" The three men found an empty room close by.

"I understand that you are in the same unit as Colonel Mabbitt?" said Gallagher.

"That's right."

"I'd like to talk to you about the explosion this morning. Our forensics people have had a look at the generator at the scene and have confirmed that there are traces of Semtex in the debris. Do you have any idea who would want to kill Colonel Mabbitt, Mister Jordan?"

"Our unit is tasked to gather intelligence on IRA activity both in Northern Ireland and here on the mainland. I dare say that we've made a few enemies along the way."

"So you think that it was a revenge attack by the IRA?" Lyle asked looking up from furiously scribbling in his notebook.

"Well I don't suppose it was the Red Cross."

"It looks like you've been in the wars yourself, Mister Jordan," Gallagher said pointing to Jordan's dressing. "How did you do that?"

"Bumped into a cobweb. I must try harder with my dusting," Jordan replied glibly. Gallagher nodded. This wasn't getting him anywhere. "Well, thanks for your time. Do they know when Colonel Mabbitt will regain consciousness? It's important that we speak to him as soon as possible."

"Apparently the next twenty four hours are critical. I'm sure they'll keep you informed," Jordan said, leaving the Special Branch officers and making his way out of the hospital.

As Jordan walked across the car park to the Land Rover he casually looked about him, scanning the area for any sign of a threat. He knew that somebody was going to try and kill him, perhaps today, perhaps tomorrow but certainly soon. He was alert, ready to respond to any attempt from wherever it came.

He decided to proceed from now on as if he was on duty in Belfast. That meant adopting all the security routines that had kept him alive for so long while working in the province. Instead of going straight to the parked Land Rover, he circled it from a distance examining the vehicle and those surrounding it. Finally he approached the Land Rover and dropped to the ground examining the underside; nothing suspicious. Jordan stood up and got into the car. He paused as he was about to insert the key into the ignition. Pulling the Bonnet release he got out and walked round to the front.

Carefully he ran his fingertips along the front edge of the bonnet, feeling for wires. So far, so good. Slowly he lifted the bonnet and peered inside. Again, there was nothing. Deciding that it was safe he dropped the bonnet shut and opened the driver's door. An ambulance's siren blared out on the far side of the car park having Jordan drop to a crouch reaching for his gun. As he swore at the ambulance under his breath and himself for being so twitchy, he looked up into the cab of the vehicle. That was when he saw it. Taped beneath the dashboard, close to the clutch pedal, was a small flat box. A tiny red light blinked on and off.

"Oh bollocks," he whispered.

An hour later, with the car park cleared, the army bomb squad had disarmed the device and removed it. Needless to say Gallagher and Lyle were taking a great deal of interest in how and why a bomb had got into his vehicle. Fortunately Colonel Denison's timely arrival, with a team of Intelligence and Security investigators and military police Special Investigations Branch officers, meant that Jordan avoided having to answer any awkward questions.

Before being spirited away back to Templar Barracks, Denison had taken Jordan aside for a quiet word. "I know about the stolen files, Sarn't Major, and I'm assuming that today's events are a direct result of that. I'm certain that you and Colonel Mabbitt were handling matters in your characteristically irregular and secretive fashion. However, with this latest development is there anything you need that I can provide?" Jordan thought for a moment before replying.

"I'm going to need to operate freely for a few days so I'd appreciate it if you could run interference for me with Special Branch," Jordan said, directing Denison's attention to the two detectives standing some distance away.

"That shouldn't be too much of a problem."

"If you ask them nicely they might even sing you Heart on my Sleeve," Jordan said dryly. Denison looked at him quizzically but let the comment go.

"What will you do now?"

"I thought I'd take a little holiday. A few days at the seaside will do me the world of good. I've just got a few things to pick up from the barracks before I go."

"Fine, contact me there if there is anything you need," Denison said then added, "and Sarn't Major, good luck."

"Thank you, Sir." Jordan then noticed Gallagher and Lyle walking towards them. "If you'll excuse me, Sir, I think it's time I left." He glanced towards the approaching men as he quickly got into an army saloon car. Looking visibly annoyed as they watched the car speed away, they demanded to know where Jordan was going. It was only when Denison asked who they were and they produced their identification that the penny dropped and he said, "My wife has all of your records."

Harry Grant was wild with anger as he drove his rented red Vauxhall Astra hard up the motorway heading north. He punched the steering wheel as he recalled walking into the hospital and learning that his target was still alive. Grant didn't tolerate failure in anyone, not least himself. He regarded it as a deep and unforgivable character flaw. So the fact that Jordan had evaded his car bomb made him positively apoplectic. Knowing that it was pointless trying to get to Mabbitt now that he was surrounded in security and there was no reasonable chance of another attempt, and that Jordan had disappeared again, Grant resigned himself to moving on to the next target and return to Mabbitt and Jordan later.

Failure was the only thing that produced real emotion in Grant. Over the course of many years he had learnt to suppress them. He prided himself on being able to constantly stay in control. He dare not allow the deep rage inside him to rise to the surface and reveal itself fearing that, if it ever did, it would completely devour him and he would lose control forever.

Bannon's team in New York hadn't been able to locate Michael Prentiss. His last known address was that of his parents where he lived when he was recruited by Mabbitt four years earlier. Grant had left his hotel in Canterbury, from where he had planned the murders of Alexander and Mabbitt, and by mid afternoon was driving onto the slip road off the A1 and down the hill into the market town of Grantham in Lincolnshire.

It didn't take him long to find the house located in a quiet cul-de-sac. As he parked the Astra at the bottom of the drive and got out, he noticed the lace curtains in the window of the house next door twitching. He knocked on the door and waited. There was no movement from within. He knocked again. With still no response, Grant peered through a large sitting room window.

"They've gone on 'oliday," came a voice over the fence. It was the curtain twitcher next door. Grant turned and smiled at the old woman whose expression was fierce and her tone unfriendly. Crossing to the fence he stood looking down at her.

"Won't be back till next week," she continued "Taken the caravan to Weymouth, they 'ave. Gone for a fortnight."

"Has Michael gone with them?" Grant asked.

"Who?"

"Michael, Michael Prentiss."

The old woman screwed her face up so it was even more wrinkled than before.

"They don't live there no more. Moved to France two years ago. The Hendersons live there now. She's alright but he's got some funny ways about him, if you ask me. My Timmy doesn't like him at all. He's about 'ere somewhere, probably got his nose into something he shouldn't. Are you Australian?" She looked Grant up and down but he ignored her question.

"Did Michael go to France with his parents?"

"No he moved to Norfolk. Become a bloody undertaker of all things. I ask you, you'd think he'd want a proper job wouldn't you?"

"Where in Norfolk?" Through his white smile there was a hard edge to Grant's voice. The woman shrugged.

"Oh I can't remember. Why do you want to know anyway?"

64

"Would Timmy remember? It's very important that I find him." The woman looked at him curiously.

"Of course he won't remember, he's a bloody cat! You're not very bright, you Australians, are you?" Grant's smile vanished. He bit his bottom lip with frustration and began to walk away.

"Cromer!" the woman shouted as she remembered.

"What's a Cromer?" Grant said.

"Not what, where. That's where Michael Prentiss moved to. He's an undertaker in Cromer."

Prentiss woke suddenly. Since meeting Colonel Mabbitt two days before, he had been preoccupied and unsettled. He had spent a second restless night reliving a seemingly endless week in 1980 that he spent in Northern Ireland. It wasn't killing the three men that disturbed him; he had long since come to terms with that. Nor was it the beating and agonising torture he had endured at the hands of Liam Donnelly. He was mentally much stronger than that. It was the face of Orla Duncan, a young Irish nurse, who had selflessly done so much to help him, that left him screaming night after night soaked in sweat. For months after the operation Prentiss, racked with guilt, endured the nightmares of how the girl he had fallen in love with, who he had promised to protect, had died in his arms.

Prentiss sat up in bed and looked at the bedside clock, six forty-two. As he ran his fingers through his blonde hair, damp with perspiration, he was aware of movement at the end of the hallway in the living room. Wearing only his underwear he got out of bed and tentatively walked out of the bedroom and towards the living room's partially opened door. Prentiss slipped into the kitchen and, taking a carving knife from the rack, proceeded back into the hallway. He paused for a moment outside the door, ready to face whoever was on the other side, before kicking it open and bursting into the room.

Prentiss stood motionless, the knife raised above his head, as he saw a man sitting in the armchair, his face obscured by a copy of the *Funeral Director* magazine.

Slowly the figure lowered the magazine and without looking up from the page said, "Morning Michael, it's been a while." Jordan lifted his eyes from the magazine at Prentiss who was staring at him with an expression of astonishment and rage.

"Richard? What the bloody hell are you doing here!?" Prentiss said finally, lowering the knife and tossing it onto the table.

"You're looking well, keeping fit lifting all that dead weight?"

"Look, Richard if you're here to take me back to Ashford I'll tell you the same as I told the Colonel." Jordan interrupted Prentiss abruptly with a matter of fact tone.

"They tried to kill him yesterday morning; they still might for all I know. As I'm talking to you now he's in a coma fighting for his life. Then yesterday afternoon they put a bomb in my car wired to the ignition. Fortunately I spotted it so I thought I'd better come and pay you a little visit. Whoever it is will be coming after you next and I'm not prepared to sit on my arse and wait for it to happen or pretend that it's all going to go away because trust me, it won't."

"What happened?" Prentiss asked sitting down.

"Remotely detonated roadside bomb. Don't worry I've known the Colonel for a long time. He's a tough old bird, he'll be okay. Now go and get dressed, I'll make some coffee. The sight of you in just your pants is too disturbing, even for me, this early in the morning."

An hour and a half and two cups of coffee later Jordan had told Prentiss as much as he knew about the situation in which they now found themselves. As he had listened to the veteran intelligence man, Prentiss observed just how tired he not only looked but also sounded. He still had the same professional focus and note of urgency in his voice but there was now a trace of weariness and fatigue in his superciliousness, absent four years before.

"Do you live here alone?" Jordan asked. Prentiss nodded. "No girlfriend?"

"No, no girlfriend."

"You can't mourn her forever you know. You're a young man, Michael don't let what happened eat away at you. You need to move on."

"I'm fine!" Prentiss snapped irritably. "At least I was. I like being alone, it's simpler this way. I don't need to be reminded about who I was then. What I did."

"I need you with me, Michael. Together we stand a chance of getting whoever it is before they get us. I know it's the last thing you want right now but I don't see that you have any choice. Not if you don't want to be laid out in one of your own coffins by the end of the week."

"I don't know what you think I can do."

"Four years ago you were one of the most naturally intuitive intelligence operators I had ever met. You managed to stay alive in circumstances that most experienced officers would never have coped with. You not only completed your mission but you also stopped an assassination attempt on the Prime Minister. You were given the George Cross for bravery for Christ's sake."

"Oh, yes that's right. My George Cross from a grateful nation. A medal that's so secret I'm not allowed to tell anyone I've got it. I have to hide the bloody thing in a drawer! No secret medal is going to bring Orla back. What did her bravery get her?"

"Oh bloody hell, Michael, will you drop this woe is me crap. I'm asking for your help, I can't do this alone. Are you with me?" Prentiss looked intently at Jordan after his outburst before replying.

"Okay I'm with you but when this is over that's it. I'm finished with all this secret squirrel shit for good."

"Fair enough," Jordan said reaching into his jacket pocket. "You'll be needing this." He placed a small Beretta automatic on the table and slid it towards Prentiss. I thought I'd bring you a gun you were familiar with. I know it's been a while; are you still okay with that?" Prentiss picked up the weapon and looked at it in his hand. It was the same weapon he had used to kill Donald Boyle. He removed the magazine and, confirming that it was loaded, pushed it back in with the heel of his hand.

"I'll manage. So," Prentiss said, pulling the slide back to cock the gun, "what do we do now?" Jordan sat back in his chair.

"Well, we have no idea who these people are, what they look like or even how many we're talking about. So we do the only thing we can do."

"Which is?"

"Wait for them to try and kill us."

Chapter Nine

In a cheap bed and breakfast close to the sea front in Cromer, Grant attempted to make himself comfortable on the bed. His heavy frame sank into the exhausted mattress, a stray rusty spring digging painfully into his lower back. It was mid Sunday morning. Having left his Grantham hotel before dawn, he had driven the hundred miles to the Norfolk coast. Once there he then spent a couple of hours reconnoitring the town and the surrounding area. With the three funeral businesses located, Grant was satisfied he was getting closer to his next target.

Steve Bannon had been pleased with his progress when Grant had telephoned New York the previous evening. He had insisted that Grant ring in every forty-eight hours to update him personally on his progress and to arrange delivery of any new additional information Grant would need. The former SEAL was ahead of schedule which, as it transpired, was fortunate. Earlier that day Thomas Fisher had contacted Bannon demanding an update and giving him an ultimatum. Fisher had been forced to begin his election campaign sooner than he would have wished thanks to his wife revealing his intentions to a prominent local journalist.

Thomas Fisher hated interviews. Although he knew that they were a necessary and crucial part of his campaign, until he had the confidence of knowing that all six names on the list had been silenced, he lived in fear of exposure. The man was in a constant state of anxious irritability which he was increasingly failing to conceal. That morning he had endured a television interview with one of the most aggressive political commentators around. Managing to remain both calm and affable, Fisher had responded to the interviewer's questioning sincerely and knowledgeably. His warm smile and relaxed manner had projected itself well on the television and the interview was hailed by his campaign team as a great success.

Driving back to his office, Fisher decided that he would give Bannon a week to finish the job. After all, he was paying a great deal of money for this contract and he would dictate the time scale. He'd had enough of waiting for the sword of Damocles to fall. He was enjoying his rising popularity and the thought that it could be jeopardised by something as toxic as Boyle was, quite simply, unacceptable.

As Bannon spoke to Grant, having been given the ultimatum by Fisher, he jotted down Grant's requirements needed to complete his assignment. Informed that he now only had one week, Grant demanded a bonus for Bannon changing the terms of his contract. Bannon had anticipated this, having told Fisher he wanted another million as compensation for the increased difficulty. Agreeing to an additional two hundred and fifty thousand dollars being immediately put into his account, Grant satisfied Bannon that it could be done.

As Grant pushed a stained pillow behind his head he re-read Michael Prentiss' file. Although Richard Jordan as an experienced professional was going to be difficult, it was Prentiss that Grant had the greatest reservations about. He stared at the file picture of a sixteen year old Prentiss. He was intelligent and unpredictable, a dangerous combination in an opponent. He wasn't going to over complicate this one. He didn't have time for finesse or an elaborate accident. Tomorrow he would find him and kill him on sight.

There was a gentle knock on Steve Bannon's apartment door in Concord. At a little after ten on a Sunday morning, Bannon was sound asleep in bed. The knock came again, louder and longer this time, rousing him back to life. As he fell out of bed and put on a towelling robe the knocking continued.

"Alright, alright I'm coming, keep your shirt on," he called, reaching the door and opening it. He looked visibly surprised as Grace Fisher stood in front of him.

"Can I talk to you?" she said anxiously. Bannon invited her inside. She waited as he threw on some clothes and rejoined her in the lounge.

"What's the problem?" he asked as they sat together on the sofa.

"Tom doesn't know I'm here, Steve and I'd appreciate it if it stayed that way. He's playing golf with Joe Espinosa and the Mayor." Bannon agreed to Grace's request cautiously intrigued as to what she was doing there.

"I'm really worried that Tom might be mixed up in something dangerous."

"Dangerous? Tom? Why would you think that?"

"Well, he's changed. He's become secretive; he flies into a temper at the slightest thing. We used to talk all the time but since he decided to run for the senate if I ask him anything he accuses me of prying into his affairs." As she spoke her voice became shrill with emotion. Bannon took her hand.

"I'm sure it's just the stress of the election campaign and he'll return to the old Tom when he wins."

"But that's not all," Grace persisted. "That man you and Tom were talking about, Brad Mason." Bannon stiffened.

"What about him?"

"Not long after you were talking about him he was killed, murdered. I'm scared, Steve. Scared that Tom has got himself involved in something..." Grace hesitated, aware that she was beginning to sound hysterical. Bannon smiled compassionately.

"That was nothing more than a coincidence, Grace. Tom couldn't have had anything to do with that. He didn't even know Brad Mason." Grace looked confused.

"If Tom didn't know him, what did he want you to talk to him about?"

"It was just a case that Tom had. He asked me to talk to Brad to get some background information on his client. Trust me, Grace; there is absolutely nothing to worry about. If it will help I'll have a quiet word with him, see if I can get him to relax a little."

"No," Grace replied quickly. "That's okay. I'm sure you're right. I'm just being silly." Feeling a little embarrassed that she had brought such wild and unfounded accusations about her husband to Bannon, she hastily said goodbye and left.

As Bannon closed the door he paced thoughtfully then poured himself a small whiskey. "Oh, Grace," he said, "I do hope you're not going to be a problem."

As Sunday afternoon wore on, Prentiss and Jordan sat looking at each other in silence. "I don't like this, it doesn't feel right. This flat is a nightmare to defend; only one way in, one way out and nowhere to run to," Prentiss said.

"I was just thinking the same. While we're sat here twiddling our thumbs there's nothing stopping them putting a bloody great bomb in the funeral parlour downstairs and raising this whole place to the ground with us in it. We need to get out of here. But the question is, where?"

"I think I know just the place," Prentiss replied. "There's a cottage a few miles along the coast road from here near Bacton. I did a funeral a couple of weeks ago of a widow who lived there alone. No family. The solicitors are planning to sell it after they've wound up the estate so it's empty at the moment."

"Is it defendable?"

"Perched on the edge of a cliff, access via a quarter of a mile single track through open fields."

"Sounds perfect." Jordan said standing up. "Michael m'boy, you've got a phone call to make then we're getting the hell out of here."

Old Mrs Stannett's brick and flint cottage smelled damp and fusty. The elderly widow had lived alone during her final years despite her declining health and poor mobility. Fiercely independent, she had steadfastly refused all offers of help by social services and would fly into a rage if the subject of a nursing home was ever tentatively broached. She died alone, emaciated and dirty sitting in her chair, undiscovered for almost a week.

It was early evening when Jordan and Prentiss unloaded Jordan's pale blue escort estate. Fortunately the power, water and telephone were all still connected so it was just about habitable, but the unmistakable odour of death hung heavily in the air. Jordan looked around the small dingy living room disapprovingly. "Another shit hole," he muttered under his breath as he threw down a large black holdall.

An hour later, as Prentiss carried a plate of sandwiches into the living room, Jordan finished his phone call and replaced the receiver. Prentiss had packed some supplies from his flat to last them a couple of days.

"Well, I've got some good news. That was Colonel Denison, 'I' Corps CO. Colonel Mabbitt has been brought out of his coma and, although his injuries are serious, he's off the critical list. Told you he was a tough old sod," Jordan announced. Prentiss looked relieved as the two men sat down and began to eat.

"How long do you think we are going to have to stay here?" Prentiss asked. "You know, before they make their move?"

"I don't know," replied Jordan shaking his head "Somebody certainly appears to be in a great hurry to see us all dead so I don't suppose it will be very long."

"Have you any idea who?"

"Michael, I've been over it and over it and I can't think who. If it is a revenge thing by the IRA, why start with killing a CIA man who had nothing to do with Northern Ireland?"

"What was his involvement with Ares?"

"From what I remember, someone in the NI section of MI5 asked the CIA to lean on Boyle to pass on information about Donnelly's terrorist activities."

"And it was this chap Mason that did the leaning?" Prentiss said.

"That's right."

"So if it's not the Irish, who is it?"

"I'll tell you one thing, whoever these people are, they're well funded and very well informed." Jordan sat back in his chair and closed his eyes. His head was throbbing thanks to a combination of one of Merseyside's finest and what seemed like forever without any proper sleep. "I don't imagine anything will happen tonight, nobody knows we're here," Jordan continued, his eyes still closed. "If I'm right, and I usually am, they'll take the bait tomorrow and come for us then."

"Just like that?"

"Oh yes. Trust me; they won't be able to resist it," Jordan said opening one eye.

Before leaving his flat, Prentiss had telephoned Daniel Fearnley at home to explain that regrettably he had to go away for a couple of days. Prentiss was genuinely sorry for having to leave at such short notice but told him it was a family emergency and that he really had no choice. Fearnley accepted the explanation without question or enquiry, even when Prentiss said that he had left an envelope marked 'Charles Mabbitt' on the reception desk downstairs should he come into the office asking for him.

"Nevertheless I'll take the first watch. You look shattered," Prentiss said. Jordan's only reply was a quiet and rhythmic snore as he fell deeply to sleep.

Harry Grant rose early the following morning. Despite numerous valiant attempts, and a great deal of cursing, he was unable to generate any hot water and so had endured a cold weak shower in a filthy pink bathroom that was barely fit for purpose. Returning to his room, he dressed quickly and took his gun from a small overnight bag. Expertly he stripped down the .45 automatic, cleaned, oiled, reassembled it, screwed on the silencer and placed the loaded weapon on the bed. Taking the page of local funeral directors he had ripped from a phone box's Yellow Pages the day before, he went downstairs to use the public phone in the empty reception. It was the second of the three possibilities that produced the response to his polite enquiry to speak to Michael Prentiss he was hoping for. Although the woman had said that Prentiss wasn't there at present, she had told him what he wanted to know. Grant had found his next target. He read the address of 'Daniel Fearnley Funeral Director', screwed up the page and tossed it on the floor as he made his way back to his room.

Monday morning was always a busy time for Daniel and Audrey Fearnley. Daniel conducted the funerals he had arranged during the middle of the previous week and Audrey arranged the funerals of the deaths that had taken place over the weekend. Today was no exception. At eleven thirty the phone hadn't stopped ringing since just after nine o'clock. They had been notified of four funerals that needed arranging and taken countless enquiries regarding the details of the two funerals Daniel Fearnley was conducting that day.

As Audrey replaced the receiver and returned her attention to the pile of forms on her desk, she became aware of a large figure standing in the reception. Her normally warm smile became nervous as the man stared at her and, in a thick New York accent, said, "Good morning." There was something about the American that she found unsettling and she began to feel vulnerable as she sat behind her desk alone in her small office. Grant held her gaze as Daniel Fearnley walked into the reception from a door marked 'Private'. Audrey looked visibly relieved as her husband approached the American from behind.

"Can I help you?" Fearnley said, having noticed Audrey's concerned expression and deciding to deal with this character himself. Grant casually turned to face Fearnley.

"I'm looking for Michael Prentiss. Is he here?" Fearnley eyed the stranger suspiciously. It wasn't unusual for people to come in asking for Prentiss by name but they were normally bereaved families that he was arranging funerals for. Fearnley didn't know this man and was automatically protective of his assistant.

"No, he had to go away for a couple of days. Is there anything I can do?"

"No," Grant said acidly "It's a personal matter. Did he say where he was going?"

"Afraid not." Then Fearnley remembered the envelope. "Are you Mister Mabbitt?" Grant raised a single eyebrow on hearing the name.

"Yes."

"Michael said you might call in," Fearnley said reaching for the white envelope on the reception desk and handing it to the American. Grant took it, still holding his stare. He looked down, read the name on the envelope and slipped it into the inside pocket of his jacket. Then, looking at them both in turn, turned and left without saying anything more, leaving the Fearnley's speechless and feeling more than a little disturbed.

Grant walked the hundred yards down the busy road to where his Astra was parked. Ripping open the envelope, he took out a folded sheet of paper on which there were directions to an address of a cottage near Bacton and just four words in capital letters written underneath it;

"I'M WAITING FOR YOU!"

Chapter Ten

At the cliff side cottage Prentiss and Jordan had been awake since before dawn. Jordan had left just before seven and driven into Cromer, parking his Escort estate in the same small car park Colonel Mabbitt had used a few days before. From there he was able to discreetly observe the funeral parlour and all its comings and goings. Prentiss had remained at the cottage. There he had taken up position with a pair of binoculars in a front upstairs window that afforded him an uninterrupted view of the approach from the main road.

As he sat three feet from the window on a rickety wooden stool he'd brought up from the kitchen, concealed behind a dirty net curtain, Prentiss scanned the open ground. He had no idea how long it would be before an attempt would be made. Jordan's experience and instinct said it was going to be today and Prentiss had no reason to doubt the man's tactical intuition.

As Prentiss looked down at the Armalite rifle leaning against the wall and felt his Beretta pressing into the small of his back, he became aware of feeling something that he had tried so hard to forget and hoped he would never experience again. The combination of fear and adrenalin excited him. It was precisely this feeling that had sustained him during Operation Ares. The danger made his mind sharp. He felt attuned to the situation he now unexpectedly found himself in and, now that he had accepted it, part of him felt guilty for beginning to almost enjoy it.

As the morning wore on and the streets began to fill with holidaymakers laden down with beach paraphernalia, Jordan was beginning to find it difficult to remain alert. He had been sitting in his car for more than four hours. Although he felt sure that his as yet unidentified enemy would turn up here sooner or later, doubt was beginning to creep in. As he was about to get out of the car and stretch his legs, there was something about a tanned muscular man walking up the road that attracted his attention. Something about the way he moved. Jordan watched him carefully. The figure didn't take his eyes off the funeral parlour as he approached it. Jordan picked up the camera, complete with telephoto lens, that lay on the passenger seat and began snapping at the suspicious looking stranger. Without altering his stride, he walked inside. He was totally unlike the dozen or so people that had entered or left the funeral parlour during the last two and a half hours. This one had a predatory, almost visceral, air about him and his whole demeanour was completely wrong for a small English seaside resort. Jordan undid the retaining strap on the shoulder holster that held his Browning 9mm automatic securely in place and waited.

Less than five minutes later the same tanned figure appeared and walked back down the road. Jordan got out of the car and stood at the edge of the car park and smiled as he watched Grant walk to a red Astra. From his safe distance, Jordan saw him produce Prentiss' envelope from his pocket, rip it open and read it.

"Got you," Jordan murmured as he watched his prey angrily punch the roof of his car. Taking a small telescopic sight from his jacket pocket Jordan focused on the car, memorising the registration number. He noted that the car was empty. It was fairly safe to proceed on the assumption, therefore, that this man was working alone rather than as part of a team. As Grant got into his car, slamming the door shut, Jordan returned to his and prepared to follow.

Grant drove around the town for half an hour as he considered the consequences of the note. He had lost the element of surprise which complicated his job exponentially. Finally he parked outside his unspeakable accommodation and went straight up to his room. He paced around the bedroom like a caged animal, reading and re-reading the note. It was taunting him, daring him to try and attempt the hit. Grant fought to control his anger. He needed to think clearly now. This was a fundamental change to the dynamic of his assignment. Somebody had put the pieces together and realised what he was doing, anticipating that Prentiss would be his next mark and warning him. Grant concluded that, in light of this, Jordan would almost certainly be with him.

As Grant ruminated in his room, Jordan had parked across the road and was walking into the reception downstairs. A fat, middle-aged man with greasy receding hair and wearing a tatty grey cardigan stood behind the desk. He eyed Jordan as he noisily slurped his tea from a chipped mug.

"Yes?" he asked lethargically. Jordan looked around him as he approached the desk.

"I believe my friend is staying here. He came in just a few moments ago, big chap, short dark hair. Can you tell me what room he's in?"

"And why should I do that?"

"Because if you tell me I won't have to kick your nasty flabby great arse all round this sorry excuse for a hotel," Jordan said, menacingly.

"You mean the Yank, Mister Morse. Up the stairs, end of the corridor on the left, he's in room four," he replied, speaking faster than he almost certainly had done for years.

"Is he alone?" Confirming with a vigorous nod that he was, the manager put down his mug and wiped his sweaty palms on his cardigan. "Pass key," Jordan said holding out his hand. Fumbling in his trouser pocket for a moment he produced a small bunch of half a dozen numbered keys and put them into Jordan's hand. "Why don't you go and put your feet up for ten minutes. You don't want to over tire yourself, do you?" The manager didn't need to be told twice and disappeared through a door behind the reception desk. Alone in the reception, Jordan pulled his gun from its holster and climbed the stairs.

In his room, Grant was now calm and controlled. He sat on the edge of the bed examining a detailed map of the local area. He located the cottage and studied the surrounding geography. As he considered his options he heard the floorboards creaking in the corridor. This wasn't unusual as all the floorboards creaked on the upper floor. What was unusual, and had him reaching for his gun, was that he couldn't hear any footsteps that normally accompanied the creaking when somebody was walking down the corridor.

Grant folded the map and stuffed it into his jacket then, crossing to the tall mahogany wardrobe, pulled it away from the wall where it stood opposite the door. Standing behind it he pulled the wardrobe into the corner at an angle so there was just enough room in the small triangular space to conceal him.

There was the tiniest click as Jordan turned the key in the lock then the door was flung open. As the door banged against the wall, Jordan crouched low in the corridor. Only his head and gun arm were exposed as he scanned the room for movement. There was none. Holding his gun steady in both hands, his arms outstretched, Jordan slowly entered the room. Kicking open the bathroom door, he burst inside only to find it empty. The only sound was the steady dripping of the shower. He returned into the bedroom and stood motionless, looking, listening, searching for the smallest clue as to where the American could be. The room was small. The only other place to hide was in the large wardrobe in the corner. Jordan approached it cautiously. Holding his pistol in his right hand he raised his left to open one of the double doors. Taking a deep breath he pulled at the door stepping back as he did so. He barely had a chance to look inside when the whole wardrobe tipped forward and fell on top of him. Grant had pushed it, as heavy as it was, quite easily. With Jordan buried underneath it, Grant fired a couple of shots into the back of the wardrobe with his silenced .45 then ran out of the room making good his escape.

As Grant sped away, Jordan hauled himself out from beneath the wardrobe. The two shots Grant had fired had missed him and were embedded in the floor. Getting to his feet, he kicked the wardrobe in anger. Jordan had sustained a few cuts and bruises but was generally unhurt. As he replaced his gun in the shoulder holster beneath his jacket and walked back down the corridor, he couldn't believe that he had allowed himself be overpowered so easily by such a simple manoeuvre. It just reinforced his belief that it really was time to pack it all in.

"Oh shit," he said as he reached the bottom of the stairs. The body of the manager lay beside the reception desk. Thick red blood pooled on the floor beneath him from the two bullets Grant had put in his chest on the way out. As Jordan looked over at the body the front door opened and an elderly couple entered. Taking a second or two to register what she saw, the woman began to scream hysterically, shaking uncontrollably. Jordan decided it was time to leave and, pushing past the couple, ran for his car as a small crowd began to gather.

It was just before one o'clock that afternoon when Michael Prentiss saw Jordan's blue Escort turn off the main road and drive towards the cottage. Picking up the Armalite he ran down the stairs and was outside the front door as the car came to a stop. "What happened to you?" Prentiss said as he saw Jordan's bruised face.

"Somebody thought I'd look better wearing a wardrobe."

"What?"

"Let's go inside and you can make me a strong coffee in that toilet of a kitchen and I'll tell you," Jordan said, dabbing a cut lip with the back of his hand.

Ten minutes later Jordan had recounted the morning's events finishing with the murder of the B and B manager.

"Sounds like Colin Whittaker. Not what you would call a popular bloke. If you wanted to hide something from him the safest place was under the soap. The Co-op will probably end up doing his funeral. Why was he killed, he couldn't have been much of a threat?" Prentiss said.

"No, he wasn't. I suspect he planned to kill him when he left in any event. Our American friend clearly didn't want to be identified. Which is too bad," Jordan reached into his pocket and pulled out a roll of film, "because I've got some very nice holiday snaps of him. All we need to do is to get this to Colonel Denison and see if he can put a name to the face. I'm sure Mister Morse is going to be on file somewhere."

"Interesting he's chosen to go by the name of Morse, don't you think?" Prentiss mused.

"What do you mean?"

"Because, my dear Sergeant Major, in Roman myth and literature, Mors is the personification of death." Prentiss smiled at Jordan who sat tutting and shaking his head.

"You're as bad as bloody Mabbitt with your myths and your gods and your..."

"I think the word you're stumbling for is education," Prentiss interrupted.

"Oh chuckle, chuckle." Jordan reached for the phone. "I'll ring Denison. We'll get this film to him and then we can disappear until our Roman god is found."

"No," Prentiss said firmly.

"What?"

"I'm not coming with you. I'm staying here. It could be days or weeks before he's caught, if at all. I'm not going into hiding indefinitely. I've got a life here, Richard."

"Yes, the operative word there being 'life'. You know - the opposite of death? This guy's a professional, Michael. Which means he's going to keep coming until you are dead."

"Exactly! Which is why I have to stay. This way we draw him out, we don't have to go looking for him."

"You know what you're saying, don't you?" Jordan said seriously. "You're offering yourself up as bait."

"I know, but I don't see that I have much of a choice. Look, it's important that you get this film to Denison. If we get a name we may get to find out who's behind this. It's not as if you'll be gone for long is it? A few hours at most and then you'll be back."

"Alright," Jordan said reluctantly. He knew what Prentiss said made sense but having seen this man he also knew that Prentiss was no match for him. He picked up the receiver and began to dial Denison's number.

"One more thing," Prentiss said, "can you ask Denison to arrange a press release that Colonel Mabbitt has died as the result of his injuries then have him discreetly moved to the infirmary at Templar."

"What for?"

"Two reasons. Firstly, it will stop any further attempts to kill him if Morse thinks the Colonel is already dead."

"Makes sense, and secondly?"

"If this Morse is as determined as you say he is, with Mabbitt gone and with only the two of us left, he's almost fulfilled his contract. Combine that with our little 'come and get me if you think you're hard enough' note, he'll be compelled to finish what he's started," Prentiss said assuredly, secretly relishing having to plot every move and counter move.

"You know something?" Jordan said as he waited to be connected to Colonel Denison. "You're wasted here. Mabbitt was right about you, you're a natural."

Colonel Denison agreed to help and suggested that they meet at a roadside café north of Chelmsford at four that afternoon so Jordan could give him the roll of film. Jordan was relieved that it meant he didn't have to leave Prentiss alone for more than a few hours.

The two men walked out to the car together. Jordan put his hand on Prentiss' shoulder. "Remember, Michael there's no reason for anyone to come here. Suspect anybody that does, whatever they look like. Don't take any chances. You do whatever you need to to stay alive, got it?"

"I've got it. Just get that film to Denison. I've a feeling that the fact Morse is an American has got more to do with Donald Boyle than someone that makes bombs for the IRA in Belfast."

"I should be back here by six," Jordan said getting into the car. "Stay sharp."

As Prentiss watched the Escort drive away he scanned the open ground one last time before going back inside the cottage. He took out his Beretta and weighed it in his hand. It was time to accept the situation and deal with it. The time for wishing Northern Ireland hadn't happened was past. He pulled back the slide to chamber a round and flicked on the safety. He was ready.

Chapter Eleven

Richard Jordan had only been driving for thirty minutes when he noticed that he had picked up a police car behind him. It stayed well back but was definitely keeping pace with him. Jordan overtook a couple of cars just to be certain. Sure enough, a few minutes later, there it was again closing the gap.

As he neared the little market town of Diss, Jordan watched carefully as a white Ford Granada appeared from a side road and tucked in behind the patrol car. For the next couple of miles, as the three car convoy continued towards Diss, Jordan watched in his rear view mirror as one of the two stone-faced officers in the patrol car was in constant radio contact with somebody. Almost certainly, Jordan guessed, one of the four men in the Granada. Some well meaning citizen in the crowd had obviously got the registration number at the B and B and given it to the plods, Jordan decided, and the white Granada was clearly the armed support. He took the roll of film from his jacket pocket and slipped it into his left sock.

The patrol car's blue lights and two tones came on as it made its move, drawing level with Jordan. Signalling for him to pull over, the patrol car pulled in front and began to slow as the Granada pulled up close behind. Jordan had little alternative than to comply and pulled over sandwiched between the patrol car and the Granada. The three cars had barely stopped moving as three armed men leapt from the car behind, weapons drawn, and surrounded Jordan's Escort.

Having been dragged out of his car, disarmed, arrested and bundled into the back of the police patrol car, Jordan was taken to Diss police station. The station buzzed with excitement as Jordan was brought in and put in a cell. The custody sergeant, more used to the itinerant labourers being brought in drunk and disorderly, peered through the cell door at his notorious prisoner.

Jordan looked at his watch impatiently as he sat at a table alone in a stark interview room. It was three-thirty; he had been in the small provincial police station and kept *incommunicado* for over an hour and a half. He was conscious of the fact that Colonel Denison would be at the rendezvous in less than thirty minutes. What concerned him even more was that the longer he was kept detained, the longer Prentiss would have to face Morse alone.

Ten minutes later the door opened and two familiar faces entered the interview room. Chief Inspector Gallagher and Sergeant Lyle pulled out the chairs opposite and sat down. Jordan forced a smile. "Well if it's not Simon and Garfunkel. No, I'm mistaken, it's Peters and Lee." Gallagher didn't respond to Jordan's sarcastic attempt at humour.

"Mister Jordan," Gallagher began, smoothing his long greying hair back with his palms.

"I prefer Sergeant Major," Jordan interjected still smiling. "I've had to work hard for my rank."

"Sergeant Major," Gallagher began again "You are in a great deal of trouble." Jordan looked at him innocently "Oh?" he replied.

"Can you tell me why you were found to be carrying a concealed handgun?"

"Chief Inspector, I have a constant carry authorisation. In my line of work it's not only advisable, it's necessary. You're more than welcome to check it with my unit." Jordan and Gallagher looked at each other intently. Then Jordan continued. "Let me save us some time here. You want to know why I was at a Bed and Breakfast in Cromer earlier today where the manager was found shot dead. Well, the truth is I wanted to get away for a few days. You know, take a quiet holiday. That business with the bomb I found in my car was all very upsetting. I was just about to check in to the B and B when I found this poor chap dead on the floor. Obviously I was shocked. I thought Cromer was a quiet little place but, to be honest, it was all a bit too rough for me so I decided to leave. Somebody has clearly got entirely the wrong idea and gone jumping to conclusions when they saw me leaving." There was silence in the room for a moment before Gallagher spoke.

"Can you smell that Sergeant?"

"Sir?" Lyle said, his arms folded.

"Unmistakable. I can smell bullshit a mile off. Now you listen to me..."

"No, you listen!" Jordan growled, leaning into Gallagher's face. "I'll tell you what's bullshit. Dragging me in here on some bloody stop under suspicion charge without a shred of evidence of me having committed any crime whatsoever. I didn't kill that unfortunate in Cromer and when your ballistics people dig the bullets out of him you'll see that they weren't fired from my gun."

"So why did you leave in such a hurry?"

"Because, you dickhead, I'm a covert army intelligence officer. Covert means not openly acknowledged or displayed."

"So?" Lyle said.

"So I don't reveal myself unless I really have to. I've found that I live longer that way."

Gallagher continued to question Jordan for a further hour but without success. Jordan had undergone extensive interrogation resistance training over the years involving standing in stress positions, exposure to white noise and prolonged beatings. If he could withstand all of that, there was nothing that a plod from the Special Branch could do or say to make him talk. Having failed miserably, Gallagher had Jordan taken back to his cell to stew, while he waited for the post mortem results on Colin Whittaker.

Harry Grant punched the air with delight as he turned off the television having watched the BBC six o'clock evening news. The newsreader had solemnly reported that the senior army officer, injured when a faulty generator exploded in Kent on Saturday morning, had died of his injuries. He jumped back onto the floral chintz sofa and put his feet up on the polished coffee table in front of it. Grant stretched his arms out then put his hands behind his head. The news of Mabbitt's death had raised his spirits from the dark sombre mood of earlier in the day. The two thirds of a bottle of malt whisky had also been quite instrumental in lifting his gloom.

He looked around the sitting room of the large detached house on the main road in the village of Sparham near Norwich. He had selected it because it was set well back from the road and almost completely hidden by large hedges and fruit trees. Grant had no idea who or how many lived at the house as he pulled up outside and lifted the fox's head black wrought iron knocker on the front door. Fortunately for him it was an elderly couple who had recently moved up from London to enjoy a quiet retirement in the country. They now lay motionless together on the tiled floor of the small boiler room located off the kitchen. Grant had herded them in and put a single bullet into each of them having first ascertained that they were alone in the house.

He looked up at the ticking clock on the mantle above the open brick fireplace. It was six thirty which meant it was one thirty in the afternoon in New York. As he poured himself another malt he rang Bannon at his office. With his usual arrogant self confidence he reported that everything was going well and fully expected to be completed by tomorrow. As Bannon praised Grant for his work thus far there was something in his voice, an inflection, a subtle change in his tone that made Grant feel uneasy. Although Grant had been discharged from the navy on medical grounds, having been diagnosed as a paranoid psychotic with sadistic tendencies following increasing incidents of torturing prisoners during combat operations, he was extremely intuitive, calculating and had an IQ far above average. Grant got the feeling that he was about to become not only expendable but a liability. He decided it was time he got a little life insurance for himself.

In his office in New York, Steve Bannon put down the receiver and looked across at Thomas Fisher. "We're almost there, Tom. By this time tomorrow there won't be anyone left alive that knows about your connection to Boyle's activities."

"And your man?"

"Like I said, there won't be anyone left alive," Bannon replied intently. Fisher smiled. "You've done well, Steve. I'm grateful to you." Fisher got up to leave.

"There is just one more thing, Tom. It's about Grace," Bannon said.

"What about Grace?"

"I'm concerned that she may potentially pose a problem."

"Why?" he asked coldly.

"She came to see me at my apartment, worried about your erratic and uncharacteristic behaviour. She seems to have linked it with overhearing our conversation when she heard the name Brad Mason. Then when he was reported dead in the newspapers a few days later she thought you might be mixed up in his murder somehow."

"Damn it!" Fisher said his eyes wide as he ran his fingers through his hair nervously. "What did you tell her?"

"I just told her that you asked me to talk to Mason to get some background on a case you were working on as I knew him and you didn't."

"Did she buy it?"

"Maybe; for now. There may come a time when we need to be sure," Bannon said. Fisher looked at him, swallowing hard.

"Grace is not going to be a problem. You don't need to concern yourself with her."

"That's good to hear, Tom, because I like Grace, really I do. But it does become my concern if she starts looking into my connection to Mason's death. So you'd better make sure she just forgets about it or I might have to review the situation. And that really would be a shame, wouldn't it?" Bannon said menacingly.

"I'll take care of it."

"Make sure you do. And for God's sake pull yourself together. Relax a little. We're nearly there. Just hold your nerve a little longer and you'll have everything you want." Fisher nodded as Bannon showed him to the door.

Once he was alone Bannon dialled the long international telephone number to one of the more downbeat hotels in London's Bayswater. Asking to be put through to Mister Kitter, Bannon waited as the receptionist connected him with the man's room. It only rang twice before he heard Kitter answer.

"It's almost time for you to take care of that awkward problem we discussed, Mister Kitter. Stay by the phone, I'll be in touch soon."

Harry Grant took out the scrap of paper he had carried with him since he had arrived in England. On it was written a name he had found in the Operation Ares file, and a telephone number. Grant was a great believer in tactical advantage. Never accepting anything or anyone at face value, he constantly sought anything that may give him an edge either at that moment or at some point at a later date.

It was with this in mind, as he had waited at Heathrow for his flight home following the burglary at the Mabbitt residence, he had spent the four hours carefully reading the stolen file. The contents were clearly valuable and not just to whoever had paid Bannon to acquire it. As Grant strolled around the airport he thought deeply about what he had read. How useful, he considered, the information this file contained may prove in the future. Thirty minutes later Grant had emerged from a photography shop having had the entire file photocopied.

Once back in New York, and having accepted Bannon's assassination list, Grant had sat in his apartment cross referencing the first four profiles of the six with his secretly photocopied Ares file trying to get an insight as to who would want these six people dead in such a hurry.

As he studied the plethora of information it was one name, a single brief reference in the original Ares file that stood out. Calling in a few favours from some of his numerous underworld contacts, Grant was able to get a location for the name and obtain a telephone number for him.

Now as he sat on the chintz sofa looking at the scrap of paper and finishing the last of the cold chicken he had found in his search of the refrigerator, Grant decided that the time had come. It was just before nine fifteen and the sun was setting behind the fruit trees at the front of the house. Licking the grease off his fingers he reached over and turned on the large table lamp then dialled the number and waited. A woman answered. In a polite, cheerful voice Grant asked to speak to Niall.

By nine thirty Grant was pouring himself a third very large cognac from a Waterford crystal decanter into a huge brandy balloon. His conversation with the man, who up until fifteen minutes ago had only been a name in an operation file, had gone exactly as he had envisaged. Giving him just enough information to whet his appetite, Grant had arranged for Niall to come to the house in Sparham the following morning at eleven. His self-satisfied smile disappeared as his thoughts turned from his conversation with Niall to that of Steve Bannon. He felt more disappointed than angry that, if his suspicions about Bannon were correct, someone would be coming to kill him in the next few days. Although it made perfect sense to assassinate the assassin, Grant had always held Bannon in high regard, thinking of him not as a friend but certainly more than just an employer. He felt aggrieved that he should be considered just as expendable as someone with a fraction of his expertise.

Grant drained the balloon and tossed it into the open fireplace resolving to attend to Mister Bannon's betrayal in the fullness of time. His prime concern was Jordan and Prentiss. First though he needed some sleep. The brandy was beginning to make him feel groggy as he laid his head down on the sofa arm. Tomorrow was going to be a busy day Grant thought, as he gave in to the effects of the alcohol and drifted off to sleep.

A few miles away in a cell in Diss police station, Richard Jordan lay on the padded bunk staring at the ceiling. He had been held for over six hours by Chief Inspector Gallagher under the special powers terrorism act and had not been permitted to make contact with anyone. Jordan knew that they hadn't got anything other than circumstantial evidence connecting him to the B and B manager's murder. It was only a matter of time before forensics proved the bullets that killed him didn't come from his gun. Unfortunately time was the one thing that Jordan didn't have. He had failed to keep his rendezvous with Colonel Denison who presumably now assumed he was dead. And then there was Michael. For all he knew Morse could have already killed him by now. He punched the wall with the side of his fist in frustration. Special Branch coppers, Jordan seethed, were just like trench-foot, got in the way while trying to do your job and smelled bloody awful on a hot day. He had to get out. For the moment though he had no choice. All he could do was wait.

Chapter Twelve

As Grant studied the map of the area around Bacton deciding how best to approach the cliff side cottage, there was a knock at the door and an unexpected opportunity presented itself. As Grant opened the door a uniformed postman stood before him clutching a package. His cheerful smiley expression changed to one of curious surprise as he saw Grant in the doorway. Before he could ask where Ted and Joan were, Grant swiftly and unemotionally produced his silenced .45 automatic from behind his back and shot him in the forehead. The single shot propelled the postman backwards, falling like a felled tree onto the driveway beside his van. Grant looked around to see if he had attracted any attention but, as it was only just after seven in the morning, the road beyond the fruit trees was quiet.

Taking him by the ankles, Grant pulled the dead man into the house and kicked the door shut. First removing the dead man's uniform jacket, Grant carried the body and put it in the boiler room with those of the elderly couple. He squeezed his big frame into the jacket and hat and, stuffing the gun into his front waistband, picked up the map and left the house.

Tossing the hat onto the passenger seat he climbed into the bright red Royal Mail Morris Ital postal delivery van. The roads were quiet as Grant drove the van steadily for half an hour the twenty miles to the cottage. He slowed as he caught sight of the remote brick and flint house across the fields, stopping just before the turn. He studied it carefully. There was no movement either outside the building or at any of the windows. There were no vehicles visible or a garage to conceal one. The open ground between the road and the cottage was empty and Grant couldn't see anybody hiding in it.

He looked at his watch, seven thirty-five. He put on the grey cap, pulled the peak of it down to just above his eyes and, taking out the silenced .45 automatic and resting it on his lap, turned onto the single track that led to the cottage.

He drove slowly, constantly watching the cottage for signs of movement as he hummed quietly to himself.

From his upstairs observation point, Prentiss watched the van approach through the binoculars. He was almost relieved that at last there was something to break the seemingly endless tedium of inactivity. He had barely slept, catching the occasional few minutes periodically through the night then waking with a start at the slightest sound. When Jordan hadn't returned by ten o'clock the previous evening Prentiss had telephoned Colonel Denison at Ashford who, having waited for two hours, confirmed that Jordan hadn't shown up at the rendezvous and feared the worst.

As the Royal Mail van approached, Prentiss began to feel the adrenalin surging through his body. After almost forty-eight hours without sleep it was good to feel re-energised rather than having a constant headache and the sensation of wading through treacle. He focused the binoculars on the driver.

"You look legitimate enough," Prentiss said to himself. "But why are you making a delivery to a woman who's been dead for several weeks?" Prentiss knew that it was usual practice for the solicitors to put a stop on all mail to the deceased's residence. He put down the binoculars and picked up the Armalite. The tingling up the back of his neck told him this was no postman.

In Diss police station Jordan's cell door swung open and the custody sergeant stepped in. "You're free to go," he said bluntly. Jordan got to his feet.

"About bloody time." He pushed past the sergeant and into the corridor where Gallagher was waiting for him.

"Forensics put you in the clear as far as the B and B manager is concerned so you can leave, for now. I don't know how or what you're mixed up in, Mister Jordan, but be assured I've got my eye on you."

"How reassuring. Now with your permission, or without," he said contemptuously, "I need to make a phone call." Jordan barged Gallagher out of the way as the custody sergeant followed him hastily down the corridor. "You," he barked at the sergeant, "take me to a telephone, now!"

At the cliff side cottage, the Royal Mail van had stopped some twenty feet from the front of the house. Prentiss took a deep breath and threw open the front door. Crouching in the doorway, he pointed his rifle at the van. The driver had got out and the double doors at the back of the van were open. With the doors open, Prentiss couldn't see behind the vehicle. Keeping his gun trained on the van he slowly started moving towards it. Cautiously, he looked through the windscreen and through to the open back doors. There was no sign of the postman. His finger hovered over the trigger as Prentiss tentatively walked round to the rear. There was nobody there. He swore under his breath. He must have got into the house somehow, Prentiss thought.

Warily, Prentiss went back into the cottage. His throat was dry and his heart beating against his chest. He hesitated outside the living room then eased the door open with his foot. As Prentiss entered, his rifle raised, the telephone started ringing. Distracted momentarily by the unexpected and recurring noise, he was unaware of Grant emerging silently from the kitchen behind him. Having rapidly scanned the room and confident that it was empty, Prentiss turned to go back into the hallway. He had barely moved when he felt a sharp heavy pain to the side of his neck. Prentiss' legs buckled and he crumpled to the floor. "Amateur," Grant said as he picked up the Armalite and, stepping over the unconscious Prentiss, crossed to the phone. Throwing the rifle onto the sofa he picked up the receiver and listened.

In Diss police station Jordan's relief quickly turned to unease as there was no reply when he asked, "Michael, are you okay?" He could hear the calm, controlled breathing on the open line. "Who is this?" Jordan finally asked coldly. Again, there was no reply. "Have you killed him?" Jordan asked, praying he wouldn't hear the inevitable answer.

"He's alive, at least for the moment," Grant replied in his strong New York accent as he glanced over at Prentiss lying unconscious in the doorway.

"Mister Morse, I presume," Jordan said.

"Yes, Mister Jordan. It is Richard Jordan isn't it?"

"Yes, I'm Jordan."

"I'll bet it was you in my hotel room yesterday, wasn't it? Yes of course it was. Sorry about the wardrobe, no hard feelings I hope?"

"What do you want?"

"There's something I want you to do for me. It shouldn't be too difficult for a soldier with your experience."

"What?"

"I'll let you know. Come back here and wait. Don't do anything cute, Richard. Not if you want to see Mister Prentiss again, alive."

"Why should I? You're going to kill us both anyway."

"Let's just say that my priorities have changed. Killing you and Mister Prentiss is no longer my prime concern. I'll be in touch." Grant replaced the receiver taking a note of the telephone number as he did so.

In the small office in Diss police station, Jordan checked his belongings with the custody sergeant and signed to say it was all correct. Chief Inspector Gallagher entered holding Jordan's Browning automatic.

"I suppose you'll be wanting this back?" Jordan held out his hand to take it but Gallagher withdrew the gun sharply. "This isn't finished, Mister Jordan. I don't like bombs in cars and dead bodies in Norfolk hotels. Nor do I like secret soldiers who carry concealed weapons. Trouble seems to follow you around, doesn't it? And I'm going to make it my business to find out why." Gallagher slapped the gun into Jordan's outstretched hand. Jordan didn't respond but simply left the room. He was too tired and had more important things to think about than to waste any more time talking to a thick frustrated policeman.

Michael Prentiss came to, being jolted amongst assorted packages and mail bags in the back of the Post

95

Office van. His wrists and ankles were bound tightly with
parcel string, cutting off the circulation to his hands behind
his back and causing them to swell and burn. As the
dizziness subsided and his eyes focused once again, Prentiss
looked up at the tanned bull neck and short jet black hair of
his captor behind the wheel. From the way his frame filled
the driving seat Prentiss could see that this was a formidable
enemy. The way he had silently and so easily overpowered
him was proof of that. Grant had angled the rear view mirror
so he could see Prentiss in the back and impassively watched
him struggle in vain to free his hands.

"Where are you taking me?" Prentiss asked. Grant
didn't answer. "I thought you just wanted me dead?!" he
shouted, looking at the pair of eyes staring back at him. The
van lurched sharply to the left and came to a stop. Grant got
out and Prentiss was left alone in the back of the van. He
rolled onto his back and waited for the rear doors to open,
planning to kick out with his tethered feet. The sounds of the
footsteps however, were walking away becoming fainter and
fainter, then nothing.

Prentiss looked about him. He had to find something
to free his hands. Unlike in the films he had seen, there were
no convenient sharp edges he could use to cut through the
string. There was however a packet of Marlboro cigarettes
and a battered Zippo lighter on the dashboard. Any thoughts,
no matter how impossible, of somehow reaching the lighter
and burning through the string were short-lived as he heard
the footsteps returning. Prentiss resumed his position ready
to strike out. The doors opened, Grant, anticipating such a
move, immediately stepped back a couple of paces safely
avoiding Prentiss' futile kick. Leaning into the van Grant
grabbed the front of Prentiss' shirt with his left hand pulling
him up, and punched him hard in the face with his right.
Prentiss felt a moment of searing pain then blackness.

"You're proving to be a real disappointment," Grant
said in a condescending voice as Prentiss regained
consciousness a few minutes later. "I thought you were going
to give me real trouble. I mean, I've read your file. Four years
ago you killed three men without mercy. One of them you

drowned in his kitchen sink after you'd been tortured with a power drill!" Grant said incredulously. "I was expecting some stone cold killer, but just look at you. My Grandmother could take you and she's in a wheelchair for Christ sake."

"I'm a bit out of practice but I'm sure it will all come back to me when I kill you," Prentiss said glaring at him disdainfully. He was lying on the chintz sofa in the Sparham house, his hands and feet still bound. Thick blood poured from his nose and tasted sweet in his mouth. He spat it out and pressed his face to a cushion wiping most of the blood away.

Grant laughed. "Save it boy. Whatever you were you ain't no more." He got up and grabbing Prentiss under the arms pulled him off the sofa and dragged him into the boiler room. "Now if you'll excuse me I need some privacy as I've got a few phone calls to make before my guest arrives." He dropped Prentiss next to the bodies of the elderly couple and the postman. "You just lay there and bleed quietly." As Grant closed the door he laughed. "It must be just like being back at work with all these dead people around."

A few minutes later the phone rang in the cliff side cottage near Bacton. Jordan had just arrived having first telephoned Colonel Denison from outside Diss police station. He had requested that the Colonel send someone from the intelligence section from the nearby Royal Anglian Regiment Headquarters in Bury St Edmunds to collect the roll of film. Forty minutes later a green army motorcycle arrived ridden by a soldier wearing combat dress. Confirming the corporal's orders to deliver it to Templar Barracks, Jordan had handed the film over to him.

"Ah, Mister Jordan. I'm glad to see you made it back safely," Grant said brightly as Jordan answered the phone. "Now listen carefully, there's something that I want you to do for me."

"How do I know that Prentiss is still alive?"

"Oh he's just fine. I've introduced him to a few friends I've met here. They're a bit quiet; you know how stiff you Brits can be?"

"I want proof."

"All in good time. First I'm going to give you some instructions which you will carry out precisely. I want you to check into the Savoy hotel in London under the name of David Morse, go to your room and wait."

"Wait for what?"

"For the person that's going to try and kill you. Once you have taken care of them for me I'll contact you as to where to find Michael."

"Let me speak to him, now!" Jordan demanded. Grant picked up the phone, the cable just long enough to reach the boiler room door.

"Michael, Richard wants to say hi," Grant said holding the receiver towards Prentiss.

"Piss off!" Prentiss shouted. Grant laughed and spoke to Jordan.

"Did you get that, Richard? I'm afraid Michael isn't feeling very, how do you Brits say, chatty at the moment? It's ten fifteen now, I want you checked in and relaxing in your room by one." Grant hung up before Jordan could reply. Jordan swore under his breath. Less than three hours to get to central London. He gathered his things together, got back in his car and sped away from the cliff side cottage and headed south for London.

While Grant was busy on the phone Prentiss was searching the dead postman's trouser pockets. A particularly difficult task as his hands were still tied behind his back and made even more so as he had all but lost the feeling in his fingers. The search proved fruitless. Then he noticed a small pair of scissors hanging on a nail on the wall next to the boiler. It was among a number of gardening tools; a trowel, hand fork and a ball of garden twine. Prentiss struggled to his feet using the postman's body for support and, raising his arms as high as he could behind him, took the scissors off the nail. Manoeuvring the blades into position over the string took a few minutes. He grimaced with the pain as he tried to move his fingers, but that was nothing compared to the pain Prentiss felt when he finally cut through the string. He dropped the scissors as the blood surged back into his hands. With no time to wait for the pain to subside, Prentiss freed his ankles. Putting the scissors into his pocket he grabbed the hand fork from the wall. He was now armed. It wasn't much but it was a start.

Sat on the chintz sofa in the sitting room, Grant had woken Steve Bannon with his phone call. It was almost five thirty in the morning in his Concord apartment when he had blearily answered the phone.

"It's done," Grant said in a monotone voice. Bannon sat up in bed and began to congratulate him on a job well done. "I want the rest of my money transferred as we agreed."

"It'll be done as soon as the banks open at nine," Bannon said. "Are you coming straight back?" Grant raised an eyebrow at the seemingly innocent question.

"No, I thought I'd spend a few days having some R and R at the Savoy in London. It's been a busy kinda week." As Bannon went on to say how much he thought that was a good idea, Prentiss quietly opened the boiler room door. From across the hallway he could hear the American's voice.

"And Mister Bannon, I'll be checking my account this afternoon at two. I hope I won't be disappointed." Prentiss heard the ting of Grant replacing the receiver as he stepped out into the hallway. He had only taken a couple of steps when he heard a loud knocking at the front door. He ran down the hallway away from the sitting room and up the stairs as Grant walked to the front door and opened it.

From the landing Prentiss could hear Grant and another male voice move into the sitting room. Armed with only a garden hand fork, Prentiss decided that discretion was the better part of valour and that it was time to leave. He quickly moved into a front bedroom and opened the window. Swinging out onto the drain pipe he began to slide down. As he did so the rusting brackets holding the pipe to the wall broke away. Prentiss fell to the ground landing on his shoulder leaving the drain pipe swinging precariously at forty five degrees from the house.

Prentiss lay on the drive for a moment, the breath knocked out of him. As he staggered to his feet Grant's powerful arms grabbed Prentiss' from behind and held him securely. Grant spun Prentiss round until he was facing a man in his fifties with receding grey curly hair. There was something vaguely familiar about him but Prentiss was certain he had never met him before.

"Michael, don't run off. There's someone here who has been wanting to meet you for a long time," Grant said playfully in Prentiss' ear. The man's granite face moved closer to Prentiss' and stared deep into his eyes and, in a harsh Belfast accent, said, "My name's Niall Donnelly. I think you knew my little brother, Liam."

Chapter Thirteen

Steve Bannon waited until seven thirty that morning before ringing Thomas Fisher at home. As Fisher sat on the edge of the bed to take the call, Grace watched her husband's face become more relaxed than she had seen in weeks. There was a tangible sense of relief in his tone and posture. It was as if a dark shadow that had concealed his true character all these weeks had now been lifted, revealing once again the man she had fallen in love with.

He put down the phone and ran round the bed and kissed Grace passionately. "I love you," he said grinning with excitement like a small boy.

"What's happened? Who was that?" she asked, smiling at Fisher's infectious mood.

"That, honey was the call I've been hoping for. I have just been informed that a contract I've been waiting for has been completed."

"What sort of contract?"

"What?" Fisher checked his excitement. In his exuberance he had said more than was advisable.

"What sort of contract was it?" Grace said again.

"Just something to do with a case I've got on at the moment. It's been proving to be a rather difficult one."

"Is this the same case that involved that man who was murdered, Brad Mason?" She asked. Fisher got up from the bed and walked towards the door saying innocently, "Yes, that's right." He then quickly changed the subject. "I'm going to grab a quick shower before I go in to the office, do you want to join me?" He smiled playfully.

"I'll be there in a minute," Grace said. As she watched Fisher go through to the bathroom an uneasy feeling gripped her stomach. She was wrong, his dark shadow was still there and it frightened her to think what it might really be concealing.

As Steve Bannon finished his conversation with Fisher he immediately started dialling the international number to England. It was a short conversation lasting less than a minute. Arnold Kitter was a foot soldier: a mindless thug whose sole talent was for intimidation and violence. Bannon had found him three weeks earlier, fresh out of Sing Sing having just finished a three year stretch for armed assault and demanding money with menaces. At just over fifty, Kitter had spent thirty years of his miserable life behind bars having neither the wit nor the perception to not get caught.

Bannon always knew that Grant would have to be killed once he had completed his assignment. After all, he knew too much. Once he had accepted the job he had become a problem that required a permanent solution. It was a pity. Grant had been a valuable employee having successfully carried out some extremely difficult and unsavoury jobs. It was, therefore, with a little regret that Bannon was sacrificing his best man. But this was business and, sadly for Grant, there was no room for sentiment in business.

Bannon had sent Kitter to London the day after Grant had killed Caroline Rawlins with orders to book into a small hotel and wait for instructions. Only too delighted to make ten thousand dollars for killing some poor schmuck, Kitter gratefully accepted Bannon's job offer.

It was twelve forty-five when Kitter left his Bayswater hotel and took a black cab to the Strand, arriving at the Savoy hotel a little before one. Just minutes before, Richard Jordan had checked in as instructed under the name of David Morse and been shown to his room on the fourth floor.

Kitter walked through the front hall open mouthed at the opulence surrounding him, from the artwork on the walls to the black and white chequerboard marble floor. Approaching the reception desk he took a small white envelope from his jacket pocket. The young blond man behind the desk watched him approach.

"How may we help you, sir?" he said in a rather officious and superior tone as he looked Kitter up and down.

"I wanna leave this for Mister David Morse," Kitter said handing over the envelope.

"Any message, sir?"

"No, no message, just that." He nodded towards the envelope. He watched as the pompous young man turned and slipped it into one of the pigeon holes in the rack behind him. Number Four-One-Two; that was all he needed. Kitter walked across to the elevators and went up to the fourth floor. Alone in the elevator he took the .357 magnum revolver from the leather shoulder holster concealed beneath his jacket. He smiled at himself in the full length mirror as he checked the cylinder was fully loaded then replaced the gun, adjusting his jacket slightly to reduce any sign of a bulge.

Reaching the fourth floor, the doors parted with a 'ding' and Kitter got out and padded down the beautifully carpeted corridor. This was going to be the easiest ten grand he had ever made, he thought to himself. Maybe things were starting to look up for him. Standing outside Four-One-Two he looked up and down the empty corridor then pulled out the revolver and held it under his jacket at waist level.

As Kitter rapped on the door he cocked the hammer of the revolver. His plan was simple. Two slugs to the chest as soon as the door opens then beat it. He waited but there was no reply. He knocked again, harder this time. As he did so he felt a sharp pain as Jordan's gun butt struck the back of his head. Having picked the lock and lay in wait, Jordan had quietly emerged from the empty room opposite.

Snatching the gun from the reeling American, Jordan opened the door and pushed him inside. As Kitter lay on the floor clutching his aching head, Jordan closed the door, his Browning automatic trained on the sprawled thug. "Right, sunshine," he said, "it's time we had a little chat."

"How did you know I was coming?"

"It never ceases to amaze me what a hotel receptionist will do for twenty quid, even in a place like this. I just had him ring up if anyone came looking for me. So, you've been sent here to kill a man called David Morse, right?"

"I've got nothing to say to you," Kitter sneered.

"You listen to me, sunshine. I haven't got a lot of time so don't mess me about. Now, who sent you?"

"I don't remember," he said defiantly.

"Something tells me that you're not exactly a novice when it comes to this type of thing. So you've got a good idea how this works. You know that this is going to end very badly for you unless you answer my questions. Who sent you to kill Morse?"

"You mean you ain't Morse?"

"That's right, but he's got a friend of mine," Jordan leant forward menacingly, "and I want him back." Kitter stared obstinately back at Jordan.

"Okay," Jordan said with a resigned tone, sighing hard. "If that's how you want it." He took Kitter's revolver and looked at it. "Snub-nose Smith and Wesson .357 Magnum." He smiled approvingly. "Do you know just the shock of a magnum bullet impacting on a human body can kill?" Kitter didn't reply. "Of course you do. You've used one of these before; you know exactly what it can do, don't you?"

Jordan picked up a cushion from a chair close-by and squatted down in front of Kitter. "I was in Dhofar a few years ago and I saw a bloke use one of these things on a prisoner he was interrogating. Very unpleasant. Kept shooting bits off him. There was blood everywhere. The prisoner talked of course. Everybody talks in the end. He talked and then he died. I can still hear him screaming now." Jordan said matter of factly. Beads of perspiration began to form on Kitter's brow.

"I don't know nothing." He said nervously.

"Oh, I think you do, despite the double negative," Jordan said coldly. "In my job you get to know your way around a man's anatomy. For instance," Jordan prodded the revolver's short barrel into the top of Kitter's thigh, "just here is the Femoral artery. If that ruptures you will bleed to death in less than three minutes. So you can just imagine what's going to happen to you if I put one of your wadcutter bullets through it." Jordan's face was grey. "So let's start again. Who sent you?"

"I can't," Kitter said. Jordan slammed the cushion onto Kitter's leg and pressed the magnum into it.

"Son, I really don't have the time for this!" He cocked the revolver and pressed down hard.

"Alright! Alright!" screamed Kitter "Steve Bannon, it was Steve Bannon!" For the next five minutes Kitter blurted out everything he knew about Bannon and his consultancy company. Once satisfied that he had told him everything, Jordan left having knocked Kitter unconscious with a single blow to the back of the neck. Wiping the revolver of his fingerprints, he left the gun on the floor. An anonymous call to the police as he left the hotel would ensure Kitter wouldn't cause him any further problems.

"You're looking better, my dear fellow. You had us all worried there for a little while," Colonel Denison said as he entered the private room in the infirmary at Templar Barracks. Charles Mabbitt, his head heavily bandaged, lay in bed propped up with three large white pillows.

"I understand that I have, in fact, died," he said brightly, raising his eyebrows, wincing as he did so. The left hand side of his face was badly bruised. From his cheek to his forehead was a solid mass of green and yellow swelling.

"Yes I'm sorry about that, Charles. That was your Sarn't Major Jordan's idea. Seemed to think it was necessary," Denison replied pulling up a chair next to the bed.

"And where is the errant Mister Jordan now?"

"Good question." Denison's brow furrowed. "He made contact this morning having been detained by the Special Branch in Norfolk overnight but I haven't heard from him since."

"And Michael Prentiss? What of him?"

"He telephoned me last night from some remote cottage near Cromer where he and Jordan had been hiding out, but he appears to be missing as well."

"Do we have any idea as to where they are or, dare I ask, what they are doing?" Mabbitt asked impatiently.

"Just these." Denison took a large brown envelope from his briefcase and slid out some enlarged photographs. He handed them to Mabbitt explaining that Jordan had taken them in Cromer believing the subject to be the assassin.

Mabbitt looked at the three prints of Grant carefully, studying the face of the man that had tried to kill him. "Who is he?"

"We don't know yet. Jordan says he's an American travelling under the name David Morse, but so far a face is all we've got."

"Right," said Mabbitt decisively, "I want you to wire copies of this over to Nigel Dickinson at Aldergrove."

"Anything else?"

"Yes, get me a telephone set up in here. Those two have been out in the cold on their own far too long. I think it's time they had a little help."

"Can you do that? Use the unit for something like this, I mean? Strictly speaking you should hand all this over to Special Branch."

Mabbitt looked at Denison with a twinkle in his eye. "My dear chap, what is the point of commanding a clandestine unit if, on occasion, one can't use it to be a little mischievous? Anyway, I take it you've met Gallagher. Personally I wouldn't trust him to be able to find his own backside with both hands in a brightly lit room." Denison smiled and turned to leave. "And get young Parkes in here. He can start co-ordinating things while the quacks insist that I remain in bed. If nothing else at least he can organise a decent cup of coffee. I'm sure the stuff they're serving up in here is sourced from the ablution block."

"I was going to ask you if you were sure you were up to all this, but I don't think I'll bother."

Richard Jordan had walked out of the hotel and round the corner to a public phone box. As he dialled Templar Barracks two police cars with lights flashing and sirens wailing screeched passed him and pulled up outside the Savoy. Having told the switchboard operator who he was he waited to be connected with Colonel Denison, he was more than a little surprised therefore when it was Colonel Mabbitt's voice that came on the line.

"Richard, where are you?" barked Mabbitt. Jordan explained the sequence of events that had led him to that point.

"The man employing the monkey I've just left unconscious in the hotel room, and presumably our friend, David Morse, is a Yank by the name of Steve Bannon. Runs Bannon Strategic Solutions, a security consultancy firm out of New York."

"Mister Morse is clearly nobody's fool," Mabbitt said holding his aching face. "He has obviously anticipated that this Bannon would send somebody to have him eliminated once he had killed everyone on the list. If your unconscious friend had succeeded just now he would have reported back to Bannon who would understandably believe that Morse was dead."

"So what are we going to do about Prentiss, Colonel? Morse has got him somewhere and I haven't got a clue as to how I'm going to find him."

"Sadly I'm afraid that we must assume that Michael is dead, at least for the moment. Morse has no reason to keep him alive and, as he expected you to be killed in that hotel room, certainly would have had no intention of releasing him to you. Without any current leads, if Michael is still alive, he's very much on his own."

Jordan fell silent for a moment. "What do you want me to do?"

"Come back here. There's nothing more you can do there. Hopefully by the time you arrive I'll have some information on Morse from those holiday snaps you took in Cromer and I'll have Mister Parkes work up a profile of this Steve Bannon."

"Yes, Sir," Jordan said quietly. Mabbitt could hear the frustration in Jordan's voice.

"Don't blame yourself, Richard. I'm sure you did all you could to protect Michael. But I wouldn't write him off just yet. He's not going to give up without a fight. He's too bloody-minded for that."

"It's Londonderry all over again isn't it?"

"And he got through it," reassured Mabbitt. "Now get yourself back here. We're about to go on the offensive."

Chapter Fourteen

Having taken a couple of hard punches to the stomach and with his hands tied in front of him with butchery string, Michael Prentiss was thrown into the back of a refrigerated butcher's transit van by Donnelly and Grant. He was then driven south to central London. Once the rear double doors were slammed shut he was plunged into pitch darkness inside the back of the van. Although empty except for a few steel meat hooks hanging from a central ceiling pole, the smell of raw meat was overwhelming. The only sound was the gentle hum of the refrigerated unit located at the centre of the cab wall close to the roof blowing out ice-cold air.

Donnelly had said nothing to him before they began their journey. He had just looked at Prentiss with contempt and then given him a fast one, two with the speed and technique of a professional boxer. Prentiss kept himself fit but the two blows, one to the solar plexus and the other just under his ribcage, brought him to his knees gasping for air.

Prentiss lay in the darkness shivering uncontrollably as the temperature began to drop. He attempted repeatedly to get to his feet but as the van careered through the Norfolk country lanes he was sent crashing into the steel lined van sides, first one way then another. Finally Prentiss crawled, feeling his way in the darkness, to a corner and curled up tightly. The only advantage of the numbing cold was that he could no longer feel the deep contusions in his wrists caused by the tightly bound string. He had never felt so cold. His throat burned as he swallowed and his limbs were set fast, no longer able to move. Sleep began to creep over him. Prentiss was overcome with the combination of the severe cold and days of being alert without rest. He knew he had to stay awake. Hypothermia was a real danger now. Prentiss was aware that he was exhibiting many of the symptoms; slow shallow breathing, increasing difficulty in concentration and acute lethargy. All he could do was to try and hang on and hope that they would reach their destination soon.

It was almost three hours before the rear doors were flung open. Prentiss opened his eyes a fraction as the light poured in. By now he was almost unconscious and was barely aware of being hauled out of the van by two men and taken across a small enclosed brick courtyard and into a meat store. His feet left two tracks on the sawdust floor as Prentiss' inanimate body was dragged face down across to one of the meat hooks suspended from the ceiling. Donnelly lifted him from the waist while the second man put the hook between Prentiss' wrists suspending him by the string. As Donnelly let him go and Prentiss was left hanging by the wrists the searing pain of his bodyweight causing his bonds to cut deeper into his already seriously injured flesh quickly brought him to a semi-conscious state.

Donnelly looked at Prentiss as he hung there like just another piece of raw meat amongst the sides of pork and beef that were suspended from meat hooks in the small store. Donnelly smiled a self satisfied smile. "Take the van, Freddy," he said to the second man without looking away from Prentiss. "And get down to the meat market and pick up a couple of lambs. We need them for chops, we're right out." The second man muttered an acknowledgement and left. Prentiss squinted as he tried to focus on Donnelly standing in front of him.

"Why don't you just kill me and have done with it?" Prentiss said weakly. Donnelly laughed with his eyes wide.

"Oh no, Mister Prentiss we're going to spend the next few days getting to know just how much pain you can take. I'm not going to kill you today, tomorrow or even the day after that. By the time I'm finished with you I promise you'll be begging for me to kill you for what you did to my wee brother. You just think on that for a while, Michael. I'll leave you to get settled in and make yourself comfortable." Prentiss closed his eyes and tried to ignore the pain as Donnelly left the store, shutting and bolting the door as he went.

Niall Donnelly had been a butcher in Clerkenwell for almost twenty-five years. He had moved to London from Belfast with the proceeds of a bank robbery in Newry,

County Down. Now, at fifty years of age, he was an established and well liked member of the local community. Playing on his public persona of the cheerful jolly Irishman he had built up a thriving business. His shop was located in the centre of town in a prominent position just off the High Street. The meat store was across a small Victorian courtyard behind the shop accessed by an adjacent side alley.

Physically he was big. Standing just shy of six feet three and weighing two hundred and fifty pounds, he had a large bald head with a long face permanently covered in untidy stubble. His grey eyes sparkled constantly in a roguish, playful manner that belied his true nature. Donnelly had a reputation for being someone not to be crossed. He had a cruel and sadistic side to his character and relished inflicting pain on those unfortunate enough to invoke his wrath.

Four years earlier he had stood by his brother's open grave in Londonderry and sworn vengeance on whoever had murdered him. When the phone had rung therefore and an unknown American voice had offered Liam's murderer, wanting nothing in return, Donnelly found the opportunity irresistible. Now he'd got him and four years of hatred and rage could be meted out on the young man strung up like a piece of meat in his store. He was going to enjoy making him suffer. Finally he could take his revenge for his brother and he was going to make sure that he savoured every minute of it.

It was almost four o'clock that afternoon when the bolt to the meat store was drawn back as Donnelly returned. As Prentiss hung helplessly, his feet some six inches off the floor, he rested his head on his right shoulder and upper arm. He opened his bloodshot eyes as Donnelly closed the door behind him.

"I'm sorry you've been kept hanging around, Michael. You don't mind if I call you Michael, do you?" Donnelly said glibly. "I've waited a long time to meet you." He looked up at Prentiss' wrists and winced. "Now they look as if they're smarting a little. Still shouldn't bother a hard man like yourself. You being a military assassin and all." Prentiss stared at him impassively.

Donnelly took a blue and white butcher's apron from a hook on the wall and put it on. He crossed to a long wooden table that was covered in all manner of butchery tools. "I want to introduce you to the tools of my trade," he said brightly picking up a large saw. "Take this, for instance," he said holding it up. "This is a twenty inch meat and bone saw." Donnelly held it up to Prentiss' face before replacing it on the table. "You'll become better acquainted with that in a few days. Then there's this," he said triumphantly, holding up what resembled a small axe. "This is a double-edged meat cleaver. It'll cut through just about anything." Once again he returned it to its position on the table.

Prentiss slowly turned his head and looked at the meat hanging around him then looking back to Donnelly said, "Any chance of a bacon sandwich? I haven't eaten for ages." Donnelly stared for a moment then threw his head back and laughed uproariously.

"Excellent!" he bellowed. "This is going to be more enjoyable than I could have imagined. I thought you were going to be a snivelling little shite begging for his life but no, you've still got some fight left in you, haven't you? Good!" Donnelly clapped his hands and rubbed them together in anticipation.

"I'm so glad I haven't disappointed you," Prentiss replied sarcastically.

"Oh I don't think you're going to do that, Michael. In fact, I'm sure of it." Donnelly walked along to the end of the table and picked up a long steel tubular spike by its worn wooden handle. "This is what I wanted to introduce you to first. It's an eighteen inch larding tube although the word tube doesn't really do it justice. It's really a hollow needle, or spike if you will, and it's designed to inject lard into the meat." He held it up in front of Prentiss' eyes and ran the tips of his fingers up and down its length. "Beautiful isn't it?"

"I use something similar for embalming called a trocar."

"Yes of course you're an undertaker now aren't you? Ah well you've probably got some idea as to what's going to happen to you then. Just so there's no misunderstanding I'll tell you anyway." Donnelly's tone changed. It was now hard and vicious. "I'm going to push the spike through your abdomen and inject the lard into your stomach. And when I've done that I'm going to do it again and again." Donnelly allowed himself a smile. "I wouldn't be much of a host if I let you go hungry now would I?"

As Donnelly loaded the lard tube a real sense of fear gripped Prentiss. Nobody knew he was there and therefore there was no chance of anybody coming to save him. He considered his options as Donnelly approached him. There was no way he could fend off the big Irishman from his present position let alone overpower him. Donnelly ripped open Prentiss' shirt exposing his torso already bruised from the earlier punches. Donnelly lifted the spike and pressed it to Prentiss' skin just above the navel. Prentiss struggled to control his breathing as Donnelly taunted him by applying just enough pressure to the spike to prevent the tip piercing the skin.

"Now don't be shy, Michael. You can scream as much as you like there's nobody around to hear you. Just in case, I think we'll have a little background noise. He switched on a radio on the corner of the table and turned up the volume. As the sound of thumping rock music filled the room Donnelly drew the long spike back a few inches. "This is for Liam," he whispered. Prentiss shut his eyes and waited for the pain. A loud banging on the store door made him jump and open his eyes.

"Niall, Niall it's the police. They're in the shop now," a cockney male voice called through the half open door.

"What do they want, Freddie?" Donnelly snapped.

"Don't know, they wouldn't say. You'd better come," he said nervously. Donnelly cursed under his breath and turned off the radio.

"No matter," he said. "You'll keep." He stuffed a handkerchief into Prentiss' mouth and, putting the polished steel spike back on the table, walked to the door. "Now don't go away, I won't be long," he said slamming and bolting the door. Prentiss let out a long slow breath. He had to get out, take advantage of the temporary reprieve. As the fear subsided, replaced by a new sense of hope, Prentiss looked about him. "Think, damn it, think," he thought angrily to himself. He knew he didn't have very long and then there would be no second chances.

As Donnelly walked through into the shop from the rear entrance the two plain clothes officers were waiting for him. Freddie hovered in the doorway as one of them reached inside his jacket and produced a warrant card.

"Mister Niall Donnelly?" he asked "I'm Detective Chief Inspector Gallagher, Special Branch. Donnelly looked suspiciously at the two men.

"Yes, I'm Donnelly. What does the Special Branch want with me?"

"We're investigating three murders up in Norfolk. An elderly couple and a postman were found shot in a house in the village of Sparham."

"What's that got to do with me?"

"Earlier today a white transit van with your name painted on the side was seen leaving the house in something of a hurry. In fact, it almost knocked over a neighbour out walking his dog. It was him that reported it to the local police who then discovered the bodies. We believe that the deaths are connected with another murder we are investigating, that of a hotel manager in Cromer. Do you own such a van, sir?" Gallagher stared at Donnelly looking for any signs of a reaction but there were none.

"Well I do have a refrigerated van used for transporting meat, but I can assure you that it hasn't been any further than the meat market today. Certainly nowhere near Suffolk was it?" Donnelly said earnestly.

"Norfolk. Do you think we could have a look at it?" Gallagher asked. Donnelly smiled broadly and said that they could. Telling Freddie to watch the shop he showed Gallagher and Lyle through the back and into the courtyard.

The van was parked in the small courtyard. Sergeant Lyle noted down the lettering on the side in his notebook

N. DONNELLY HIGH CLASS BUTCHER- CLERKENWELL

From inside the meat store Prentiss could faintly hear the three men talking outside. Gallagher asked to look inside the back to which Donnelly happily obliged. Two lamb carcasses were hanging from meat hooks inside.

"Is this your only van?" Gallagher asked.

"Yes, I've had this one about six months. I get a new one every couple of years and have the lettering put on. I suppose it's possible your dog walker could have seen one of the old ones," Donnelly replied in a matter of fact tone.

"And you've been here at the shop all day?"

"All day, Freddie can vouch for that. To be honest, I don't really think I can be of much help to you, Inspector."

"What's in there?" Lyle asked nodding towards the meat store.

"Beef, pork, poultry. It's a meat store; these lambs will be going in later. Do you want to have a look?"

Inside, hearing this Prentiss tried to call out but was unable to spit the handkerchief out of his mouth, only managing a muffled grunt. Hearing the voice say that wouldn't be necessary, Prentiss realised that they were leaving as the voices grew fainter and fainter. He was filled with an intense and overwhelming feeling of panic. Looking up, he saw that the 'S' hook he was hanging from was suspended from a large steel ring in the ceiling. If he could only reach that he would be able to unhook himself. He tried to stretch his fingers to pull himself up the hook. The intense pain in his hands and wrists made him cry out, his gag stifling the sound. Prentiss fought back the tears that welled up in his eyes. He bit down hard on the handkerchief ball in his mouth and tried again. The pain he felt now was nothing to that which Donnelly was going to inflict upon him once he returned. Slowly, very slowly he reached up once again. Trying to block out the pain he focused on trying to get his fingers through the ring. Finally he did it; first one hand then the other. Then with a last supreme effort Prentiss pulled himself up towards the ring freeing himself from the meat hook.

He dropped to the floor both relieved and delighted at his achievement. Every part of his upper body hurt but there was no time to rest. He pulled the gag from his mouth and staggered to his feet. Crossing to the table and grasping a huge cleaver by its blade he sliced through the string. As he pulled the last of the string out of the deep contusions in his wrists he heard the familiar sound of the bolt being drawn back. With his hands free and the adrenalin surging Prentiss snatched up the lard tube and stood next to the door. As it opened he plunged the long steel spike upwards into Donnelly's stomach. Reeling round Donnelly lurched sideways and fell to the floor inside the meat store. Kicking the door shut Prentiss knelt astride Donnelly pinning the man's arms with his legs. He pulled out the spike. Blood was beginning to pool in Donnelly's mouth and trickle down his cheek. Prentiss looked down at him consumed with hate. All the feelings and memories he had spent so long trying to repress had returned. He raised the spike above his head with both hands. "Say hello to your brother for me." Using all his strength Prentiss thrust the spike into Donnelly's chest.

A few seconds later, Prentiss climbed off Donnelly's lifeless body and opened the door a little. The courtyard was empty. Cautiously he emerged from the store and, running to the van, opened the driver's door. No keys. Prentiss knew he looked battered and dishevelled but he had no alternative than to make his escape on foot. He ran down the alley and into the street buttoning his shirt as best he could as he went. He emerged onto a busy street bustling with shoppers. Prentiss walked away from the butcher's shop and, having no idea where he was, disappeared into the late afternoon crowd.

Chapter Fifteen

Having watched Donnelly's van drive out of the driveway at the house in Sparham, Grant had wasted no time in packing up and driving the short distance to Norwich railway station. Catching the London train just before eleven he had arrived at Liverpool Street station at one o'clock. It was then a short cab ride to the Savoy hotel arriving just in time to see Jordan leaving. He watched Jordan walk away from the safety of the taxi before casually strolling into the hotel smiling at the liveried doorman holding the door for him. Discovering David Morse's room number from reception he took the elevator and forced the door of room Four-One-Two.

As he silently closed the door behind him Grant saw the motionless heavy lying on the floor. Listening acutely for signs of anyone else in the room for a moment, he satisfied himself that he was alone. He bent down and felt for a pulse in the man's neck. He raised an eyebrow and sneered as he detected a faint but steady beat. "You're getting soft, Richard." Kitter began to stir. Grant cupped the man's chin with his hand and in one swift movement spun the helpless thug's head until he heard his neck break with a loud crack. Dropping the dead man's head to the floor, Grant left the room and took the elevator back down to the lobby as the police arrived. Coolly he stood and watched the manager escort the uniformed officers upstairs before nonchalantly walking out of the hotel.

"I'm very disappointed in you, Mister Bannon. Not so much that you wanted to have me killed, that I can understand. After all I'm the last loose end to be tied up. What gets to me, what really sticks in my throat, is that you send some stupid, incompetent asshole to do the job." Grant stood in an Islington Pub and spoke acidly to Steve Bannon on the phone. "Did you really think that would-be hoodlum could take me?" Bannon sat back in his chair and listened intently. He considered himself something of a tactician but he had played this completely wrong. Grant was his best man; he should have known that eliminating him would take cunning and finesse, not some blunt instrument with a gun.

"I'm sure we can resolve this," Bannon said calmly.

"Yes we can, Stevie boy. The time here is now two fifteen. I'm going to check my account in exactly fifteen minutes. If the remainder of my money isn't there I'll have to send the photocopy of the Ares file I have here to some of the TV networks over there. I'm sure they'll be interested in Thomas Fisher's dirty little secret. Which would be a shame. I understand that it's pretty much a certainty he'll be elected to the Senate." Bannon said nothing. He had gravely underestimated the former SEAL and he was going to have to pay the price for that. That was, of course, until he could find a more satisfactory and permanent solution to the problem of Harry Grant.

"It'll be done."

"Make sure that it is because if your involvement ever became known, well let's just say your reputation would be somewhat...sullied." Grant hung up the phone and ordered another whiskey, confident that Bannon would have his money transferred before he could finish his drink.

At four thirty that afternoon, in a large open plan office in New Scotland Yard, Detective Chief Inspector Gallagher sat back in his chair sipping coffee with his feet in his worn brown shoes resting on a pulled out drawer. Across the desk Sergeant Lyle flicked through the pages of his notebook. Gallagher was trying to make sense of the events of the last few days. He had been in the Special Branch for two years having spent the previous five in the Anti-Terrorist Squad and had a reputation for dogged tenacity.

"Alright, Ray," he said to Lyle "Let's start from the beginning and see what we've got. Colonel Charles Mabbitt, the commanding officer of a secret army intelligence unit has his wife murdered during a burglary at his house. The safe is emptied and the family valuables stolen. Then somebody kills him with a remotely detonated bomb."

"Then there's Richard Jordan," added Lyle.

"Yes, Richard bloody Jordan," he said scornfully. "A Sergeant Major in Mabbitt's unit finds a bomb in *his* car and then miraculously turns up at the scene of a shooting in bloody Cromer of all places. Connection?"

"It might help if I knew a little more about Mabbitt's unit, Guv."

Gallagher put down his cup. "The Fourteenth Intelligence Company, commonly known as The Det."

"The Det?" said Lyle curiously.

"Short for The Detachment. They're one of the funny ones, have almost complete autonomy and they are ultra secret. I first came across them when I was in SO15 a few years ago. Their sole purpose is to combat the IRA and the little I've seen of them; they're bloody good at it."

"Then surely it must be something to do with the IRA. Some kind of revenge campaign, maybe?" Lyle said then thought for a moment. "What about our Irish butcher, Niall Donnelly, do you think he's connected to the Sparham murders?"

"I don't know. There's something going on there. He was a bit too confident for my liking. Cocky Irish sod."

"Do you think it was his van in Norfolk?"

"Oh yes, it was his van alright. That story about it could have been one of his old ones is just a load of old bollocks. Check it anyway, though. We're missing something, Ray. Chase up ballistics and find out if it was the same gun that was used on the B and B manager and the three at Sparham. Also, run a background check on Donnelly. I want to know everything from the day he was born to what he had for lunch today. And Ray," he added thoughtfully, "check the computer; see if there have been any other murders during the last twenty-four hours that might, no matter how tenuously, be connected to all this."

The army charge nurse bristled disapprovingly as Richard Jordan smacked her playfully on the behind as he entered Colonel Mabbitt's room.

"Mister Jordan, I'll thank you to keep your hands to yourself.," she said primly.

"And after all we've meant to each other, Sister. I suppose a cup of tea is out of the question? It is nearly four-thirty," Jordan said buoyantly. She strutted out of the room secretly suppressing a smile.

"Richard, please don't bait the staff. They have a rather punctilious demeanour that really is best avoided." Jordan apologised and pulled up a chair next to the bed. "There's been a rather interesting development while you've been making your way here. Your friend in the hotel room, are you sure you only left him unconscious?"

"Yes, checked him before I left."

"Only we've been snooping on the police radio, as they do occasionally have their uses, and he appears to have been found dead in the room with a broken neck."

Jordan nodded angrily. "It must have been Morse making sure I did the job. The police arrived within minutes of me calling them. He must have done it as soon as I left the hotel. He was there and I didn't see him, I must be slipping."

"Don't reproach yourself, Richard. I've got our people watching all the ports and airports with Morse's photograph. We'll find him."

"And Michael? Has there been any word?" Jordan asked. Mabbitt shook his head solemnly.

"On a more positive note, however, the name you extracted has proved to be very useful."

"Steve Bannon."

"Yes, I've got a team working up a profile at the moment. Hopefully it should give us more of an idea as to who is orchestrating all this and why," Mabbitt said trying to adjust his pillows. "Now be a good chap will you and go and see if you can appropriate a small bottle of whisky, for medicinal purposes of course. For some inexplicable reason those harpies out there seem to be adverse to me having the occasional glass."

Sergeant Lyle handed a typed two page report to Chief Inspector Gallagher. "What do you make of this, Guv?" Gallagher read it then re-read it.

"And this was earlier today?" he asked.

"The body was found about three hours ago at one-thirty following an anonymous phone tip. Although there was no ID on the body, the receptionist distinctly remembers him being an American. He arrived just before one o'clock asking which room a David Morse was in."

"David Morse?" Gallagher said. "That name sounds familiar." He began furiously searching through the reams of paper that covered his desk saying the name over and over under his breath. Opening a folder he turned the pages until he found what he was looking for. "Got it!" he said holding up the page. "There was a David Morse booked into the Cromer B and B but no sign of him when the local boys interviewed the guests."

"There's just one more thing that might just make your day, Guv. The receptionist gave a description of David Morse and you'll never guess who it sounds like?"

Gallagher shrugged. "Well go on who do you think I am, Ali bloody Bongo?" he said impatiently.

"Only Sergeant Major Richard Jordan, secret agent and royal pain in the arse," he said excitedly. A broad grin crept across Gallagher's face.

"Well, well. What about that. Issue a warrant for Jordan's arrest. Find him, I want him behind bars by bedtime and no secret squirrel crap is going to prevent me getting some answers. I've got him this time."

"Yes, Guv." The phone rang on Lyle's desk. Answering it he listened without speaking, his face fixed with a sober expression.

"What is it?" Gallagher asked when Lyle eventually finished the call.

"Niall Donnelly has just been found murdered in his meat store. Stabbed twice, once straight through the heart."

Gallagher looked at him nonplussed. "What the bloody hell is going on?"

Colonel Mabbitt dozed lightly, his bed still covered with papers from a busy afternoon's work. Finally, however, he had submitted to the will of the fearsome charge nurse and taken a break. As his racing mind searched for a little peace and tranquillity to ease, albeit temporarily, the pounding in his head the silence was shattered by the telephone ringing. Wearily he opened his eyes a fraction and put the receiver to his ear. In a public call box in Euston railway station Michael Prentiss said, "Colonel, is that you?"

"Michael!" Mabbitt said pulling himself up. "It's good to hear your voice again. Where are you?"

"I'm in London, Euston Station."

"Are you alright?"

"I'm okay, but I need picking up. Can you send somebody?"

"Stay where you are. I'll send Richard to get you," Mabbitt said urgently.

Prentiss hung up. It was just after five o'clock, rush hour and Euston station was crowded with commuters. Nevertheless he felt very conspicuous with his dishevelled appearance and ripped, dirty shirt. He needed somewhere to hide until Jordan arrived. Deciding that the safest place was probably the public lavatories, he went into a cubicle and locked the door. He put the lid down and sat on the toilet. For the first time in what seemed to be an eternity he felt he could relax a little. Reaching into his pocket he took out his watch. The injuries he had sustained to his wrists made it impossible for him to continue wearing it. It would be a couple of hours before he would be picked up. Leaning his head against the cubicle wall Prentiss closed his eyes. He was tired and hungry. The food he could wait a little longer for, it was sleep he needed now. Barely even noticing how uncomfortable he was, within seconds Prentiss drifted off into a deep sleep.

Richard Jordan wasted no time making his way back to London. He had spent less than five minutes with Colonel Mabbitt. Just long enough to be briefed and ordered to take one of the unit's Range Rovers fitted with communications and a full weapons pack. Minutes later the white Range Rover with civilian number plates was tearing up the road heading for London.

It was just after six-thirty by the time Jordan crossed the Thames and made his way in heavy traffic up the East India Dock Road towards Whitechapel High Street. Jordan didn't like cities and he hated London in particular. How anyone could get all misty eyed about somewhere that was so congested, polluted and stressful remained a complete mystery to him. He longed for the fresh air and big skies of South Wales where he could walk without being jostled, run over or stopped and ever so politely demanded to contribute to this week's charitable cause.

Twenty minutes later Jordan nosed the four wheeled drive into a parking space outside Euston railway station. He walked inside and, standing by the entrance, began to scour the station for Prentiss. It was still a hectic mass of commuters which made it difficult for Jordan to find him. He began walking around casually, his eyes scanning the area, looking for that one familiar face.

One of two uniformed police officers patrolling the station noticed Jordan and nudged his partner. They stopped, watching him as he got nearer to them in the crowd. Satisfied that he was in fact the subject of an arrest warrant issued that afternoon, the first one radioed it in. Then they made their move. Warned that he was to be considered armed and dangerous, they split up and circled round behind him. Flanking him on either side they drew their truncheons. Without warning, one hit Jordan in the ribs while the other forced him to the ground shouting that he was under arrest. As they both pounced on him struggling to put him in handcuffs, Prentiss sprinted through the startled crowd and kicked one of the officers sending him sprawling along the ground. From his prone position Jordan elbowed the other in the side of the head knocking him sideways. Prentiss punched the officer hard on the bridge of the nose knocking him unconscious.

"I thought you were supposed to be rescuing me?" Prentiss said to Jordan sarcastically as they both got to their feet.

"Come on, they're bound to have called for backup. The car's outside." As they began to leave a few of the braver members of the crowd stepped forward. Jordan pulled out his gun. "No heroes please; we're a little pushed for time." There were screams as the crowd scattered at the sight of the weapon. Running from the station Jordan and Prentiss got to the car and took off down Euston Road.

Negotiating the traffic with one hand on the steering wheel, Jordan picked up the radio handset with the other. "It's good to see you, Michael," Jordan said looking across at Prentiss and smiling. Then the radio crackled to life with the disembodied voice from the communications room at Ashford. As he tried to drive as unobtrusively as possible so as not to attract any more police attention Jordan said, "This is Sergeant Major Jordan, I've got a bit of a problem."

Chapter Sixteen

"He's been spotted, Guv," Lyle said rushing into the office. "Jordan managed to escape two uniforms as they were trying to arrest him."

"Idiots! Where was this?"

"Euston Station, about ten minutes ago. Thing is, he seems to have got himself some help. They both got away in what is believed to be a white Range Rover. I've put out an all cars alert."

"Right, draw a gun and one for me too and have the car outside in ten minutes ready to go," Gallagher said sharply.

"Go where? Listen, Guv. Don't you think you ought to leave it to uniform? I think you're letting this Jordan..."

"What!?" Gallagher barked. "Jordan's out there running round the country thinking he's above the law, that it doesn't apply to him somehow. Well I'm not having it, right? And if I wanted to be nagged, Sergeant, I'd have stayed married!"

A few miles away in a small car park behind a small office block on Pentonville Road, Jordan was being connected with Colonel Mabbitt.

"Richard, do you deliberately go out of your way to antagonise the police forces of this country?" Mabbitt asked in an exasperated voice.

"No, Sir; it seems to be a natural gift I have."

"Have you got Michael?" Jordan looked across at the battered Prentiss and confirmed that he had. "Is he alright?"

"He's a bit of a mess but he always was a scruffy sod," Jordan replied jocularly.

"There appears to be a warrant out for your arrest so I think you had better disappear for a while. Can you get to Chelsea Barracks?" Mabbitt asked.

"Yes, I'll get there."

"Good. I'll tell them to expect you. And Richard," Mabbitt added seriously, "you and Michael take the utmost care. The plods are pursuing you with extreme alacrity."

Standing in line at the British Airways check-in desk, Harry Grant lifted his sunglasses to get a better look at the smooth tanned legs of the girl in front of him. He was feeling good, relaxed. In a couple of hours he would be in the air bound for Thailand and looking forward to enjoying all the pleasures that a million dollars would most definitely bring him. He smiled a broad white smile at the check-in girl as he put his suitcase on the conveyor. Returning the smile she attended to his bag and handed him a boarding card.

"I hope you enjoy your flight, Mister Grant." Grant nodded his thanks and winked at the pretty girl whose attention had already moved to the next passenger. With time to kill, Grant decided to see if the bar was stocked with a decent bourbon. Choosing a secluded corner that afforded him a good view of the whole bar and particularly the entrance, he sat with two fingers of Wild Turkey over ice and a copy of The Times.

Grant watched the comings and goings, looking for recurring faces as he pretended to read the newspaper. After thirty minutes and a second large bourbon, a young man in his mid twenties wearing a tan leather jacket and jeans entered the bar and stood waiting to be served. He was lean and athletic, more greyhound than bulldog but definitely military thought Grant as he turned the page of his newspaper. Casually the young man looked around the bar. Grant watched him carefully, his eyes returning to the newspaper as the man looked across in his direction. Grant could feel his eyes on him just for a moment. Then he was gone.

Grant tossed the newspaper on the table and finished his drink, crunching the last of the ice as he watched the bar entrance. This was going to be inconvenient he thought to himself. He was unarmed, having ditched his weapons before travelling to the airport as there was no possibility he would be able to get them aboard the plane.

He left the bar and walked out onto the concourse. Browsing in a book shop, he scanned the area. Then he saw him. Tan leather jacket and blue jeans, this time with another man. This one was older, late thirties maybe, stocky with a thick brown moustache. Putting down the book he left the shop walking away from the two men. Grant strolled slowly looking in each of the shops as he went. Ahead of him in the middle of the concourse stood an advertising board. As he approached it he could see the two men behind him reflected in the glass. Clearly following him, Grant decided he had no alternative. Unfortunately he was going to have to take care of them.

Fifteen miles east of Heathrow, Richard Jordan and Michael Prentiss drove past the Houses of Parliament and headed south down Millbank. Jordan looked over and noticed the wounds on Prentiss' wrists.

"Are you okay?" Jordan asked. Prentiss glanced down at the dried blood and the deep contusions. "I'll be alright. Nothing a dab of Germoline and a plaster won't fix."

"What happened?"

"I've just been hanging around with Liam Donnelly's brother. Enjoying that Northern Irish hospitality I've come to expect from that particular family. At least I managed to keep my teeth this time."

"Did you kill him?" Jordan asked.

"Oh yes." Prentiss replied coldly staring ahead. "He got what he deserved." The unadulterated hatred in Prentiss' face was clear.

"Be careful, Michael. Killing gets to be like eating a huge meal. It's not too difficult if you've got the stomach for it. The problem is, you get to like it."

"Speaking from experience?"

"No, not me. Not ever. But I've seen it happen too many times. You're a good lad, Michael. Just make sure it doesn't happen to you."

A police patrol car approached them from the opposite direction. Jordan and Prentiss pulled down the sun visors to help obscure their faces. The patrol car had barely driven passed them when the siren and blue lights came on and it did a U turn and began to pursue. Jordan cursed and put his foot hard on the accelerator pulling out into the oncoming traffic. Swerving violently the Range Rover mounted the pavement scattering terrified pedestrians as they ran for their lives. Driving back onto the road, Jordan once again pulled out across the road this time into the path of an oncoming routemaster. Continuing onto the opposite pavement, the bus slewed sideways and came to a screeching halt blocking the road in both directions.

Jordan glanced in his rear-view mirror and smiled at the chaos he had left behind and the patrol car unable to continue pursuit. He pulled the car back onto the road and drove down Chelsea Embankment. Minutes later they were at the security gate of Chelsea Barracks. Jordan flashed his ID at a Scots Guardsman who nodded and climbed onto the vehicle's running board. Shouting for the barrier to be raised, he directed Jordan as they sped into the barracks and towards the parade ground.

Waiting for them at the edge of the parade ground was a Captain from the Scots Guards. Jordan pulled up next to him and both he and Prentiss got out.

"Sarn't Major Jordan? Captain MacNeesh. I understand you're in a spot of bother with the rozzers," he said with the merest hint of a supercilious smirk that one only finds with the Brigade of Guards officer class. Jordan nodded. MacNeesh looked across at Prentiss then back to Jordan. I have a message for you from your Colonel Mabbitt. "Apparently the man you're after is at Heathrow Airport and you are to proceed there straight away. The Colonel has laid on transportation for you." A Gazelle helicopter circled overhead. "And, unless I'm very much mistaken, here it is."

As the Gazelle landed in the centre of the parade ground, MacNeesh continued. "My orders are to have Mister Prentiss driven back to Templar Barracks immediately."

Prentiss recoiled. "I don't think so, I'm coming with you. If you think you can leave me behind now you can piss off. You got me into this and I'm going to bloody well see it through," Prentiss said to Jordan indignantly.

"My orders are quite specific," MacNeesh insisted. Jordan looked briefly at Prentiss then at MacNeesh.

"He comes with me." Prentiss and Jordan ran to the waiting helicopter and climbed aboard. The pilot handed them each a headset and flicked a switch on his control panel. "It's Colonel Mabbitt for you, Sir."

"Yes Colonel, go ahead," Jordan said as he fastened his safety belt.

"Ah Richard there you are. We've got our man under surveillance at Heathrow Airport. I want you to get over there and take charge," Mabbitt said. "And Richard, I would appreciate it if you could avoid killing him. There are a number of questions I'd like to have answers to. Am I clear?"

"Understood."

"Good. Is Michael on his way here?"

"No, Colonel; I'm going with Richard," Prentiss interjected.

"I'd much rather you didn't. I need you to come back here; Richard is quite capable of taking care of our American friend. I've got something else for you." Prentiss fell silent at Colonel Mabbitt's orders. Frustrated that he wasn't permitted to go with Jordan while at the same time intrigued as to what the Colonel wanted him to do. Eventually he replied into his headset. "Alright Colonel, I'm on my way."

"I'll see you later," Jordan said as Prentiss climbed out of the helicopter. Prentiss nodded and, closing the door, ran back to where Captain MacNeesh was waiting.

"It looks like I'll be needing that lift you offered me after all."

Detective Chief Inspector Gallagher had monitored the havoc Jordan's journey through Westminster had caused over the radio. From the front passenger seat he yelled obscenities both at his police driver to go faster and into the radio at the incompetence of the traffic officers allowing Jordan to evade them. At last there was a confirmed sighting of Jordan's vehicle driving into Chelsea Barracks. Gallagher was elated. "That's only round the bloody corner!" he yelled and, picking up the radio, stated that they would be there in five minutes.

The unmarked Granada screeched to a stop at the front security gate of Chelsea Barracks as a rather dour Scottish corporal stepped forward. Gallagher leapt from the car holding up his warrant card and ordering the soldier to raise the barrier. A somewhat heated argument then ensued ,resulting in the corporal telephoning the adjutant for instructions.

"Sorry for the delay, sir," the corporal said in a monotone voice as the barrier was raised. Gallagher muttered something about the man's lack of intelligence and dubious parentage as he got back into the car. Two patrol cars followed the Granada onto the camp with their lights flashing. As the three vehicles roared onto the parade ground, Gallagher watched as a Gazelle helicopter took off. As he got out of the car he could just make out Richard Jordan's smiling face before the helicopter turned and climbed heading west. Angrily Gallagher punched the roof of the car swearing furiously.

As Gallagher was raging on the parade ground, a Ford Fiesta was being driven out of the main gate with a guardsman in civilian dress behind the wheel. Next to him was Michael Prentiss who watched the Gazelle helicopter until it was nothing more than a tiny speck in the distance.

At Heathrow Airport Harry Grant stared into a shop window. The two men following him stood some distance away and watched as unobtrusively as they could. He smiled to himself as he saw them mirrored in the window. They were obviously under orders to just observe and not apprehend him. He had been forced to re-think his travel arrangements which, although it was not going to be too much of a problem, irritated him intensely. This assignment had gone on for too long. All he wanted to do now was to relax on some remote little island in the Andaman Sea off south central Thailand and disappear.

Grant had had enough of playing follow-my-leader and decided it was time he made his move. As he approached the escalator he sprinted up it barging his way to the top, knocking over passengers as he went, blocking it behind him. Caught unawares by Grant's speed, the two intelligence men gave chase attempting to climb over those trying to get to their feet. By the time they reached the top Grant had disappeared. They split up, a move that Grant had not only anticipated but desired. He watched from his hiding place behind the curtain in a photo booth as the two men began their search in opposite directions. It was the young greyhound that made his way towards Grant.

Grant slipped out of the booth and walked into a café. Unobserved, he picked up a knife from a table holding it, blade upward, against his wrist. The dinner knife wasn't particularly sharp but it did have a tapered point adequate for the task. He left the café and stood next to an advertising board. His young pursuer had entered a duty free shop and was scouring the busy aisles for his target. Grant moved towards the shop maintaining a fixed gaze on the back of the tan leather jacket as it moved down the shop. Quickly Grant walked down the next aisle parallel with the intelligence man. He stood at the end and waited the few seconds for him to appear.

"I think you're looking for me?" Grant said as he stood face to face with his opponent. Mabbitt's man took a second to react then reached inside his jacket but it was too late. With one single powerful movement, Grant grasped the back of the man's neck with one hand and thrust the knife between his ribs and into his heart with the other, killing him within seconds. Taking the dead man's weight, Grant lowered him to the floor. Pulling the Browning nine millimetre pistol from the shoulder holster hidden beneath the man's leather jacket, Grant called out.

"I need some help here!" A number of customers began to gather round the body. As the crowd grew he slipped away, hiding the gun in his waistband. In the confusion amidst the screams from inside the duty free shop, Grant walked unnoticed down the escalator towards the main exit.

Richard Jordan's Gazelle had touched down on the emergency helicopter landing pad and he was now being driven to the main terminal area by airport security. The security man's radio notified all security staff of a stabbing in the duty free shop. Hearing this Jordan told the driver to take him straight to the front of the terminal building. He didn't need to know any more details. Jordan knew that this was the work of his American, David Morse and at that very moment he would be trying to escape.

A couple of minutes later Jordan was out of the car and running into the main terminal building. As he reached the doors a squeal of tyres close by made him turn. Stopped in the road was a silver Ford Capri. The female driver was being forced out screaming from behind the wheel and thrown onto the tarmac. Jordan stopped as he recognised the woman's assailant. "Morse," he murmured as he started running towards the car. Grant had no sooner got in and slammed the door than the car roared away leaving a cloud of white smoke and the stench of burning rubber.

As Jordan stood in the road attempting to read the Capri's registration number the security man arrived panting at his shoulder. Jordan turned and grabbed the wheezing guard by the arm. "I need to get back to my helicopter, now!"

Chapter Seventeen

It was nine-thirty that evening when Michael Prentiss walked into the infirmary at Templar Barracks. Declining repeated offers of medical treatment for his injuries, he was shown straight to Colonel Mabbitt's room.

"Michael, my dear boy I'm delighted to see you looking so well," Mabbitt said looking up as the door opened and seeing Prentiss standing wearily in the doorway.

"Hello, Colonel. How's the head?"

"There's a bit of a dent but don't worry, I'm not quite ready for one of your business cards just yet. Now come and sit down before you fall down."

"Has Richard got Morse yet?"

"No, he killed one of my surveillance team at Heathrow before Richard arrived. Corporal Megson; he'd only been with the unit six months. The slippery bastard managed to get away in a stolen car. Richard is currently trailing him in the helicopter. That's the bad news. The good news however is that we have learned his true identity. His name is Harold Robert Grant," Mabbitt said opening a folder. "According to our colleagues in American Naval Intelligence he spent ten years as a US Navy SEAL, their equivalent of our Royal Marines Special Boat Service. Not as good of course but they try their best. He specialised in both explosive ordnance and advanced special operations. One of their best men apparently, brave, fearless, chest full of medals; you know the type of thing. Which is why they were so sad when they were forced to let him go."

"Why?"

"Expediency, really. The navy decided that it was in everyone's best interests that they quietly discharge him on medical grounds for..." Mabbitt quoted from the file "displaying increasing signs of psychosis combined with violent and sadistic episodes."

"You mean he's a nut-case?"

"Oh yes, absolutely barking but very clever and quite, quite deadly," Mabbitt said earnestly. "Still, we'll let Richard deal with that little problem. I've got something else that requires your attention, if you're up to it that is?"

"What do you want me to do?" Prentiss asked. Mabbitt handed him a folder.

"This is all we know about a man called Steve Bannon. Former CIA officer and now a respectable security consultant as principle of Bannon Strategic Solutions with rather swanky offices in New York. We now know that it was him who paid Grant to kill us all. What I want you to do is to find out who paid him and why."

"You don't think this Bannon is the one ultimately behind it then?" Prentiss asked opening the file.

"No, not for a minute. I'm certain that he is just a middle-man in all this. There's got to be someone else with a very personal connection with Operation Ares." Mabbitt squeezed the bridge of his nose. His vision was beginning to blur and his head was thumping.

"Are you alright, Colonel?" Prentiss asked.

"Fine, fine. I'm just flagging a little. Anyway, go and get yourself cleaned up, have a hot meal and a good night's sleep. When you've read the file we'll continue our discussion in the morning." Mabbitt was looking tired. He had pushed himself much harder than he should and he knew that he had to get some rest if he was going to see this through. He closed his eyes. Prentiss took the file and quietly opened the door. Without opening his eyes Mabbitt said, "And get those wrists looked at before they get infected. You're no use to me in hospital!"

"Yes, Colonel. I'll see you in the morning," Prentiss said, but Mabbitt was already asleep.

Harry Grant had been driving for half an hour, heading south then east into Kent. Deciding that he had pushed his luck far enough, he pulled into a roadside café car park. The police would certainly be looking for the stolen Capri and so he urgently needed to abandon it and find another car. As Grant turned off the engine he was unaware that Richard Jordan's helicopter, which had been tracking him from Heathrow, was now circling high above. Jordan instructed the pilot to land as close to the café as possible without being detected. Unfortunately for Jordan, because of the combination of electricity pylons and uneven terrain, he had to jump from the Gazelle while it hovered ten feet above a field almost half a mile away.

Grant looked around the car park in the gathering darkness. There were a couple of lorries and a handful of saloon cars. An overweight figure wearing overalls and smoking a cigarette lumbered out of the café and, puffing hard, crossed the car park to one of the lorries. Grant watched him carefully. Perhaps, he thought, if he asked the fat roly-poly man very nicely for a lift he wouldn't have to kill him. It was worth a try.

As the driver unlocked his lorry fumbling with the keys in his large squidgy fingers, he turned on hearing the American voice.

"Any chance of a lift to Dover?" Grant asked cheerfully, lighting a Marlboro.

"American, eh?" he said in a broad West Country accent.

"That's right. So, Dover?"

"Yep, I'm bound for Dover. I suppose I could give you a lift as far as the ferry."

Grant smiled "That'll do just fine." Running round the front of the lorry he climbed into the cab. "Cigarette?" Grant said offering the pack of Marlboro to the driver.

"Don't mind if I do."

As the two men made small talk in the lorry Richard Jordan climbed over the fence behind the café and edged towards the car park. From the side of the café building he could see the empty Ford Capri. Some distance away a lorry's engine shuddered into life. In the half light he could just make out Grant's face in the cab. Jordan drew his pistol and training it on Grant, ran into the car park and took up a firing position twenty feet in front of the lorry.

"'Ere, what's he doing?" the driver shouted.

"I think he's trying to stop me," Grant said pulling out his gun and digging it into the driver's ribs. "Run him down." Flustered, the driver tried to protest but Grant pushed the gun in harder. "I said, run him down." Crunching the gearbox into first the terrified driver started to move the lorry. Grant flicked the headlights on to full beam, blinding Jordan as he tried to take aim. With the lorry bearing down on him and unable to get a clear shot he leapt out of the way onto the safety of the bonnet of a parked car.

As Jordan put away his gun and clambered off the dented bonnet, a brown suited man came running out of the café. "Look what you've done to my car!" he yelled angrily, his face scarlet with rage.

"Yes, I'm sorry about the damage. I'll make sure it's put right," Jordan replied wearily.

"You'll do more than that!" he said grabbing hold of Jordan's arm. Jordan twisted the man's hand and spun him round until he was face down on the bonnet and held him tightly in a wrist lock.

"Listen mate," Jordan said in the man's ear. "If some days are diamonds and some days are stones, today I'm having a real fucking pebble. I am tired, hungry and very, very pissed off. Now unless you want to make my day any worse than it already is you'll give me the keys to your car and I'll go and get it mended for you."

"Jacket pocket," squeaked the reply. Jordan found the car key and pulled the man to his feet.

"Thank you for your co-operation." Jordan released him and got into the car. "Do have a pleasant evening."

Chief Inspector Gallagher slammed the phone down and shouted a long string of abusive profanity. "No joy then, Guv?" Sergeant Lyle observed when Gallagher had finally finished. Gallagher looked at him, breathing hard.

"Apparently Sergeant Major Richard bloody Jordan is on active service at present and therefore details of his whereabouts cannot be divulged at this time. A matter of security you understand. Security, my arse!"

"What about the character who was with him in the car?"

"Details of current operations or personnel cannot be divulged due to the extremely sensitive work of the unit."

Gallagher mimicked pointing to the telephone. "I'm telling you, Ray, this bloody army unit. Now, to top it all, another one of their secret bloody squirrels gets himself murdered at Heathrow bloody Airport while on some kind of top secret operation, the details of which we are not even allowed to bloody know!" Gallagher threw his pencil across the desk in frustration and rubbed his face vigorously with his palms. "Okay, so what have we got?"

"Ballistics has confirmed that it was the same gun used at both the Cromer and the Sparham murders, a .45 automatic. I was thinking, Guv," Lyle said. "What if our Norfolk murderer is also the same man who killed Colonel Mabbitt and planted the bomb in Jordan's car?"

"David Morse. And you think Jordan's after him, leaving death and destruction in his wake?" Gallagher said, then nodded thoughtfully. "It makes sense, and our dead soldier at the airport was..."

"Killed by Morse when he tried to stop Morse leaving the country," continued Lyle.

"Right!" Gallagher said excitedly "Get me a copy of the Heathrow incident report. There's got to be something in there to give us a lead. We've got ourselves a terrorist on the loose, Ray, and it looks like he'll do just about anything to get away."

"What about Jordan? Do you want me to lift the arrest warrant? If we're right he's not guilty of anything more than doing his job."

"No," Gallagher replied. "Put out an alert not to approach if sighted, just report his whereabouts. We'll use him to find Morse. I'll bet my bunions that wherever Morse is, Jordan won't be far behind."

In a lorry park near the docks in Dover Grant sat with the driver and lit another Marlboro. It was a few minutes before midnight and it had been raining heavily for almost an hour. Arriving a couple of hours earlier, having taken a longer more convoluted route to the port, Grant was satisfied that they hadn't been followed. He now sat in silence as he watched the rain beat down hard on the windscreen.

The end of Grant's cigarette glowed brightly in the darkness of the cab as he took a long slow draw. "My Grandparents lived by the sea," he said quietly. "In Maine; a little place just outside Portsmouth. I used to visit them every summer. Grandpa would take me fishing in this little green wooden boat and Grandma would bake her cinnamon and apple pie. I guess that's why I joined the navy. I've always been crazy about boats." The glass was starting to steam up and Grant wound down the window a fraction. "It's getting a little stuffy in here. You don't mind if I have the window open do you?" The driver remained silent so Grant continued. "Things seemed a lot simpler in the navy. They told me who they wanted me to kill and I went and killed them. They even gave me medals for it. I was an SCPO. Do you know what that is?" Grant looked at the driver but didn't wait for a reply. "A Senior Chief Petty Officer."

As Grant continued to speak nostalgically about his past his mood suddenly grew darker, more bitter. "Then when I'd finished killing for them the navy decided to cut me loose, just like that. They took away everything that I was, that I had become and left me with nothing. It wasn't my fault. I did what they ordered. I wanted to keep doing it, I loved it you see. But they said I was crazy, that I was enjoying it too much. You do see that it wasn't my fault, don't you? It was them that made me do it. It's like Richard Jordan. He just had to show up back there. All I wanted was a friendly ride to Dover with you but he had to try and stop me. So he left me no choice, do you understand?" Grant looked across at the driver sitting behind the wheel staring vacantly straight ahead. A trickle of blood came from the small bullet hole in his left temple and had dripped onto his overall. Grant looked at the dead man and shook his head sadly. "It wasn't my fault," he said to him apologetically. Then getting out of the lorry, he walked away into the night.

Richard Jordan had driven the commandeered Saab 99 along the A2 as far as Canterbury but there was no sign of Grant's lorry. He pulled over and punched the steering wheel angrily. It was dark and the heavy rain made driving difficult. A road atlas lay on the back seat. Jordan flicked on the interior light and turned to the page showing his location. Where were you going? Jordan pondered as he followed the A2 with his finger on the map. "If I wanted to get out of the country where would I go?" Jordan said as his finger stopped at Dover. He smiled. "I'd get over to France and just continue to my intended destination from a French airport."

Tossing the map onto the back seat, Jordan set off for Dover. As the rain lashed against the windscreen Jordan longed for a hot bath and a good night's sleep in a comfortable bed with clean sheets. His mind wandered as he stared at the road ahead as he considered what his army career had cost him. A failed marriage, an empty room and a life spent either fighting or pretending to be the sort of people nightmares are made of. The time had come to call it a day. To try and salvage the little that was left of his humanity while there was still time. The young brave adventurer he had once been such a very long time ago had long since gone. All he wanted now was to be left alone in peace.

A large white sign at the side of the road brought Jordan sharply out of his melancholic thoughts and re-focused his mind on what he had to do. He gave a wry smile as he drove past the road sign that read, WELCOME TO DOVER. This time he wasn't going to let him get away.

Chapter Eighteen

Grace Fisher had spent a sleepless night watching the luminous digits on the bedside LCD clock. She was growing increasingly anxious that her husband, Tom, had become involved in something sinister. Something that had led to Brad Mason's murder, of that she was certain. She prayed that whatever it was he was an unwilling participant. His secretive, almost furtive, behaviour however, together with his uncharacteristic sudden and aggressive outbursts, only reinforced her suspicions that he had become mixed up in something terrible.

Tom Fisher rose early that morning. It was less than three months to the elections and he was campaigning hard. Grace pretended to be asleep as he showered and dressed. She didn't want to speak to him, not this morning. She had arranged to meet somebody who she hoped could help her. Somebody to whom her suspicions wouldn't sound either paranoid or ridiculous.

Fisher left the house at seven-thirty after kissing the 'sleeping' Grace lightly on the cheek. Once he had gone Grace quickly dressed and after slipping a small fat white envelope into her purse, drove towards Concord.

It was an hour later when her silver Mercedes convertible pulled off the road in front of a diner near Turtle Pond, a few miles north of the city. She checked herself in the mirror then got out of the car and went inside. Standing for a moment in the entrance she looked at the sparsely occupied diner. As a smiley waitress stepped forward to show Grace to a table a man got up from his and approached her.

"Mrs Fisher? Frank Garner. I've got a table right over here." He gestured to a table next to the window and Grace obediently followed. She sat down tentatively opposite a large half eaten plate of ham and eggs. Garner resumed his seat.

"Please forgive me, Mrs Fisher. I've been up most of the night and I was ravenous. Can I get you something?" he said as the smiley waitress appeared.

"Just some coffee please," Grace said quietly. Garner nodded to the waitress and asked for his own cup to be refilled. As the young bubbly blonde girl went to fetch the coffee pot Garner looked at Grace and smiled. He had a large kind face. His thinning grey hair was combed straight back making his thick grey eyebrows appear even more bushy.

Grace immediately felt at ease with this man. At around sixty years old, Garner reminded her of her own Grandfather when she was a little girl. She began to speak but Garner smiled and held up his hand for her to be quiet. They looked at each other in silence as the waitress brought their coffee. "Now Mrs Fisher, how can I help you?" Garner said once she had gone. Grace took a sip of her coffee as she tried to decide where to begin.

Frank Garner listened without speaking for the next ten minutes as Grace poured out her suspicions of her husband Tom, his connection with Steve Bannon and the murder of Brad Mason. Finally she finished, acutely aware that she had nothing more than an uneasy feeling to go on.

"You think I'm crazy, don't you?" she said sheepishly. Garner beamed reassuringly and shook his head. A single rebellious long eyebrow hair waved as he did so. "No, I don't think that you're crazy." Garner had an instinct for when someone was telling the truth. Over twenty-five years as a detective in the Chicago Police Department had taught him that. A career brought suddenly and unexpectedly to an end when he was shot in the chest while on a drugs raid in the notorious Englewood district. Retired with a full pension, he had moved to New Hampshire seven years earlier and started his own one man private detective agency. This was very different from the usual matrimonial and missing person cases that took up most of his time. He was intrigued by the beautiful young girl's story and captivated by her vulnerability. He knew of Thomas Fisher, of course. There couldn't be anyone in the state that didn't. His popularity was increasing by the day and he was considered the sure front runner amongst the pundits.

"Will you help me?" asked Grace.

"What is it you want me to do exactly? I mean, your husband isn't your average man in the street now is he?"

"That's why I've come to you. There's nobody else I can talk to about this."

"Not even your father?"

"Especially not my father. Tom can't do a thing wrong in his eyes." Grace waited for Garner to reply but he just looked at the young woman carefully. She grew impatient and got up to leave. "I'm sorry you obviously think I'm just some neurotic woman."

"Of course I'll help you," Garner said calmly as he took her hand. "And just for the record I don't think you are at all neurotic; just very scared." Grace sat down again and thanked him. "My fees are one hundred dollars a day plus any expenses I incur," Garner said. Grace produced the envelope from her purse and placed it on the table saying that it contained a thousand dollars. Garner put the envelope into his jacket pocket without opening it. "I'll be in touch in a few days. Try not to worry." Grace smiled weakly then went back to her car.

From a brown sedan at the far end of the parking lot, a man in his thirties watched Grace Fisher drive away. Having photographed the two through the diner window with a telephoto lens as they talked, the camera clicked again as he took more shots of Frank Garner returning to his car. As Garner headed back to Concord the driver of the brown sedan put on his mirrored sunglasses and, discreetly and quite expertly, began to follow him.

In his Manhattan office, Steve Bannon replaced the receiver and sat back in his leather executive chair. The call his secretary had put through to him fifteen minutes earlier had interrupted his lunch but now he had little appetite to finish it. Rick Novak was lured away from the CIA by Bannon a year or so before and was formerly one of the agency's covert surveillance officers. It was to him Bannon had just been speaking.

Concerned that Grace Fisher was becoming a potential threat to his operation following her visit to his apartment, Bannon had assigned Novak to watch her. Sadly his concerns, it seemed, had been justified. Novak had followed Garner back to his small office in Concord and having identified him was now requesting further instructions. Bannon told him to switch his surveillance from Grace Fisher to Garner and give him constant updates on his movements.

"Grace, Grace, Grace, why couldn't you just leave things alone?" Bannon said to himself mournfully. It was all beginning to fall apart. First Grant and now this. Grant he could take care of at a later date but Grace; she was more of an immediate problem. Perhaps, he thought, the moment had arrived for him to re-think his future. Although he had promised him a great deal, Bannon decided it was time to consider an alternative strategy that didn't involve Tom Fisher. Maybe a relocation; he enjoyed the time he spent in South America. It was time to look for somewhere warm with a favourable exchange rate and, of course, with no annoying little extradition agreements.

He picked up the phone and spoke to his secretary. "Get hold of Sam Williams for me. I've got a little job for him in Concord." Then he thought for a moment and added. "On second thought forget that, I'll take care of it myself."

As Bannon sat in his Manhattan office Michael Prentiss was walking into the infirmary building at Templar Barracks. He had spent a couple of hours the previous night reading the Bannon file from cover to cover before, completely exhausted, falling asleep. It was six o'clock and he hesitated before he knocked on Colonel Mabbitt's door. Prentiss needn't have worried about waking him. As he opened the door Colonel Mabbitt greeted him with his customary exuberance and beckoned him to come in.

"Good morning, Michael. Did you sleep well?" Mabbitt said pointing to a chair.

"Surprisingly well thanks, Colonel. And you?"

"Like a top, dear boy, like a top." Prentiss sat down and put the file on the already crowded bedside table. "So, what did you make of Mister Bannon?" Mabbitt asked nodding towards the file.

"Ex-CIA, recruited straight out of Harvard, now a successful security consultant. Indeterminate financial status but the fact that he has an expensive office in Manhattan and lives up in New Hampshire I think it's probably safe to assume that he's absolutely loaded. On the whole, Steve Bannon is a thoroughly reputable and respectable businessman without so much as a blemish on his character," Prentiss concluded.

"And yet he sends one of his employees, Harry Grant, with a list of people he wants killed quickly. Not only that, he then sends another of his employees, one Arnold Kitter, to eliminate Grant thus ensuring Grant's silence regarding the list."

"I should imagine he's feeling decidedly twitchy that Grant is still alive and trying to get away having killed Kitter at the hotel. Has there been any word from Richard?" Prentiss asked. Mabbitt shook his head.

"Nothing yet but don't worry. I have every confidence that Richard will prevail," Mabbitt replied, winking assuredly.

"So what is it you want me to do?"

"I'd like you to pop over to New York. Have a bit of a poke about. Take a closer look at our Mister Bannon."

"Colonel, I really don't think that I'm going to achieve much in New York. I'm a Funeral Director not a trained investigator," Prentiss said.

"Oh I think you'll manage, Michael. I have every confidence in you."

"But Colonel, I don't even have my passport." Prentiss' protestations were cut short as Mabbitt raised his finger for quiet as he picked up the telephone and asked Lieutenant Parkes to come in.

"Michael, whoever is paying Bannon has got to be intimately connected with Operation Ares and has very personal reasons for wanting us all dead. I can't think of anyone more qualified to investigate Steve Bannon. After all, who knows Ares better than you do?" Before Prentiss could answer the door opened and a young officer in barrack-room dress came in carrying a holdall.

"That's my bag!" Prentiss said snatching it from him and peering inside. Lieutenant Parkes pushed something into Prentiss' hand. "And my bloody passport!" He turned and faced Mabbitt. "These were all in my flat, Colonel. I wonder how they got here?"

"I wonder?" Mabbitt said innocently. "There's just one more thing, Michael. As time is of the essence rather than send you on a regular commercial flight you'll be flying out of RAF Brize Norton with some paratroops going on a two week exercise with the Americans at Fort Dix. Therefore I think it would be more seemly if you were officially part of Her Majesty's armed forces. Just for appearances sake you understand." Parkes handed Prentiss a military identity card. Prentiss looked up at Mabbitt open mouthed. "Welcome to the unit, Lieutenant Prentiss."

Richard Jordan had had a miserable night. He had driven for hours through the streets of Dover in the pouring rain checking every lorry park, supermarket car park and piece of waste ground he could find. Finally he drove to the docks and grabbed a couple of hours sleep in the car. He woke to a clear blue cloudless sky and the screech of the seagulls circling the boats heading into the channel, chartered for a day's fishing.

As he sat alone Jordan now had serious doubts as to whether Grant had come to Dover at all. He didn't like playing hunches; they were too imprecise for someone that spent his life dealing in facts. But at the moment his instinct was all he had to go on. Turning on the radio he tuned into the local radio station. He laughed ironically as Gallagher and Lyle's 'Breakaway' was finishing. As the last few bars faded away Jordan reached to turn the radio off when the news came on. His hand hovered over the knob, his eyes flashing towards the radio as the newsreader announced that a man had been found shot dead in his lorry. Jordan listened; his heart began beating faster with optimism, as the monotone voice reported that the victim had been discovered an hour earlier near Dover's marina in what appeared to be a motiveless attack. That was all Jordan needed to hear. Grant was here and he would have to move fast if he was going to stop him getting away.

Deciding to leave the car, Jordan pulled up his collar and began walking towards the marina. The Saab was sure to be reported as stolen and he could well do without any more inconvenient entanglements with the local plods. Reaching the marina at a little after eight o'clock, Jordan found a call box and rang Colonel Mabbitt. Updating the Colonel as concisely as he could, Jordan listened carefully as Mabbitt considered what he had heard.

"If I were Grant and I knew that the ports were being watched," Mabbitt said, "with my naval background the only reason I would make for Dover would be to..."

"Find a boat," Jordan said quietly finishing Mabbitt's sentence as he looked across at the hundreds of vessels berthed in the marina. "I'll be in touch. I've got to go and find a needle in a haystack."

"You sound tired, Richard. Are you alright? I can send you some help if you need it."

"No thanks, Colonel. After the airport incident I think that the fewer people involved in this, the better. This Grant, he's very good, probably the best I've ever seen. If I'm going to get him I'll have to do it alone."

"Very well, Richard. As you wish." Mabbitt fell silent for a moment. "Just one more thing. It's in connection with the murder of Corporal Megson at Heathrow. You may remember that I previously told you I needed to question Mister Grant when you found him. That is no longer the case. Am I clear?"

Jordan closed his eyes, relieved at finally being given Mabbitt's unspoken order. "I'll take care of it."

Chapter Nineteen

The Salty Spray was a twenty-five year old wooden fishing boat and had been owned by Captain Sam 'Cuddy' Mercer for almost ten of them. At forty-two feet long and thirteen feet at the beam, and despite its age, it gleamed in its berth at Dover Marina.

Standing in the blue and white painted wheelhouse located near the stern, Cuddy Mercer examined the charts and plotted a course south into the Channel. Having left school at fourteen in 1935, Mercer had spent all his life as a fisherman as his father had before him. He had been given his nickname 'Cuddy' by the rest of the crew on his first fishing trip. In particularly foul weather conditions he had spent most of the three day voyage in the small cabin or 'cuddy', being so violently sick he actually thought he was going to die. From that day on the nickname continued although mercifully the seasickness didn't.

In 1939 at the outbreak of the war, Mercer was conscripted into the Royal Navy. As many fishermen were at that time, he was directed into the Royal Navy Patrol Service. Sometimes referred to as the navy within the Royal Navy, Mercer served aboard a minesweeper off the coast of Scarborough. It was dangerous work and losses of both vessels and men remained extremely high for the duration of the conflict. Although he had been sunk three times before the end of the war in 1945, Mercer was thankful he had come through relatively unscathed. This was more than could be said for the two thousand, three hundred Patrol Service officers and men that lost their lives in the seas around Britain.

With a lifetime of fishing behind him Mercer, at the age of fifty-five and increasingly troubled by arthritis in his hands after years of exposure to the freezing rain, decided it was time for a gentler, slower pace of life. He bought *The Salty Spray* from a Brixham fisherman and sailed it round the coast to its new home in Dover. He now spent his days just about eeking out a living operating as a charter fishing vessel, taking small groups and individuals for a day's fishing for the princely sum of ten pounds including rod and bait hire.

Mercer looked at his watch and tutted, eight thirty. He was due to take a party of three out to the Varne Sandbanks for the day and they were already half an hour late. He looked up, suddenly aware of somebody on the quayside.

"That's a fine boat you have there. Are you taking her out today?" the stranger said in an American accent. Mercer came out of the wheelhouse and squinted at the stocky American as the early morning sun rose behind him.

"Mid channel, if they ever turn up," he replied irritably.

"Mind if I come along? It's a great day for fishing. The name's Harry by the way," Grant said as he looked up at the clear blue sky. Mercer, never one to turn away work, gestured for him to come aboard. Eagerly Grant boarded the fishing boat with all the visible excitement of a small boy embarking on an adventure.

Mercer took Grant's ten pounds and lifted the lid on the live bait tank on the deck. "Dungeness Black Lug worm," he said to Grant. "Best bait around for catching the fish in these waters." Grant peered into the tank of water and nodded approvingly.

"I used to use something similar back home when I went fishing with my Grandfather in Maine as a boy." Mercer liked the American's friendly approach and infectious smile. It wasn't long before they were both chatting like old friends. Their cheerful banter was interrupted only by the eventual arrival of the three corporate bankers ready to begin their day's fishing.

As the trio of bankers came aboard they carried between them a large case of beer which they threw down on the deck. Despite the early hour they had clearly enjoyed a liquid breakfast before they arrived. Mercer and Grant looked disapprovingly at each other as they watched the men uproariously stumbling towards the wheelhouse. Mercer asked if any of the three had been to sea before only to be asked by the one the other two called Bertie, "Been to see what, old chap?" This was met by more guffaws as the three collapsed in a group of chairs located near the prow.

"Do you ever go further than mid channel? France, for instance?" Grant asked. Mercer replied that he'd go just about anywhere if the money was right.

"Inshore, the sandbanks like today, even to some of the deep water wrecks off the French coast."

"So you know the French coast pretty well?" Grant asked casually.

"Like the back of my hand," Mercer replied to Grant's delight. "Why do you ask, Harry? Do you want to go?" Grant looked at him slyly, his eyes twinkling.

"That would be great but what about the three wise men over there?"

"Once we leave the harbour they won't have the slightest idea where we are. Anyway, it's my boat, we'll go where I say," Mercer said adamantly. Grant grinned and winked conspiratorially.

"Aye, aye, Skipper."

As Bertie, Charles and Nigel opened the first three bottles from the case of beer and tossed the bottle tops over the side, Mercer fired up the 150 horse power Gardner engine and prepared to cast off. Grant went astern having offered to help with the aft mooring rope as Mercer, from the wheelhouse, began to raise the anchor. The low hum of the hydraulic winch vibrated as the anchor slowly began to rise out of the water.

"Ahoy, there! Have you got room for one more?" came a man's voice sounding slightly out of breath as if he had just been running. Richard Jordan didn't wait for an answer and jumped aboard. Mercer came out of the wheelhouse as Jordan approached him.

"This is turning into a busy day," Mercer said laughing. "Yes there's room for you Mister...?" Before Jordan could answer Grant appeared from behind the wheelhouse smoking a Marlboro and wiping his hands saying he had cast off aft. He stopped and stood motionless as he saw Jordan. The two men looked at each other intently.

"Richard Jordan," he replied maintaining his icy stare into Grant's eyes.

"Glad to have you aboard, Richard. I'm Captain Mercer, this is Harry and those other three are... best left alone. Like as not they'll be unconscious by lunchtime," Mercer said returning to the wheelhouse. For the first time the two men faced each other. Neither wanting to make the first move but remaining tensed, prepared for the other to do so at any moment.

"Hello, Richard. So you're here to get yourself a big fish?"

"Not really, more pest control," Jordan replied acidly. The boat jolted and as the engine revved, it made its way through the Marina and out into the Channel. Jordan and Grant maintained their positions standing ten feet apart in front of the wheelhouse.

"I don't want to kill you, Richard. I just want to get away. All you've gotta do is let me go, look the other way and nobody else needs to get hurt. It's up to you."

"I can't let you do that."

"So you want your revenge, is that it?"

"No," Jordan said quietly. "It's not about revenge, it's about justice."

"Don't give me that bullshit, Richard. We're both professionals, soldiers trained to kill the enemy. We are the same, you and I."

"Those people in Norfolk, the lorry driver last night. They weren't the enemy; they just got in your way. We're not the same," Jordan said contemptuously. "My Commanding Officer, Colonel Mabbitt, you may remember him from your little hit list, he's a great one for famous quotations. He's got one for almost every occasion, actually. I suppose that's the officer class for you, you know all that private education and being flicked with wet towels in front of the fire by the seniors. Anyway, there's one by Aristotle. He was Greek, you know. The Colonel uses it a lot. It goes something like, '*At his best, man is the noblest of all animals but separated from law and justice he is the worst.*' So you see, Harry I can't let you go. You're nothing more than a rabid dog that needs putting out of everyone's misery."

Grant's face hardened for a moment then he looked out at the open waters of the English Channel and took a deep breath of sea air. "I wish things could have turned out differently. It's a pity I've got to kill you. You're a good soldier and a brave man but you must realise that you can't possibly win. Your conscience makes you weak. Your preoccupation with protecting these four innocents will be your downfall. The first move is yours, Richard," Grant said menacingly, slowly backing towards the wheelhouse and stepping inside. Jordan watched him as he laughed with Cuddy Mercer. Grant was right about one thing. The thought of these civilians being what the Americans liked to call 'collateral damage' was unacceptable.

In a small first floor office just off North Spring Street in Concord, Frank Garner had spent the morning making a dozen or more phone calls to try and get some background on Steve Bannon. All his contacts both in the police department and the FBI had said the same thing. Bannon's character was squeaky clean and Bannon Strategic Solutions' exclusive client list ranged from multi-national corporations and the US Government to high net worth individuals and A-list celebrities. However, nearly all of Garner's contact's conversations had finished with a 'but'. Bannon and his company had something of a dark shadow with regard to the way it had operated from time to time. Nothing had ever been proved and was always from unsubstantiated rumour and conjecture. There had been incidences however where burglary, intimidation and, on at least two occasions, unexplained sudden deaths had been tentatively linked to employees of Bannon's company. Garner was left feeling distinctly uneasy about Steve Bannon and his evidently not quite so squeaky clean activities.

His meeting with Grace Fisher earlier that day played on Garner's mind. The young woman was clearly terrified, fearful that her husband and Bannon were somehow involved with the murder of a CIA Deputy Director. Following the morning's unofficial calls to friends he trusted in the law enforcement community, Garner had the distinct feeling her suspicions may well have some substance.

He drained the last of the cold bitter coffee in his mug and sat back in his chair. Deep in thought he turned away from his battered wooden desk and gazed out of the window onto the street below. Then he noticed it again. He couldn't be certain but the brown sedan parked a little way up the street looked like the one that was in the diner's parking lot earlier. He had only noticed it because he had had the same model and colour sedan in Chicago and although commonplace there, they were much less so on the affluent streets of Concord.

Pulling open a bottom drawer Garner took out a small pair of binoculars and took a closer look at the car. The driver sat alone reading a newspaper wearing mirrored sunglasses. If this was the same man from the diner, thought Garner, he had obviously followed Grace Fisher there and observed their meeting and was now tailing him. He decided it was time to find out for sure and, tossing the binoculars back into the drawer, he left the office.

Luigi's Deli was a popular delicatessen and café a couple of streets from Garner's office. He often went there for a pastrami on rye with a large black coffee to go and catch up on all the local gossip. As he emerged from his building, Garner walked up the street away from the sedan. Casually he strolled the ten minutes to Luigi's saying hello to familiar faces as he went. As the traffic cleared he crossed the street, glancing around him. Sure enough the driver of the brown sedan, still wearing his mirrored sunglasses, was walking unobtrusively in the midday crowd some distance away already on the other side of the street.

Luigi looked up as Garner opened the door and came in and greeted him with his usual Mediterranean ebullience. Garner smiled as he slipped round behind the counter and slapped the fat Italian playfully on the cheek saying, "Can't stop and I was never here okay, Luigi?"

"Okay," Luigi replied with a confused smile as he watched Garner go through to the back, out of the kitchen door and into the alley. A minute or so later the door opened again. Novak stood in the doorway and, snatching off his sunglasses, scanned the deli then cursed under his breath and left. "Is nobody hungry today?" Luigi said to himself as he picked at some rather tasty Italian salami, closing his eyes as he savoured it.

Garner wasted no time in making his way back to the brown sedan using a short cut from the other end of the alley. As he reached the car he knew that he wouldn't have very long before the driver returned. He stood next to it and after having a furtive look around him to make sure nobody was looking he unlocked the passenger door. The set of skeleton keys he used he had 'confiscated' from a Chicago criminal who successfully stole cars to order. That was, of course, until Garner shot him dead with a pump action shotgun when he tried to resist arrest.

Once inside Garner quickly checked the door pockets and glove box but they were all empty. The car was spotless, not so much as a chocolate bar wrapper was left lying around. He pulled down the sun visors but again there was nothing. He was running out of time. The driver would appear at the end of the street at any minute. He felt around under the passenger seat. His fingers touched a small piece of paper. Grabbing it he pulled it out and looked at it. It was a credit card slip from a gas station in New York. He read the name, Rick Novak, and put it into his pocket. Time to go, he thought, getting out of the sedan. After locking the door and taking a note of the licence plate he returned to his office to add to his ever increasing telephone bill and call in a couple more favours.

It took him just over an hour to learn that Rick Novak was employed as a special security consultant at Bannon Strategic Solutions and was based in New York. Garner sat with his feet resting on the desk mulling over the information. The fact that Novak had been following Grace Fisher, he thought to himself, meant that Bannon and or Fisher were concerned that she may not keep her suspicions about them to herself. Now that they knew that she had spoken to him at the diner they would have to assume that she had told him everything. That being the case, Grace was in very great danger. It would only be a matter of time before they found it necessary to ensure her silence, permanently. A cold feeling came over Garner as he realised that, by the same token, he too was now a threat.

Chapter Twenty

The Hercules C130 touched down at Fort Dix six and a half hours after taking off from RAF Brize Norton. Prentiss had sat apart from the other passengers, eyed with curiosity and suspicion as he was the only one wearing civilian dress. The huge transport plane was filled with a platoon of fifty men of the second battalion, the Parachute Regiment. Once airborne the platoon's officer, a young lieutenant in his mid-twenties, came and sat next to him full of exuberance. "Timothy Ash," he said with a cheerful curtness removing his maroon beret and extending his hand. Prentiss spent the remainder of the flight avoiding his questions and listening to him prattle on about what an ordeal his Sandhurst experience had been.

Prentiss waited quietly while the soldiers disembarked before he picked up his holdall and headed for the door. As he walked down the steps and away from the climate controlled aircraft the summer New Jersey heat hit him. He looked up into blue cloudless sky as the last of Lieutenant Ash's troop made their way to the rear of the Hercules to get their kit. Although it was only nine thirty in the morning eastern standard time, the temperature was already over seventy degrees.

At the bottom of the steps stood a very serious looking US army soldier wearing combat fatigues. "Lieutenant Prentiss?" he said abruptly. "Lieutenant Travers, US Army Military Intelligence. My orders are to give you any assistance you require." Travers took the holdall without prompting and gestured towards a Jeep. Not really knowing what to say, Prentiss nodded and walked towards the vehicle adopting an air of quiet authority.

Travers started the engine, glancing at Prentiss intrigued as to why the young Englishman was there. As a counter intelligence officer based at Fort Dix he had been called into his CO's office an hour before and ordered to facilitate the requirements of a British military intelligence officer who would be arriving that morning. Despite asking for more information regarding the visitor, he was bluntly told that it was classified.

"So," Travers said finally. "I have made some quarters available for you. I'll get you settled in." Prentiss had spent the flight trying to formulate some kind of plan of action. Having no real idea as to what he was going to do regarding Bannon, the one thing he was sure of was that he would be much happier on his own.

"That won't be necessary. Just take me to the nearest railway station." Travers looked at him questioningly, irritated that Prentiss wanted nothing more from him than a taxi ride.

"The railway station," Travers repeated. "That's all, nothing else?" Prentiss looked at the ambitious young officer's irked expression and allowed the corners of his mouth to form a smile.

"No, that's all," Prentiss said then added, "There is one more thing." Travers looked at his passenger without speaking. "You can forget you ever saw me."

Thomas Fisher was a man reborn. The weight of the previous few weeks had been lifted and the spectre of Donald Boyle was now gone forever. He was riding high in the polls and his election to the Senate was as certain as it could be. Achieving almost celebrity status, Fisher had become the darling of the TV talk shows, his all American good looks and boyish smile making him universally popular.

As Prentiss' military aircraft had begun its decent on final approach, Fisher had walked into the dining room having showered and dressed. Grace was already sat at the table having been up for hours. As he entered she sipped at the cold cup of coffee she had been nursing for half an hour, lost in her thoughts. Fisher lightly squeezed her shoulders and kissed the top of her head as he stood behind her.

"I didn't hear you get up this morning," he said brightly as he took his seat at the table and picked up the newspaper. Grace looked at him as he examined the front page.

"I couldn't sleep and I didn't want to wake you," she replied softly. Since his phone call from Bannon, Grace had noticed that although her husband had become more relaxed and less irritable, almost returning to the man she knew, he had developed an arrogance, an air of superior self assuredness previously absent from his character. It was as if he knew that he was indestructible and thus exuded supreme and total confidence.

"Pour me a coffee," he said without looking up. Grace hesitated for a moment then did as she was ordered.

"There was a time not too long ago when you would have said please," Grace said handing him the cup. Engrossed in the headline feature Fisher disregarded the comment as irrelevant and continued reading. "You wouldn't have ignored me like this either." She slammed the coffee cup down on the table and began to walk away. Fisher put down the newspaper.

"What are you talking about, Grace? I simply asked you for a cup of coffee." Grace stopped and turned. "You've changed, Tom."

"Maybe I have. For the first time I'm beginning to realise my true potential. I am able to see what I am truly capable of. This childish petulance of yours is going to have to stop if you are going to be of any use to me when I am Senator."

"Any use?" Grace repeated incredulously. "I'm your wife, Tom, not some employee."

"That's right, Grace. You're my wife and as such I won't have you being an embarrassment to me," Fisher said as if he was chastising a small child. Grace seethed with anger and turned to leave. "Oh Grace, I've invited some influential people for dinner here tonight. Six of them for eight o'clock. Make sure everything's taken care of, there's a good girl." Grace marched out of the room and slammed the door. Whoever she had just left sitting at the table may have looked like Tom Fisher but was a complete stranger to her.

Frank Garner left his apartment late that morning. It was ten-thirty as he climbed into his car. He adjusted the rear view mirror. There it was; the same brown sedan parked across the street two hundred yards away. Grace wasn't the only one who had been unable to sleep. Garner had lain in bed that night and ruminated on the situation in which he now found himself. Before turning off the light he had checked his revolver and put it on the bedside table. Then with the light out and the room in darkness he was able to look out onto the street unobserved and, sure enough, Mister Novak was settling down for the night in his brown sedan.

It took just fifteen minutes for Garner to steadily drive into down-town Concord. Occasionally he would get a glimpse of Novak's car as it maintained three or four vehicles' distance from him. Pulling up outside the First National Bank Garner got out of his car and, without looking around him, went inside.

The bank was cool and airy after the summer heat, busy with people queuing for tellers and waiting for appointments. Garner walked to a payphone on the wall and began to dial. The call was short, lasting no more than twenty seconds. He hung up, looked at his watch and waited.

Outside, parked just across the street opposite the bank, Novak sat with the engine idling. With his elbow resting on the open windowed door, he carefully watched the entrance to the bank through his mirrored sunglasses. He yawned loudly. He was tired and ready to change out of his crumpled clothes, take a hot shower and get some sleep. As he contemplated asking Mister Bannon for some help three police squad cars, their sirens blaring, squealed to a halt around him blocking in his car. From inside the bank Garner heard the commotion outside and made his way out onto the street. As he got to his car he saw Novak being dragged out of his sedan by four officers and thrown face down onto the hood. Protesting loudly he was then unceremoniously arrested and thrown into the back of one of the police cars, suspected of preparing to rob the First National. The result of an anonymous telephone tip-off to the police a few minutes earlier. Garner chuckled as he drove away. Good, he thought, with Novak off his back he could start doing some real digging.

It was eleven-fifteen by the time Garner pulled up near Bannon's apartment building. If he was going to find any evidence connecting Bannon with Brad Mason's murder then the man's apartment seemed a good place to start. Garner entered through the service entrance and up the stairs to the third floor. Emerging from the stairwell he found the corridor empty. Moments later he was stood in front of apartment Three-One-One. Looking about him and confirming he was still alone in the corridor, Garner reached into his pocket and produced a battered brown leather wallet. He had owned the lock-pick set for many years and had become quite adept in its use. Taking out one of the thin steel rods he inserted it into the lock. He worked it for a couple of minutes without success. Selecting another of the little tools, he tried again. The minutes ticked by and Garner was getting nowhere. He cursed under his breath.

"Why don't you try this?" A female voice said behind him making Garner look round with a start. Grace Fisher stood in the corridor holding up a door key, smiling.

"What are you doing here?" Garner said in astonishment trying not to raise his voice.

"I thought I might be able to help," she replied sweetly. Garner took the key and unlocked the door.

"Where did you get this?" he asked looking at the door key.

"From the building manager downstairs. I told him I'd left something here when I visited the other day and I needed to get it back without Mister Bannon knowing."

"And he gave you a pass key just like that?"

"Not exactly. I told him that if he didn't give it to me I would scream the place down and cry rape. He seemed only too willing to let me have it after that." Grace smiled her infectious mischievous smile.

"Mrs Fisher, I don't think you actually need me at all," Garner said handing back the key. Grace took the key and asked what they were looking for. Garner replied that they needed to find anything to do with either her husband or Brad Mason.

The two of them spent the next ten minutes looking through drawers, cupboards and books. Garner then turned his attention to a small document shredder that stood on the floor next to a desk. Spilling the contents onto the desk top he began rummaging through the long, thin slivers of paper. Pulling up a chair, Garner sat down and began to reconstruct the shredded documents. Most of it was just a combination of receipts and letters but there was one item that warranted further scrutiny. As he pushed the scraps of paper together Garner revealed a heading followed by a list of six pairs of letters.

"Mrs Fisher, what do you make of this?" Garner asked. Grace stood beside him and looked at the assembled fragments on the desk.

"What is it?"

"These pairs of letters could be initials and look here, he pointed to the top of the list. "BM."

"Brad Mason!" Grace exclaimed. This could be something couldn't it?"

"Could be," Garner said nodding. He took out a small notebook and jotted down the heading and list of initials. "Operation Ares. Does that mean anything to you?" Grace looked at him blankly saying that it didn't. Garner decided that they had been there long enough and it was time to leave. Telling Grace to return the pass key and go home, Garner remained in the apartment to tidy up. He promised to contact her again soon.

Once Grace had gone Frank Garner spent the next few minutes making sure that the apartment was just as he had found it. As he put the last scraps of paper back into the shredder he heard movement in the corridor outside. He swore inaudibly and darted into the bedroom as the apartment door opened and Steve Bannon came in. Garner stood behind the bedroom door and held his breath. He could hear Bannon move into the kitchen and open the refrigerator door. He peered round the door into the empty living room. Unable to see the kitchen from where he was, Garner dared not break cover and make for the front door. He knew though that in such a small apartment and with no other way out it was only a matter of time before he would be discovered. He had no choice, his only option was to overpower Bannon and run. Hopefully Bannon would think that he had disturbed a burglar, which, in truth, was exactly what he was.

Garner took out his revolver and slowly began to open the bedroom door. As he started to come out of the bedroom there was a loud knock at the door. Garner retreated once more into the bedroom wondering how much worse the situation could get. He watched as Bannon appeared in the living room and crossed to the door. There was genuine surprise in Bannon's voice as he opened the door. "Grace, how nice to see you again." He invited her inside asking her to sit down. Saying she couldn't stay long she declined.

"I've just come to apologise for the other day when I was here. You must have thought that I was completely neurotic. I wanted to say that everything is just fine now. In fact things couldn't be better. Tom seems to be back to his old self again." As Grace spoke she could see Garner hiding behind the partially opened bedroom door over Bannon's shoulder. Bannon looked at her suspiciously saying that he was relieved that everything was okay again but she really needn't have taken the trouble to drive all the way into Concord. After all, how did she know that he would be at home? Grace remained calm saying that she was in town anyway running a few errands for a dinner party she and Tom were having that evening. She moved towards the door. Bannon opened it for her. As she stood in the corridor she looked nervously about her.

"Is there a problem?" Bannon asked.

"Oh it's probably nothing. There was a man hanging around when I was coming up here. He just frightened me a little that's all."

"I'll walk you to your car," Bannon said immediately. Despite Grace's protestations Bannon insisted and, just as Grace had planned when she had seen him return as she left, he walked her to her car. As the elevator doors closed, Garner walked from the apartment and left using the stairs and service door.

The phone was ringing as Bannon returned to his apartment. He sat at his desk and lifted the receiver. As he listened to Rick Novak recount his morning's events, Bannon pulled a single strand of shredded paper from beneath the phone. He looked at it carefully and under his breath murmured, "How could this have possibly got there?"

Chapter Twenty-One

Michael Prentiss sat back in his comfortable seat and closed his eyes. Lieutenant Travers had delivered him to Philadelphia's 30th Street Station following the forty-five minute journey from Fort Dix. Prentiss then caught the first Amtrak to New York. For the first time in a week he was able to relax a little. For the moment at least his life was not in danger and he didn't have to pretend to be anything other than just another tourist. As the huge silver train travelled north he opened his eyes and gazed out of the window. The cool air from the air conditioning vent above his head felt good on his face. For the next ninety minutes, he decided as he closed his eyes again, he was going to enjoy the solitude and blissful anonymity of the journey.

Climbing down from the train at Penn Station in New York, Prentiss walked along the platform and marvelled at the size and grandeur of the railway station. Serving three hundred thousand passengers every year, almost twice as many as the more famous Grand Central Station, Penn Station was the busiest in the whole of the United States.

Prentiss threw his holdall over his shoulder and walked out of the Eighth Avenue exit. Nothing could have prepared him for the onslaught on his senses. The heat, the noise of the traffic and the sheer number of moving people he found almost overwhelming. He thought for a moment about the tiny cliff top churchyard of Beeston Regis in which he had interred the small casket of ashes a few days earlier and longed for its peace and tranquillity.

Prentiss chastised himself, annoyed at his lapse in concentration and temporary loss of focus on the job in hand. He got into the yellow cab at the head of the dozen or so in the long line of the taxi rank. Having given the driver the address, the cab set off with a sudden jerk and was soon absorbed into the sea of slow moving traffic. As the cab made its way down East 34th Street the Hispanic driver, much to Prentiss' concern, spent much of the journey looking over his shoulder at him chattering incessantly in almost impenetrable broken English. The licence on the dashboard identified him as Juan Carlos Rodriguez. Unable to understand what he was saying, Prentiss just smiled politely attempting unsuccessfully not to look at the man's brown stained broken teeth. The cab veered sharply left and Rodriguez barged his way into the Lexington Avenue traffic to a cacophony of indignant car horns. It was with some relief therefore that, five minutes later, the cab came to a shuddering stop outside the glass tower block where Bannon's company occupied the fifteenth floor and Prentiss was able to get out.

During his long transatlantic flight, Prentiss had thought hard how best to, as Colonel Mabbitt had so eloquently put it, have a bit of a poke about. He had considered all manner of elaborate strategies and disregarded them all, ultimately deciding that the direct approach would be the most effective.

It was two in the afternoon as he strode through the glass double doors and into the large marble floored lobby. The air was cool after the heat of the day. Behind the huge reception desk a round-faced man smiled warmly and asked how he could help. Directed towards a pair of elevators, Prentiss had only taken a few steps when he was stopped by a uniformed security guard who politely but firmly asked him to submit to a routine security search. With nothing to hide, Prentiss readily obliged. Before leaving Ashford he had discussed with Colonel Mabbitt whether he should be armed. They had both agreed that it would be far more prudent if he wasn't. The search was brief but thorough. The security guard, thanking Prentiss for his co-operation, walked with him to the elevators.

As the doors opened the elevator announced in a female voice that he had arrived at the fifteenth floor. Prentiss took a deep breath and stepped out into the reception of Bannon Strategic Solutions. The first thing that struck him was just how quiet it was. The girl behind the desk twiddled with her long blonde hair as she spoke on the telephone. Prentiss waited as she looked up at him with her big blue eyes and smiled demurely. Finishing her conversation with the ubiquitous 'have a nice day', she asked how she could help. Prentiss leant forward confidently on the desk and asked to see Mister Bannon.

"Is that an English accent?" she said excitedly in a harsh New York dialect. Prentiss smiled and said that it was. "I would just love to go to England. See all those simply wonderfully quaint places. My cousin lives in Sunderland. Do you know it?"

"I'm sure it's quite charming although I have never been lucky enough to visit," Prentiss replied then tried again. "Mister Bannon?"

"Oh I'm afraid he's not in the office for a few days. Mister Bannon rang in this morning He's at home taking some personal time. I can contact him if it is important." Prentiss held her gaze as he thought for a moment.

"Perhaps you could tell him that Michael Prentiss called to see him on Harry Grant's recommendation and that I'll be in touch." The blonde girl stopped writing on hearing Grant's name.

"You know Harry?" she asked in surprise. Prentiss rubbed his taped left wrist which had suffered the severest injuries.

"Yes, he very kindly introduced me to someone I thought I would never get to meet," Prentiss said with a fixed smile then thanked her and asked her to make sure that Bannon got his message. She assured him she would and told him to have a nice day.

Because of the time difference it was early evening in Templar Barracks when Colonel Mabbitt answered the telephone. "Michael, my dear boy; it's lovely to hear from you. How are things out in the colonies?" he said cheerfully on hearing Prentiss' voice.

"I've just been to pay Bannon a visit at his office but he appears to be taking some leave at rather short notice."

"That was very bold of you, Michael. You haven't got yourself into any bother have you?"

"No, not yet but give me time. Can you find out Bannon's home address for me?" Prentiss could hear a flurry of loose papers being gone through as Mabbitt rifled through his files. Eventually Mabbitt came back on the line having found the address. Prentiss jotted it down.

"It's in Concord, New Hampshire. Rather splendid scenery this time of year, I'm told," Mabbitt said.

"Any news from Richard?" Prentiss asked. Mabbitt sighed.

"Nothing since this morning. Not that that should give us any cause for concern. I have learned through many years of exasperating experience that Richard will make contact when he's good and ready."

Prentiss hung up the payphone and looked at his watch, Two forty-five. He decided to head for the airport and take a flight to Concord. As he stood on the pavement, a sense of foreboding came over him as he reluctantly raised his hand to hail a yellow cab. "Please God," he thought as one pulled up next to him, "don't let it be driven by Juan Carlos Rodriguez."

The Salty Spray was on fire and listing heavily to starboard. The flames were licking at the blue and white painted wheelhouse as the acrid black smoke rose high into the evening sky. The three drunken bankers were heaved exhausted out of the water by the crew of a French trawler out of nearby Dunkerque as the ageing fishing boat suddenly and dramatically exploded. *The Salty Spray* slipped angrily beneath the oil covered burning sea. Before the wheelhouse finally disappeared, Captain Mercer's lifeless body could be glimpsed briefly, a single bullet hole in his chest. Unable to communicate with the French fishermen, Bertie Tomkins, Charles Fanshaw and Nigel Chandler were wrapped in blankets, supplied with hot coffee and taken to Dunkerque.

It was nine-thirty that evening when Chief Inspector Gallagher received a telephone call at home from the Gendarmerie in Dunkerque. Minutes later he was excitedly barking down the phone at Sergeant Lyle to grab his passport, they were going to France. By seven o'clock the following morning they were met off the cross channel ferry in Calais by *Adjudant-Chef* Claude Blanchet.

Standing at five feet, ten, Blanchet was dressed casually in a pale blue shirt open at the collar, dark chinos and a grey leather blouson jacket. A broad smile appeared beneath his thick black moustache as he saw the two men approaching. He extended his hand having first, in excellent English, established their identities. Gallagher was surprised at the firmness of the handshake from such a wiry man. He could have no idea that Claude Blanchet was one of the elite GIGN's best officers. At thirty-three, Blanchet had been in the National Gendarmerie for ten years, the last six of which serving with GIGN. Trained to perform counter-terrorist and hostage missions both in France or anywhere in the world, the *Group d'Intervention de la Gendarmerie Nationale* were alerted when the three English bankers were questioned by the local police in Dunkerque.

As Blanchet drove the two detectives the short distance from Calais to Dunkerque in his black Peugeot saloon Gallagher briefed him on Harry Grant. Forty minutes later they were all seated in an interview room opposite three very disgruntled English gents.

"About sodding time!" Nigel Chandler, the elected spokesman for the three, declared vociferously when Gallagher introduced himself. "Perhaps you could tell us why we've been held prisoner here by these sodding frogs. They seem to have forgotten who it was that bailed them out when they surrendered to the sodding Germans." Blanchet stared at him raising his eyebrows slightly in contempt. Chandler stood, the other two following suit, all three looking condescendingly at Blanchet.

"Sit down and be quiet!" Gallagher roared. As one, the three sat down hard on their chairs, startled at the policeman's ferocity. "Now then, I need to know exactly what happened on that boat." The three sat in silence as Gallagher prompted Sergeant Lyle who produced two photographs from a briefcase. He slid them along the table in front of the three men. "Were these two men on the boat with you?" Gallagher asked. They looked at each other having examined the pictures of Jordan and Grant and all agreed that they were.

Gallagher tapped the still from a CCTV camera with his finger. "Was this man an American?" Again they nodded enthusiastically, confirming that he was. Blanchet watched the questioning intently without speaking, his arms folded. "His name is Harry Grant; the other man is Richard Jordan," Gallagher said. "Tell me what happened?"

Chandler began to recount the previous day's events. How at first everything seemed to be fine. They had sailed out mid-channel and begun fishing. There was clearly a tension between Jordan and Grant. They had kept apart for much of the day. Grant had stayed close by the captain while Jordan had watched him from the edge of the boat. Chandler remembered that Grant hadn't stopped smiling at Jordan as if he was taunting him, trying to goad him to do something. Charles Fanshaw then interrupted saying that it was clear to all of them that Jordan hated Grant and the more Grant smiled at him the more stone-faced Jordan became. "He was bloody scary actually. Is he some kind of a psychopath?"

"Just get on with it," Gallagher said curtly. Chandler continued going on to explain that by the end of the day the three of them were pretty drunk. So much so that they hadn't even noticed that during the late afternoon they had left the mid-channel fishing ground and sailed close to the French coast. He squinted his eyes as he tried desperately to remember the chain of events that resulted in him and his friends ending up in the water. Prompted by Fanshaw, Chandler began again recalling that Grant was in the wheelhouse with the captain. It had been quite noticeable just how well Grant and Mercer had got on, just as if they were old friends. Chandler's expression changed. Fear crept across his face as he recounted how Jordan had suddenly pulled out a pistol and pointed it at Grant. Inside the wheelhouse, Grant had instantly produced a handgun and held Captain Mercer hostage. For the next few minutes they shouted at each other as they maintained the stand off.

"We were at the front of the ship well out of the way but it was absolutely terrifying nonetheless," Fanshaw added.

"Go on," Gallagher said as Lyle scribbled furiously in his notebook. Chandler explained that the three of them were crouching behind the chairs as they watched Grant force Mercer below decks. Jordan had cautiously moved closer to the wheelhouse. When he was almost at the wheelhouse door, Jordan stopped as smoke started coming up from below, filling the wheelhouse. Grant had set fire to something in the engine room. Jordan kept shouting to Grant as the smoke billowed out of the wheelhouse and into the air. It was then he reappeared using Captain Mercer as a shield.

With the fire taking hold and flames everywhere, Jordan refused to move as Grant and Mercer came out onto the deck.

"That was when he did it," Chandler said quietly in bewilderment.

"Did what?" Gallagher asked.

"Grant whispered something in the captain's ear then shot him in the back. Just like that," Chandler said in disbelief. "He then pushed the captain's body onto Richard Jordan and jumped over the side."

"What happened to Jordan?" Lyle asked looking up from his notebook.

"Don't know. We decided to swim for it," Chandler said.

Gallagher, Lyle and Blanchet left the three men in the interview room and stood outside in the corridor. "This Richard Jordan, I presume he is your man and in pursuit of this Grant character?" Blanchet asked looking at Jordan's photograph.

"I can assure you he's not one of my men. I couldn't stand the stress," replied Gallagher. "But you're right about him pursuing Grant."

"I will help you to find this Monsieur Grant, Chief Inspector. I have a great many resources at my disposal." As Blanchet walked away Sergeant Lyle took Gallagher's arm and spoke conspiratorially to him.

"Do you think Jordan's still alive, Guv?" Gallagher thought for a moment then sneered.

"Of course he's still alive. Bloody Anthrax couldn't kill that one. Although it pains me to admit it, I think he's probably the best chance we have of catching this bastard."

Chapter Twenty-Two

Night began to fall as an exhausted Richard Jordan dragged himself out of the sea and onto the beach north of Dunkerque, close to the France-Belgium border. As he collapsed onto the sand, half a mile behind him the still burning sea glowed brightly in the dwindling light. Jordan hated the water and loathed swimming. It was only his single-minded determination not to let Grant escape that had sustained him during his long swim to the shore.

Regaining his strength, Jordan got to his feet and looked about him. A freshening cold northerly wind gusted, causing him to shiver in his sodden clothes. He pulled up the collar of his soaked jacket and trudged up the beach towards a large wooded area. He swore loudly with frustration on the empty beach. There was no sign of Grant and he had no idea where to begin looking for him.

On reaching the tree line, Jordan stood before a large board. He was apparently standing at the coastal edge of *Nature Reserve Marchand Dune*. In the gloom he examined the map of the local area. "Where have you gone?" Jordan said trying to make out the detail. The reserve was sandwiched between the towns of Zuydcoote and Bray-Dunes. Concluding that if he were in Grant's situation he would try to put as much distance as he could between him and the coast, he decided to make for the small town of Ghyvelde about a mile and a half away.

Jordan struck out at a steady pace arriving in Ghyvelde twenty-five minutes later. Finding a small hotel he checked in and went straight to his room having determined nobody else had arrived before him. It was too much to hope for; he thought as he pulled off his clothes, that Grant would head for the same hotel. He rang Colonel Mabbitt and gave him a brief report on the day's events. As he did so, Jordan had no idea that in one of the remote houses he had passed as he walked into town, Harry Grant sat in front of a roaring log fire sipping a glass of Merlot.

As a former navy SEAL, Grant had swum ashore with the speed and technique of an Olympic swimmer.

Hardly even out of breath, he had sprinted up the beach and made his way inland. While in the wheelhouse with Mercer earlier that day, Grant had studied the captain's charts and maps of the French coast and had memorised the geography.

As he had made his way inland towards Ghyvelde he found what he was looking for a quarter of a mile before the town. Approaching the isolated house he had knocked hard on the heavy wooden door. He didn't have to wait long before it opened. The huge man weighing three hundred pounds looked in astonishment at the soaked American standing before him. Grant smiled briefly before striking the Frenchman in the throat with his fist, crushing his windpipe. Hearing the big man fall, his wife had hurried to the door, her single scream arrested by another of Grant's powerful blows.

Grant poured himself another glass of red wine and smiled contentedly. A good night's sleep and then tomorrow he would be gone. There was only one more thing he had to attend to before he could settle down to a life in paradise. A task he not only relished but was going to thoroughly enjoy.

As Grant slept, Jordan had borrowed a map of the area from Phillipe, the hotel owner who, mercifully, could speak passable English. Other than a smattering of Arabic from his time in the Special Forces, Jordan didn't have any foreign languages. That he left to others.

He had sat up well into the night studying the map while stripping down and cleaning his Browning nine millimetre pistol after its prolonged immersion in the North Sea. Jordan knew that after finding somewhere to hide overnight, Grant would be making his move in the morning. Finally, Jordan concluded that Grant had two choices. Cross the border into Belgium on foot over the open countryside or get a plane from the aero club at the small airfield at Les Moeres. Jordan was beginning to get inside the man's mind, understanding the way he thought. It wasn't by accident he had left the fishing boat and come ashore here. Grant had a plan, he always had a plan. Jordan had woken Mabbitt when he rang him again at 2am with just one question. "Can Grant fly a plane?" Wearily Mabbitt had flicked through the man's file and given Jordan the answer he wanted. Jordan smiled as he circled the airfield with his pencil. "Got you," he said.

At eight-thirty the following morning, the *boulangerie* in Ghyvelde's main street was still closed. In thirty years Michel Latour and his wife, Madeleine had never failed to open. The small crowd of regular patrons that had gathered outside grew louder and louder in their concern and disbelief. Across the street, Jordan looked out of his hotel window at the agitated assembly below. As he stood and watched, a police car arrived and two uniformed Gendarmes got out and addressed the crowd.

Quickly putting on his jacket concealing his shoulder holster, Jordan went downstairs to the lobby. As he reached the bottom of the stairs, Phillipe entered from the street looking stunned. "It is Michel and Madeleine Latour, Monsieur. They have been found murdered in their home," Phillipe said in reply to Jordan's query. Jordan swore and ran into the street. Grant was already on the move which meant that Jordan was running out of time. For all he knew, Grant could have already reached the airfield and gone. Running down the street he looked desperately for a taxi without success. Jordan stopped and sighed heavily. He was going to have to act rashly again, he thought to himself, but he had no alternative.

Stepping into the street and taking out his gun, Jordan stood in front of an oncoming car. The Renault Clio squealed to a halt inches from him. Pointing his gun at the terrified driver, Jordan, without speaking, hauled the man out of the car and into the road then drove away.

In Dunkerque police station, Claude Blanchet hurried excitedly into the small canteen where Gallagher and Lyle where trying to get to grips with a cup of strong French coffee. "How can they drink this stuff?" Gallagher complained. "It's like bloody treacle." Blanchet hastily told them to accompany him as there had been reports of a double murder nearby. With echoes of the Sparham murders in Norfolk, Gallagher threw down the cup. The undrinkable coffee spilling over the table as the three detectives ran outside to the waiting car.

Blanchet's car with its siren screaming negotiated the heavy Dunkerque rush hour traffic. As the police driver expertly threaded his way through the congestion the radio crackled, alerting Blanchet to a car hijacking in Ghyvelde by an armed man. "That's got to be Grant!" Gallagher yelled as the Clio's details were relayed over the radio in gabbling French. Blanchet mobilised the four man GIGN team that he had brought into the area the night before.

"Don't worry, Chief Inspector," assured Blanchet. "He won't get away."

As the GIGN vehicle and the car containing Blanchet and the two special branch detectives neared the airfield, Jordan drove the Clio through the gates and onto Les Moeres aerodrome. The home of the *Aeroclub de Dunkerque,* two large hangars housing the club planes dominated to his right, while a number of smaller buildings and a control tower were located left. Jordan slowed the car to a crawl. Grant was here somewhere, he could feel it.

Jordan's instincts were correct. Grant had been woken at seven-thirty that morning by a heavy pounding on the door. Roused from a deep alcohol induced sleep he had leapt from the sofa and, glimpsing the police car outside, pressed himself against the hallway wall. Grant listened intently with his limited French as the Gendarme called to Monsieur Latour something about his bakery not being open. Instantly he could feel the adrenalin begin to flow as he silently made his way to the kitchen. With a splintering crash the Gendarme forced his way in through the front door while Grant made his escape unnoticed out the back. Grabbing Madam Latour's bicycle leant against the kitchen wall, he pedalled down the dirt track at the rear of the house before getting onto the *Rue Nationale* to Ghyvelde. As he cycled in the warm morning sunshine Grant laughed at his misfortune of killing the local baker and his wife. Probably the only two people in the area that would be missed this soon.

The battered red bicycle now stood propped against the clubhouse wall at Les Moeres aerodrome. Inside, Grant sat drinking coffee with a local businessman, Pierre Carron, preparing to fly his small aircraft down to Nice. Grant had bought a pack of Gauloises cigarettes having ruined his Marlboro in the North Sea. Carron lamented on the recent change made to the brand. The hitherto dark tobaccos from Turkey and Syria that gave them their distinctive strong taste and smell had been replaced by a much lighter tobacco blend and renamed Gauloises Blondes. Grant asked what type of plane Carron had and could he see it. Always delighted to show off his expensive plaything, Carron agreed and the two men walked across to the hangar.

The club ground crew had just finished fuelling the Beechcraft Baron 58's one hundred and ninety gallon tanks. The twin engined plane gleamed in the hangar as the two men approached. "She's a beauty," Grant said admiringly. "What range has she got? Two thousand kilometres?"

"Nearer two thousand, six hundred," Carron replied smugly. As he was about to say how much he had enjoyed meeting the American but really had to go, Grant asked if there was any chance he could hitch a ride down to Nice with him. It really was vital that he get there today. Carron thought for a moment and then agreed wholeheartedly slapping him on the shoulder. He enjoyed the man's company and a passenger would give him an opportunity to demonstrate his flying ability.

Slowly the aircraft emerged from the hangar. Jordan saw the plane appear and accelerated to get a closer look at the two figures on board. Jordan focused on the large frame of the man nearest him. Then, in the cockpit, the man turned and looked at the speeding car that caught his attention. The two men recognised each other instantly. "You're not getting away this time," Jordan said angrily.

The light aircraft reached the runway and, having clearance to take off, began to accelerate. Veering off the road and onto the grass, Jordan gave chase. So determined was he to stop the plane he wasn't aware of the GIGN team's Mercedes saloon closing behind him. Jordan decided to shoot the tyres of the aircraft, forcing it to stop.

Just two miles away, Blanchet's car sped towards the airfield. They listened as the GIGN team relayed what was happening at the airfield. Blanchet translated to Gallagher that the driver of the stolen car was shooting at the plane. "Have your men open fire on the car!" Gallagher shouted vehemently.

"We can't be sure that it is Grant in that car," Blanchet said looking at him with a concerned expression but Gallagher was adamant.

"It's him, I know it. Now tell them to shoot. I'll take full responsibility."

"Guv, we can't be sure," advised Lyle.

"I'm bloody sure. We've got to stop him. I'm not going to let him escape. Not again." Blanchet nodded then gave the order to open fire. Over the radio they could hear the crackle of automatic gunfire.

Five minutes later Blanchet's car stopped next to the GIGN Mercedes. Twenty feet away the Renault Clio was upside down, its wheels still spinning. With their weapons trained on it, the four GIGN men were slowly approaching the wrecked vehicle. Gallagher, closely followed by Lyle and Blanchet ran forward. Bullet holes riddled the entire length of the left side of the Clio. Gallagher reached the car and peered inside. "Oh my God!" he said, dropping to his knees as he recognised the blood stained face of the man crumpled in the wreckage. "What have I done?"

Far away in the distant sky a light aircraft was nothing more than a tiny speck heading for the south coast of France.

It was lunchtime that day when Major Nigel Dickinson rang Colonel Mabbitt from his office in RAF Aldergrove. His voice was quiet, sombre. Mabbitt put down his fork and listened in silence. When he put down the phone Mabbitt pushed away his plate of congealing shepherd's pie and stared ahead as he assimilated what he had just been told.

The French authorities had contacted Dickinson as his commanding officer to inform him that Richard Jordan had been badly wounded. Having undergone emergency surgery to remove two bullets from his back he was now in intensive care in Calais. Mabbitt picked up the receiver again and, with barely contained rage, ordered Lieutenant Parkes to locate *Adjudant-Chef* Claude Blanchet of the GIGN. I want him at the end of this phone within the next thirty minutes.

Twenty minutes later Blanchet sat in an office in Dunkerque police station and introduced himself to Colonel Mabbitt. In Ashford, Mabbitt listened without speaking to Blanchet's chronological account of events beginning with the sinking of the *Salty Spray*. It was only when he mentioned Chief Inspector Gallagher's involvement that Mabbitt interrupted.

"Is Gallagher there with you?" Confirming that he was, Blanchet did as Mabbitt ordered and passed the phone to him.

"Colonel, I was led to believe that you were dead."

"If Richard Jordan dies, Mister Gallagher I can assure you that you will wish I had." Mabbitt's voice was cold, icy. "I understand that you gave the order to open fire on my officer?"

"It was a terrible mistake, Colonel. I thought..."

"No, Mister Gallagher clearly you didn't think. With blinding incompetence you have blundered through this investigation hindering Sergeant Major Jordan's attempts to capture this assassin, Grant. Moreover it is because of your impetuous and recklessly clumsy actions our target has succeeded in his efforts to escape without trace and my best man is in a French hospital fighting for his life. Let me assure you, Mister Gallagher that your conduct in relation to this investigation together with your addled schoolboy behaviour will be brought to your superior's attention." Mabbitt slammed down the phone and narrowing his eyes muttered, "Lord, spare me from the maladroit plod."

Chapter Twenty-Three

Steve Bannon knew that somebody had been in his apartment. As he had held the scrap of shredded paper in his hand, his trained eyes scanned the room. He followed the same rules now as he did for all those years he served with the CIA in South America. Ensure that everything in each room was 'placed' and memorise it. Books and magazines that appeared to be casually put down were in fact carefully positioned. As were the drawers and cupboard doors. Bannon stood in the lounge. The room felt wrong, the bedroom too. It was no coincidence that Novak had been arrested outside the bank, Bannon thought. This private eye, Garner was beginning to be more than just an irritation.

Bannon had spent the rest of that day in his apartment, much of it on the phone. Once the police decided that he had been the subject of a malicious practical joke, Novak was released without charge. Bannon had curtly told him to continue his surveillance on Frank Garner and this time, if he wanted to keep his job, be more damn careful. He then spoke to his lawyers instructing them to sell his company quickly but quietly. The proceeds to be put into his ever growing Cayman Islands bank account.

Across town in his first floor office, Frank Garner sat behind his desk wearing a small set of headphones and operating a reel to reel tape recorder. He was the first to admit that he was something of a dinosaur when it came to technology but, through necessity, he had learnt the art of electronic surveillance. He listened attentively to Bannon's telephone conversations thanks to the small bug he had slipped into the mouthpiece of the receiver while searching his apartment. The tiny microphone transmitter was one that he had used while with the Chicago police department and had unfortunately got 'lost' after the operation. As he listened, the headphones pressing uncomfortably against his large pulpy ears, Garner made notes of the key pieces of information. Finally he took off the headphones and rubbed his ears. As he went over the scribblings in front of him, Bannon's phone rang. Switching on the tape recorder he replaced the headset. It was a woman's voice with a strong New York accent. Bannon recognised her as his secretary and receptionist, Mimi, from his Manhattan head office. She apologised for ringing but a guy had been into the office looking for him and he'd asked her to let him know.

"Who was it?" Bannon asked half-heartedly. People came in to see him all the time.

"He was English, had a great accent, said his name was Michael Prentiss and he came on recommendation from Harry." Garner listened as there was complete silence. He checked the equipment for malfunction but it was working fine. Whoever this Michael Prentiss was, he thought, had certainly caused a reaction.

"Did he say anything else, this Michael Prentiss?" Bannon asked finally. Beads of perspiration formed at his temples and his mouth became dry making it difficult to swallow.

"Just to let you know that he had called in to see you. Funny thing is he didn't leave a contact number." Bannon thought for a moment. He was agitated, shuffling uncomfortably in his chair.

"Put me through to Sam Williams," he said sharply. Mimi did as she was told and a few seconds later the smooth voice of Bannon's Vice President came on the line. "Sam, I've got a job for you, it's urgent. I want you to check the airlines for a reservation from New York to Concord in the name of Michael Prentiss. Do the same with the car rental companies. Also I need a surveillance team to watch the airport, train station and bus depot here in Concord. Get them from the office here; there isn't time to bring them up from New York."

"How will they know this Michael Prentiss?" Williams asked.

"He was in the office earlier and spoke to Mimi which means he'll be on the reception security camera footage. Pull an image off that and fax it up to them."

"What do you want me to have the team do once they find him, have him lifted?"

"No," he said quickly. "Passive surveillance only. He's not to be aware he is being followed, clear? Report to me when he's been located."

Assured by Williams that he would take care of it immediately, Bannon hung up.

Garner switched off the tape recorder and, pulling off the headset, sat back in his chair. Who was this Michael Prentiss that could put Bannon in such a panic? Then he cast his eyes down to the list of initials he had copied down in Bannon's apartment. He smiled as he reached the bottom pair of initials, MP. That's got to be him, Garner thought, circling the initials thoughtfully with his pencil. Then he heard Bannon dialling so he flicked the tape recorder back on. Garner pressed the headphones tightly to his ears as he listened to Tom Fisher answer the phone. "At last," Garner muttered as he eavesdropped on the briefest of conversations.

"Tom, it's Steve. We've got a problem. Michael Prentiss is still alive," Bannon said darkly. There was no reply from Fisher so Bannon continued "He's not only alive but I think he's on his way here." After a long silence Fisher said quietly; "I paid you a great deal of money for certain assurances, Steve; assurances that this situation would never happen. The problem is yours. So fix it. Now!" Fisher's voice crescendoed to a scream then he slammed down the phone.

It was five-thirty that afternoon when Michael Prentiss stepped off the plane at Concord airport. Anonymous amongst the excitedly expectant stream of tourists, he made his way through customs and out onto the concourse. Hailing a cab, he slumped into the back seat asking the driver to take him to a good hotel. Prentiss closed his eyes uninterested in the magnificence of the breathtaking New Hampshire landscape. He was tired and his whole body ached. The events of the last few days were beginning to take their toll on him. He had felt like this once before, in Northern Ireland a thousand years ago. Allowing his mind to drift, as the sun streamed through the window warming his face, Prentiss was transported back to The Anchor pub and a chance meeting with a beautiful young nurse with flaming red hair and liquid green eyes. "Orla," he mumbled, her lovely smile etched on his memory.

The cab swung round the turning area in front of the New Hampshire Hotel and came to a stop. Prentiss woke suddenly and quickly gathered himself. Paying the driver with a ten dollar bill from the wallet of cash Colonel Mabbitt had given him, he got out and walked through the gleaming white Grecian porticoed entrance. The blue Plymouth Voyager that had tailed him from the airport pulled into a parking space and the casually dressed driver sauntered into the hotel.

In his apartment, Steve Bannon received the phone call he had spent the afternoon waiting for. Having been pacing like a caged animal he snatched up the receiver before the phone could give a second ring. The conversation was brief; Bannon, abrupt and monosyllabic. While he had waited impatiently to discover Prentiss' whereabouts he had acknowledged his position had become fluid at best. Re-evaluating and considering his possible options, Bannon concluded that his affiliation with Tom Fisher was now detrimental to his own future. The moment had arrived to sever that tie permanently. Michael Prentiss, however, was an imminent and significant threat that would need to be dealt with before he could disappear. Putting down the phone, Bannon tucked a small automatic into his trousers and, now aware of Prentiss' location, left his apartment.

In his office, Garner tore off the headphones. If the six pairs of initials connected with the mysterious Operation Ares was some kind of hit list, then he'd bet his police pension that Bannon wasn't looking for Prentiss to buy him a friendly drink. He ran down the stairs and out into the street. His shadow in the brown sedan was parked directly across the street reading a newspaper, a plume of smoke rose from the cigarette in the corner of his mouth. Garner didn't have time for subtlety. Taking out a pack of cigarettes, he searched his pockets for a light. Visibly frustrated at being unable to find one he looked across the street at Novak. Smiling as he walked towards the sedan, he leant into Novak's open window and asked him for a match. Before Novak could reply, Garner punched him hard on the side of the head with his big fist. Novak slumped sideways across the passenger seat unconscious.

Garner just managed to glimpse Bannon entering the hotel as he pulled up ten minutes later and parked his car. Inside, Bannon's watcher sat innocuously in the lobby. Recognising his boss, he approached him, they spoke briefly then the watcher left. As Bannon crossed to the elevators Garner slowly walked through the glass double door entrance and watched him disappear into the elevator car.

Alone in the elevator, Bannon took out his gun and began to screw a long black silencer onto it. This Prentiss had some audacity, Bannon thought. Walking right into the office and identifying himself like that took balls. Then to go on and reveal that he had made the connection between him and Grant showed that he wasn't afraid of him. Was it conceivable that this young Englishman had killed Grant? If he had, Bannon concluded as the elevator doors opened, he would need to proceed very cautiously.

As Bannon walked down the thickly carpeted hallway, Garner was in the lobby having asked the receptionist to ring up to Prentiss' room. As the seconds ticked by and Bannon got closer and closer, Garner waited agonisingly as Prentiss' phone rang out. Finally he heard Prentiss pick up and, snatching the phone from the startled receptionist, said urgently "Bannon's on his way up to kill you. If you want to live you need to get out of there, now."

Seconds later there were two muffled shots and Prentiss' door flew open. Bannon stood in the doorway, arcing the gun across the room as he searched for Prentiss. The telephone receiver hung by the cord an inch from the floor. The room appeared to be empty. The only movement was the gentle waft of the long net curtains in front of the open French windows leading onto the balcony. Bannon warily entered, closing the door behind him. He couldn't see all of the balcony from inside the room but, deciding that if that was where Prentiss was hiding he had nowhere to go, turned his attention to the closed bathroom door. Pushing open the door, Bannon stood in the bathroom doorway. An opaque shower curtain was drawn over the length of the bath. Tentatively Bannon stepped forward. "Amateur," he said to himself and fired three silenced shots into the curtain. Something fell. He smiled as he walked over and wrenched back the curtain. Prentiss seized his opportunity and emerging from the balcony ran into the bathroom and punched Bannon hard on the back of the head. As Bannon fell forward onto the two shower gel bottles his bullets had perforated, Prentiss sprinted out of the room and down the corridor towards the elevator. Bannon roared with anger as he clambered out of the bath and gave chase. Prentiss had reached the elevator and stabbed repeatedly at the call button. Bannon appeared in the corridor. Prentiss furiously jabbed the button again. Bannon fired, the bullet zinging past Prentiss' head. The doors opened and Prentiss fell inside smacking the button for the lobby. Bannon fired again as he began running down the corridor. Prentiss heard the bullet thud into the closing elevator door.

Prentiss controlled his breathing as the elevator began to descend the six floors to the lobby. He watched the illuminated numbers count down. Six–Five–Four. "Come on, come on," he muttered impatiently. Then the elevator car stopped at Three and the doors opened. Prentiss waited for Bannon to appear. Instead an elderly couple stood in front of him and bustled into the elevator. They had barely got inside than Prentiss pressed the lobby button and the doors closed once again.

On the sixth floor Bannon had crashed through the door to the service stairs and was racing down towards the lobby. He was supremely fit and ferocious with anger and by the time the elevator doors opened in the lobby he had reached the first floor. The elderly couple dithered in the elevator preventing Prentiss from getting out. Eventually he managed to get past them and bolted for the hotel entrance. Bannon burst through the stairwell door and saw Prentiss as he reached the glass double doors. He tore across the lobby.

Prentiss saw his pursuer and ran out of the hotel. A car screeched to a halt in front of him.

"You Prentiss?" Garner said. Prentiss nodded. "Get in!" he ordered. Prentiss had no idea who this man was but, considering his present position, saw that he had little option. The car sped off as Bannon appeared. There were too many people around for him to attempt a shot so he held his gun, concealed under his jacket.

"You were lucky this time," Bannon said as he watched Garner's car disappear. "But you won't be next time, that's a promise."

Chapter Twenty-Four

It was a short drive to the small park on the banks of the Merrimack River. Neither Prentiss nor Garner spoke for the duration of the ten minute journey. The two men sat in silence in the small car park and watched the gently rolling river in the diminishing evening sunshine. Prentiss spoke first. "So who have I got to thank for coming to my rescue back there?"

"Frank Garner," he replied, regarding the young man curiously.

"CIA?" Prentiss asked.

"Why would you think I'm CIA? Your connection with Brad Mason, maybe?" Garner replied. Prentiss' brow furrowed. "Or perhaps, Operation Ares?" Garner continued speculatively, looking for some kind of a reaction. Prentiss studied the man's face impassively.

"No, you're not CIA. So who are you, Frank Garner?"

"I'm a private detective looking into Steve Bannon's involvement in the murder of a CIA Deputy Director called Brad Mason. So, now we're getting better acquainted let me ask you the same question. Who are you, Michael Prentiss?"

"Bannon sent someone to kill me. I'm here to find out why," he replied guardedly. If there was one thing Prentiss had learned it was that not everyone was who they appeared to be. For the moment, at least, he would have to consider this Good Samaritan as an unknown.

"Maybe we should pool our resources," Garner said. "I could sure use the help and I'm guessing that you've got several missing pieces to the puzzle."

"I haven't played 'I'll show mine if you show me yours' since I was six," Prentiss said earnestly, "but I'll take a chance."

Garner took out a small notebook and showed it to Prentiss. "This was a list I found shredded in Bannon's apartment. Does it mean anything to you?" Prentiss looked at the heading and down the six pairs if initials ending with his own. This was the first piece of tangible proof that Bannon had produced the hit list that Grant worked to.

"Yes," he said finally.

"I'm guessing that this is a list of individuals to be killed and Operation Ares is the codename for it. Right?" Garner said looking for confirmation.

"That's right," Prentiss replied. He wasn't prepared to divulge the true significance of Operation Ares at this stage and ideally not at all. "Bannon sent one of his men, a real charmer by the name of Harry Grant, to kill each one of these six people. He succeeded with three of them, Mason being the first."

"But why?"

"I don't know. It seems that we all know something that somebody doesn't want revealed. Somebody has hired Bannon to make sure that whatever it is dies with us."

"Jesus, Grace, what have you stumbled into?" Garner murmured.

"Who's Grace?" Prentiss asked looking at Garner's concerned expression.

"My client. She came to me to investigate the possibility of her husband's complicity in the Mason murder. I'm due to meet her tomorrow morning to tell her what I've found." He thought for a moment then asked, "Michael, have you ever heard the name Tom Fisher?" Prentiss repeated the name over and over in his head. He knew it was familiar to him but he just couldn't place the name as it lay tantalisingly just out of his reach. His mind kept drawing him back to The Anchor in Londonderry but all he could visualise was Orla's beautiful flirtatious eyes and smiling face.

Garner could see that the name meant something to him so reached into the back seat and picked up a newspaper. "Maybe this will help," he said handing it to him. Prentiss looked at the grinning face of Thomas Fisher at a recent election rally. As he studied the picture it was as if a bomb had gone off in his brain.

"The lawyer, it's the bloody lawyer." Everything tumbled into place as he read about Fisher's almost certain forthcoming triumph at the Senate election.

"I guess you know him," Garner said cheerfully.

"Yes, we met very briefly four years ago in Northern Ireland," Prentiss replied venomously. "He wasn't such a popular figure then. When I met him he was no more than a gopher for a man called Donald Boyle."

"So why does he want you and the others out of the way?"

Prentiss laughed wearily. "Because he wants the dead to stay that way and not come back to haunt him. Once we're all gone, the past is wiped clean and his guilty little secret will stay secret, forever."

"What secret?"

"That," replied Prentiss, "is complicated. Suffice it to say that if certain aspects of Fisher's past were to become known then he would have a very short and inglorious future in public office. I need to make a phone call. There's a wiley old Colonel in England that has been waiting for this information."

"Tell him that if he wants Bannon he'll have to move fast. He's spent the day selling everything. I wouldn't be surprised if he was about to disappear."

"How do you know this?"

"I planted a bug in the phone in his apartment. He and Fisher had a conversation about you too. If it's evidence your Colonel needs, I've got the whole thing on tape back at my office," Garner replied then added, "Getting the recordings is going to be a bit of a problem. Bannon's got somebody watching me and I had to resort to rather drastic measures to lose him and warn you."

"We'll think of something. I'm sure my Colonel is going to find those recordings very useful."

"This Colonel of yours, I guess he's got something to do with your British Secret Service?" Garner asked. Prentiss just smiled.

"Trust me when I tell you Frank, that my Colonel's job is so secret, I don't think even he knows what he does."

Thomas Fisher had slammed down the phone in his study having bellowed his instruction to Bannon. In his blinding rage he then picked up the telephone and threw it across the room ripping its cable from the wall and smashing the sixteenth century Persian vase that stood in its path. Fisher roared at the hapless butler to get out as he unwisely rushed in on hearing the crash.

Breathing hard, Fisher punched the desk with his fist, both unable and unwilling to control his anger. His eyes flashed to the door as Grace entered.

"Where the hell have you been!?" he bawled.

"You know where I've been," she replied indignantly. "I've had lunch with Miranda at the tennis club."

"No," Fisher replied suspiciously. "You've been meeting him haven't you?" Grace became uneasy. He couldn't have found out about Frank Garner, she had been so careful.

"Meeting who?" she asked desperately.

"Michael Prentiss. Don't deny it. I know he's here. What lies has he been telling you about me, huh?" He crossed the room and grabbed her arm tightly. "Tell me, tell me!"

"I don't know anyone called Michael Prentiss. I was with Miranda. Ring the tennis club if you don't believe me!" she shrieked. He stared coldly at her. "Tom, you're hurting me." Fisher released her arm pushing her away from him as he turned back to his desk.

"Get me a whiskey," he demanded. Grace rubbed her arm and, gathering her courage, said, "Don't talk to me like that. If daddy..."

Fisher spun round and slapped her hard across the face. Her bottom lip began to swell instantly and a trace of red blood appeared in the corner of her mouth.

"If daddy what? You're my wife and I'll talk to you any damn way I please."

"What's happened to you, Tom? I thought that you loved me," she said pressing her palm to her reddening cheek.

"You're useful to me," Fisher sneered. "You and that anachronism of a father of yours. I won't let anybody stand in my way so don't cross me, Grace. You just keep your pretty mouth shut." He pushed his face menacingly close to hers and whispered, "Just pray that you don't outlive your

187

usefulness. Now go and get yourself cleaned up, you look a mess." For the first time she was terrified of the monster the man before her had become. She left the study and went upstairs with an overwhelming sense that she was utterly alone.

The street lights were just beginning to flicker into life as Garner and Prentiss parked just within sight of the private detective's office. As he looked down the street in the fading light, Garner saw the brown sedan that had been a constant fixture for the past few days was now conspicuous by its absence. Agreeing that it would be safer to go in alone, Garner told Prentiss to wait for him in Hammy's, a small bar a couple of blocks away.

As Prentiss walked through the emptying streets of downtown Concord towards the safe anonymity of Hammy's, Garner warily proceeded to his office. Looking around him for a final check and content that he wasn't being followed, he went inside and up the stairs.

The first floor landing was dark and still. The single light bulb in the ceiling was out and Garner found it difficult to see in the pitchy semi-darkness. Fumbling in his pocket he eventually produced his lighter. With enough light to see he unlocked his office door and let himself inside. His foot kicked against something metallic as he entered and flicked on the light. The metal waste paper bin rolled away from him as he stood motionless in disbelief. In his absence, the office had been completely ransacked. Every drawer and filing cabinet had been emptied; their contents lay strewn across the room. The recording equipment lay smashed amongst the debris of a most thorough and merciless search.

Garner turned to close the door but dropped to his knees, winded by a sudden punch to the stomach. He was pushed backwards falling onto an upturned wooden desk drawer. As he fought to take a breath the door was quietly closed and a pair of legs stepped over him. Garner looked up as the figure walked over to the chair, turned and sat. Bannon looked at the ageing detective with the tiniest hint of a smile, a silenced automatic pistol levelled at his head.

"You've been spying on me," Bannon said matter-of-factly. "I've got to hand it to you; bugging my phone; very clever. I can see that I'll have to be more careful in future. I bet that bitch, Grace Fisher, helped you, didn't she?" Garner didn't reply. "Yes, of course she did," Bannon continued cheerfully. "When she came to my apartment with that lame apology for being a neurotic wife and, could you just walk me down to my car," Bannon mimicked in a high pitched voice. Garner went to stand up but Bannon told him to remain where he was. "Oh well, it's not important. She's Tom's problem not mine. I assume you've got a gun tucked away somewhere in there, Frank." He waved his gun towards Garner's midriff. "Take it out, nice and slowly and throw it behind you." Garner did as he was ordered throwing the snubnose revolver into the corner.

"What do you want?" Garner said acidly.

"You know what I want. Where's your new best friend? It was you that spirited him away from the New Hampshire Hotel earlier, wasn't it? Where is Michael Prentiss?" Bannon said the name in almost a whisper. Garner shrugged without reply. Bannon's tone turned cold, intimidatory. "You will tell me."

In Hammy's, Prentiss had been sat at the bar nursing a root beer for almost an hour. For the latter half of that time he had been fending off the advances of a woman in her early fifties whose slurred speech and half open eyes suggested that another drink was the last thing she needed. The thick layer of poorly applied make-up on her wrinkled and sagging face, together with the brightest red lipstick, attempted to conceal her true age with little success. She leant heavily on her elbows; the arms of her fake fur coat were matted and discoloured as they lay in the puddles of her spilt drink on the bar. Laverne was a regular figure in the local bars and could be seen most nights offering her unremarkable favours to any undiscerning man in return for a few drinks.

Prentiss had decided he had waited long enough. Something must be wrong and he wasn't going to find out what it was sitting here being the subject of Laverne the Lush's predatory advances. It was only a ten minute walk to

Garner's building. He passed Garner's car still parked in the same place as it was an hour before. Prentiss stood across the street and looked up at the first floor office window etched with 'F. Garner Private Investigator'. Although the light was on there was no sign of movement. Prentiss looked at his watch, nine-fifteen. The street was empty and he felt very exposed as he loitered under the street lights. He cursed repeatedly under his breath as he crossed the street. Slowly he ascended the stairs, the landing eerily lit by the light shining through Garner's half glazed office door.

On reaching the landing an old floorboard creaked loudly as Prentiss stepped forward. He froze momentarily and listened in the silence. Then, taking a deep breath, he grasped the door handle and pushed it hard. The door swung open revealing the ransacked room. Prentiss' eyes darted around the shambles that was Garner's office. Behind the desk, a high backed office chair was turned away from the door and faced the window. Slowly Prentiss picked his way across the room towards it. It was with a sense of grave apprehension and foreboding he turned the chair. Frank Garner was sat upright, his hands bound and a large clear plastic bag over his head. Prentiss could make out the man's face obscured by condensation, it was contorted and twisted. Pinned to Garner's tie a piece of notepaper had just two words scrawled on it;

'BE WARNED!'

Prentiss ripped off the note and screwed it up in his fist. "Sorry, Frank," he said quietly. Picking up the phone he dialled the long international number to Templar Barracks in Ashford. Colonel Mabbitt picked it up in his office having discharged himself from the infirmary earlier that afternoon saying that he'd have received better treatment if he'd been captured by the Mau Mau.

Prentiss gave the Colonel a brief account of the day's events before giving him the name he had been waiting for. "It's Thomas Fisher."

"Boyle's lawyer!" Mabbitt exploded "That little worm. What possible reason could he have?"

"It seems the worm has turned, Colonel. He's running for Senator and he wants a nice tidy past," Prentiss said as he glanced through Garner's diary on the desk. He turned the page to the following day, Friday, August 10th There was a single entry, Bear Hill Pond, 10a.m. He remembered Garner saying he was meeting Grace Fisher tomorrow.

"Be sure your sins will find you out, eh?" Mabbitt said. "What about that Bannon character, is he going to keep popping up trying to perforate you?"

"No, I don't think so, Colonel. With Garner dead and the recordings gone I expect Bannon will disappear without trace." There was a pause then Prentiss asked, "What about Richard?"

"Ah, long story there. Let's just say that through Her Majesty's Constabulary's skill and professionalism, Grant has escaped and Richard is enjoying the rustic charms of one of France's medical facilities."

"Is he okay?"

"Tough as old boots, I'm sure he'll be fine. You have done very well my boy. I'll arrange to get you home." Mabbitt said proudly. Prentiss looked down at Garner's lifeless body and then at the diary entry. The fact that Bannon and Grant had been allowed to get away made him feel sick to his stomach, only Fisher remained. There was no way he was going to allow him to flourish. Fisher was ultimately responsible and for that, he was going to pay.

"Actually, Colonel, I've got an appointment to keep for a friend."

"Michael," Mabbitt said warily "What are you up to?"

"I'm going to finish what I've started. I'll be in touch when it's done."

Chapter Twenty-Five

While Prentiss found a secluded place to spend the night in Frank Garner's car, Steve Bannon decided that he would conclude the winding up of his affairs from the safety of Central America. Taking a late flight down to New York, he booked himself a first class ticket to Nicaragua. By 4am on Friday 10th he was dozing at thirty thousand feet in the wide comfortable seat of a Boeing 747. It didn't matter that Garner wouldn't give up Prentiss' whereabouts before he died. Killing the old man would serve as a warning to him. Even if it didn't, so what? It was unlikely Prentiss would come after him. He had the security of enormous wealth in a country where it was easy to remain anonymous. Yes, Bannon thought as he drifted off to sleep, he had every reason to feel smugly content.

Prentiss had a less comfortable night. He climbed out of the car just before seven on Friday morning and stretched his aching limbs. Realising that he couldn't remember the last time he had eaten, Prentiss drove to a roadside diner and devoured a huge breakfast, even by American standards. As he left he enquired where he might find Bear Hill Pond. The constantly smiley waitress handed him a local map and directed him to Bear Brook State Park. Located less than ten miles south east of Concord, it wasn't long before he was surrounded by the natural splendour of one of the area's best tourist attractions.

Thomas Fisher had left the house early that morning much to Grace's relief. She had spent a sleepless night in one of the guest bedrooms praying that Fisher wouldn't come looking for her. When he had finally retired at around midnight, she had held her breath as he paused for a moment outside her room before continuing to the master bedroom and slamming the door. As he had begun to walk away she distinctly heard him drunkenly mutter, "Bitch," with so much antipathy, it sent an icy shiver through the already terrified young woman.

It took Grace an hour to drive to Bear Brook State Park. She came to a stop in a parking area close to Bear Hill Pond and turned off the engine. At almost half a mile long and five hundred feet wide, Bear Hill Pond was more akin to a lake than anything one might, in any traditional sense, consider to be a pond. Nervously she looked at her watch, nine-fifty. Not long to wait until her meeting with Frank Garner. Anxiously she looked all around her. There was nobody about. In another hour or so the park would begin to fill with tourists and families with dogs, the last of the joggers having left over an hour before. For the moment, though she was quite alone.

During the endless hours of the previous night, Grace had decided that, whatever her detective had to report, she was leaving Tom. Despite his thinly veiled threats as to what might happen to her if she even considered it, she knew that her life with him was so intolerable, so paralysing, that she could never go back. Two large leather suitcases were in the trunk of the car. Once she had met with Garner she was driving straight to her parent's estate near Turtle Pond to tell them everything.

While she watched the seconds tick round on the dashboard clock, Grace became more and more uneasy. Almost five past ten and there was still no sign of him as she scanned the small road that led from the park entrance down to the pond. She was now increasingly fearful that something terrible had happened. Had Tom found out that she had hired the former policeman? Was it his deranged paranoia last night or did he really suspect that she was meeting with someone in secret? Grace began to panic. She turned the ignition key and, as she put the car into gear, she saw Garner's car approaching in her mirror.

Switching off the engine, she got out of the car and waited impatiently as his car got nearer. Grace felt safe when she was with Garner. He was like the kindly uncle she never had. Someone with a quiet strength that would never let anything bad happen. It was only when the car was almost alongside her that Grace saw that it wasn't Garner driving. Instead of the familiar features she was expecting, they were those of a much younger man. A man she had never seen before. Certain that it was Garner's car and fearing that this was somebody sent by Bannon or worse, by her husband, she fumbled for her keys in near hysteria as she got back into her car. As the stranger leapt out of Garner's car and ran towards her she attempted to lock the doors but his youth and agility proved too quick for her. She screamed frantically.

"Mrs Fisher, don't be afraid. I'm here to keep Frank Garner's appointment with you," Prentiss said calmly. "Grace, I'm a friend. I promise I'm not here to hurt you. My name's Michael." Prentiss smiled and took her shaking hand. As the fear subsided she looked at the young man's face. It didn't look like the face of someone that was about to do her harm.

"Where's Frank?" she asked as she composed herself.

"I'm sorry, but I'm afraid he's dead." Grace gasped audibly as Prentiss told her as gently as he could. "He was murdered last night by Steve Bannon. Frank was getting too close to the truth about your husband's connection with a series of murders."

"What?" she replied in disbelief. "What *is* Tom involved in?"

"Why don't we take a walk and I'll tell you what I know?"

For the next thirty minutes, Prentiss told Grace everything. Beginning four years earlier when Fisher had worked for a multi-millionaire called Donald Boyle. How her husband had not only accompanied Boyle to deliver half a million dollars in cash to finance a terrorist cell in Northern Ireland, but had been ordered to remain in the province as a member of the cell. Prentiss told her of how he had been recruited to kill Boyle in a Londonderry pub and, having done so, how Fisher had pleaded with him to take the cash to spare his own life.

While Prentiss explained, Grace listened without speaking. When he finished telling her about the missing secret file, Bannon's man, Harry Grant, the hit list and that it was all instigated by Fisher, she lit a third cigarette and they both sat in silence on a wooden bench overlooking the pond.

"It sounds too incredible to be true, yet I can believe every word of it," she said distantly. "I always knew there was something Tom was hiding from me; something...dark. He's never spoken about the years before we met. He'd always quickly change the subject. It's as if those years just didn't exist." Grace looked at him anxiously. "He knows you're here, you know." Prentiss held her stare but didn't reply. "What will you do?"

"As I don't have any evidence against him I suppose I'd better get some. I think it's time I had a little chat with your husband. See if I can encourage him to own up to his nefarious activities and get it on tape." Prentiss smiled irritably as he thought to himself that he was beginning to sound more and more like Mabbitt every day.

"Maybe you won't have to," Grace said thoughtfully. "This stolen Ares file, I think Tom may have it. He didn't realise but I saw him putting something like that into the safe in his study a few weeks ago." She paused hesitantly. "I can get it for you."

"You have the combination?"

"Yes. Tom doesn't know but I can open the safe. Come tonight, about two. He'll be asleep by then. I'll turn off the alarms and let you in. There are some French windows on the south east corner of the house that lead into the study." The quiver that had been in her voice had disappeared and was now replaced by a steely edge.

"Are you sure about this? It could be very dangerous for you," Prentiss said looking at her swollen lip.

"I'll be fine. I'd better get back. I've got some unpacking to do before Tom gets home." Prentiss walked Grace back to her car, explaining that she needed to behave normally to avoid arousing suspicion. "Don't worry," she said confidently before driving away. "I know exactly what I'm doing." As Prentiss watched her car disappear he said uneasily, "I'm glad that one of us does."

Grace was standing in the dining room waiting for Fisher when he arrived home at seven o'clock that evening. She wore her hair loosely about her shoulders just as he preferred. Her ivory knee length satin dress fitted tightly at the waist accentuating her figure and a Cartier diamond choker sparkled around her neck.

With an air of seductive confidence she crossed the room as he stood in the doorway and, putting her arms around his neck, kissed him passionately.

"I'm sorry I haven't been as supportive as I should have been, Tom. You've obviously been under a lot of pressure these past few weeks and I should have been more understanding. I want to be a good Senator's wife, darling; if you'll let me." She looked up at him with her wide eyes and smiled.

"That's more like it, Grace," Fisher said haughtily.

"Good. Why don't we have dinner then, perhaps if you're not too tired, we could have an early night," Grace said stroking his cheek with her finger. Fisher allowed his lips to form a smile. Saying that he would shower and change, he left Grace in the dining room. Once alone she took a deep nervous breath. Maintaining this charade made her feel physically sick. Just a few more hours and she would be gone, forever.

It was a moonless night with a slightest suggestion of a warm breeze. Having scaled the perimeter wall, Prentiss ran across the huge expanse of finely manicured lawn towards the house. It was a fraction after 2a.m. when he found himself outside the French windows exactly as Grace had described. Large heavy curtains covered the doors so he was unable to tell if there was a light on inside. Grasping the handle firmly he began to ease it down when the curtain was suddenly drawn back and Grace appeared, startling them both.

Once inside, Prentiss could see that the safe was already open and, as he neared the desk, the Ares file lay open.

"I've read it, all of it," Grace said quietly. "And there's some kind of feasibility report there as well."

"Produced by Mister Bannon, no doubt," Prentiss said gathering up the folders. He then realised that Grace was dressed. "Are you okay?"

"I'm coming with you. I can't bear to stay here a minute longer," she said trying to forget how she had pretended to enjoy the prolonged period of tenderless, submissive sex Fisher had subjected her to a few hours earlier.

"Alright, let's get out of here," Prentiss said taking her arm.

"I don't think so." Grace and Prentiss spun round on hearing the voice. Fisher stood in the study doorway wearing a silk dressing gown, the short stubby barrel of a large calibre revolver levelled at them. "I knew it. My ever-faithful wife conspiring against me with a hired assassin!" Fisher yelled vociferously. "Put those down!" He waved the gun wildly at the files in Prentiss' hand.

"So what now, two more murders to keep your sordid little secret?" Prentiss asked tossing them onto the desk.

"Murder?" Fisher said quizzically walking towards them. "It's not murder to kill an intruder in self defence," Fisher explained. "But sadly not before you killed my lovely Grace when she came in and disturbed you." Without warning he lashed out at Grace, striking her on the side of the head with his gun. Propelled backwards, she fell to the floor unconscious. As Prentiss tried to make a grab for the gun, Fisher fired a single shot. The bullet ripped through Prentiss' right shoulder and embedded itself in the wall behind him. Prentiss dropped to the ground, his back to the wall. First he felt nothing then a searing, burning pain racked his upper body. Thick red blood began to seep through his shirt as he pressed his hand hard on the wound.

Fisher's eyes were wide with almost overwhelming triumph. He stood over Prentiss, pressing the gun to his forehead. "At last the tables have turned, Michael Prentiss. Now *I* am the one with the gun to *your* head."

"Except I'm not going to beg for my life like some snivelling little girl. The shame of that you can keep all to yourself.." Prentiss' words stabbed Fisher like a knife.

"Beg me!" he screamed manically.

"I should have put a bullet in you when I had the chance," Prentiss sneered weakly. He could feel himself slipping into unconsciousness.

"Finally I can put you out of my misery." Fisher cocked the revolver and pressed it hard against Prentiss' forehead. Prentiss stared into Fisher's sweaty eyes, determined not to give him the satisfaction of showing any sign of fear. His only consolation was that death would be instantaneous. Fisher's hand shook as he tried to pull the trigger then suddenly he cried out in agony as Grace, using all of her strength, brought a heavy cast iron statuette from the desk crashing down on his head. As he fell, she struck him again then again, pulping the back of the man's head.

Standing over her husband's body, Grace dropped the statuette and began to shake uncontrollably. Prentiss winced as he got to his feet and leading Grace to a chair, he sat her down. Kneeling down in front of her he examined the gash on the side of her head. The bleeding had already stopped and he was confident that no major damage had been done.

"What are we going to do?" Grace said tearfully. Prentiss thought hard. There was no way that he was going to allow this woman to be arrested for Fisher's murder. The police would never believe the truth.

"Is there anyone else in the house?" Prentiss asked as the seed idea began to form. Grace shook her head.

"No; not until six."

"Good." Prentiss' mind was racing. "Here's what happened. You and your husband disturbed a burglar. He got in because you forgot to switch on the alarm system. You both came in here. He killed Tom then forced you to open the safe."

"But what about you, you're hurt?" She looked at his bloodstained shirt.

"Don't worry about that now, I'll be fine. For this to work I'm going to have to tie you up and leave you in here, okay?" Grace looked at Fisher's body out of the corner of her eye. "Grace," Prentiss said gently, "don't look at him, look at me." She did as he asked. "He can't hurt you any more, I promise."

Fifteen minutes later while Prentiss emptied the safe, the contents of which he would drop on the lawn as he left, Grace got changed into her nightdress and dressing gown. Returning to the study she let Prentiss use the curtain sashes to bind her wrists behind her back and then tie her ankles together.

"You won't have too long to wait now before you're found. You'll be okay," Prentiss reassured as he tried to make Grace as comfortable as he could.

"Where will you go?" she asked anxiously, looking at the young man's pale, sweating face.

"Home." Prentiss smiled. "Goodbye, Grace and thank you," he said, picking up the files from the desk and running out into the darkness.

It was 10.15pm when Mabbitt's phone rang in Ashford. His exuberance turned to concern when he heard Prentiss' weak and breathless voice. "Got the files. Fisher's dead. Any chance of a doctor and a lift home?"

Having determined Prentiss' location and telling him to remain where he was, Mabbitt arranged for an emergency medical evacuation from Fort Dix. Two hours later a US Army Bell *Huey* helicopter landed at the entrance to Pillsbury state park carrying Lieutenant Travers and a medical team. There they found Prentiss, barely conscious, slumped in a phone booth, clutching two dog-eared and bloodstained folders.

Chapter Twenty-Six

It was Christmas Day 1984. Four months had passed since Michael Prentiss had been flown home by military jet. His recuperation had been slow. In addition to having lost a great deal of blood, the bullet had shattered his shoulder blade as it had smashed through it. Prentiss had spent weeks in a private hospital recovering from, as far as the world was concerned, the injuries he had sustained as the result of 'a terrible car crash'.

By mid November he was well enough to return home to Norfolk where the Fearnley's keenly awaited his arrival. Colonel Mabbitt had visited him the day Prentiss left the hospital. "Michael, my dear boy. All ready to go home?" Prentiss smiled as Mabbitt, who had been a regular visitor during his convalescence, came in and made himself comfortable on the edge of the bed.

"Just about. Colonel, I've been trying to find out about Richard but nobody will tell me anything."

"Ah yes," Mabbitt said ruefully, "Richard's injuries were far more extensive than first thought. He's in rather a bad way I'm afraid."

"Can I go and see him?"

"That's just not possible at the moment, Michael but I assure you as soon as he's ready to receive visitors I'll let you know."

"Thanks," Prentiss said, convinced that, as usual, Mabbitt wasn't telling him everything. "And what about Bannon and Grant?"

"The trail has gone rather chilly on those two. Pity, I have some unfinished business there. One day they'll crawl out from whatever slimy stones they're hiding under and be assured, when they do, I'll be waiting for them."

"If you ever want a hand with that just let me know."

"Thank you, dear boy. I'll keep it in mind." Mabbitt's voice became more serious. "The reason I'm here is I just wanted to have a few private moments with you, Michael, to talk to you about something important. Please come and sit down." Prentiss stopped packing and sat next to the Colonel on the bed.

"Before you say anything Colonel, if you're going to ask me to join your 'merry little band' again I'm afraid the answer is no," Prentiss said apologetically.

"I'm not," Mabbitt said matter-of-factly. Prentiss looked visibly surprised. "No. I want you to go back to your life in Norfolk burying all those quaint little Norfolk folk. There is, however, something that I would like you to do for me." Prentiss narrowed his eyes and smiled suspiciously.

"What?"

"I want you to forgive yourself for Orla's death." Prentiss shuffled uncomfortably. "It wasn't your fault, Michael. It's time to let it go." Prentiss couldn't reply as Mabbitt stood to leave. "Goodbye, my boy. You have my most heartfelt thanks." He grasped Prentiss' hand and held it. "You make me very proud."

Despite repeated impassioned pleas from both his parents and the Fearnley's to join them for Christmas dinner, Prentiss had refused them all. Although he had readjusted quickly back into his life in Norfolk, Prentiss found the secret part of his life, the part that he could never talk about to those around him, constantly weighed heavily in his thoughts. He knew that he would only be truly relaxed around someone that knew both the civilian and the secret sides to him. Only then would the lonely isolation disappear, albeit for just a little while. So when Prentiss received an invitation for Christmas from someone he least expected to hear from, he gratefully and excitedly accepted.

He got into his ageing Renault 5 early on Christmas morning and left Cromer in darkness. He had a long journey ahead of him but one he had been looking forward to making.

The heavy grey winter sky threatened snow as the sun rose invisibly behind the car. As Prentiss crossed into Wales the roads became smaller and smaller. The landscape changed from the gentle rolling hills of Herefordshire to the bare grassy moorland punctuated by dramatic rugged crags of the Brecon Beacons. Hoping that his rusting French car would make it, Prentiss turned onto a tiny country road, little more than a shale track, and began to climb steeply. Struggling to get a grip on the sliding stony surface, the wheels spun furiously as Prentiss drove almost to within sight of the summit of the ridge. Finally, as he thought his car was about to expire, clinging to the hill at the side of the track was a small stone farmhouse.

Standing behind a low stone wall that encircled the house a single figure, wearing a thick fisherman's sweater and a battered wax jacket, leant heavily on a stick. "I thought I was going to have to come down there and push," Jordan said as Prentiss got out of the exhausted car.

"Well it might have helped," Prentiss replied sarcastically. The two men went to shake hands but laughing loudly they embraced, slapping each other on the back then both wincing simultaneously with the pain from their respective injuries.

"Welcome to my retirement home," Jordan said, sweeping his hand across the front of the farmhouse. "See what twenty years hazard pay buys you?"

"Does it have running water?" Prentiss said eyeing it doubtfully.

"Yes, mostly through the roof. I do however have some sheep."

"I suppose you've got to have something to do during those long winter nights. Is it going to be just the two of us?"

"Yep," Jordan said as they went inside "I asked the Colonel but he said that there was something he had to do."

"It's good to see you, Richard," Prentiss said. For the first time in a long time he felt at peace with himself. As he closed the door he sniffed hard. "Is that turkey I can smell burning?"

Half way round the world from wintry Wales and fifty miles south of Managua near the shores of Lake Nicaragua, Steve Bannon emerged from the shower. Two local lovelies he had found in a nightclub in Masaya the previous evening still lay sleeping in his bed. Although it was barely seven in the morning the temperature was already nearing eighty degrees.

The sale of his company had almost doubled his Cayman Island bank balance which was already not inconsiderable. Within a month, Bannon had bought a ranch comprising of five hundred acres and a magnificent twelve bedroomed hacienda style house. To ensure his complete privacy on the ranch he employed a dozen men trained in personal security and two personal bodyguards that accompanied him everywhere.

Bannon dressed quickly and, wearing a loose fitting white linen shirt and trousers, went downstairs and into the dining room. Calling for his manservant he sat at the ornate marble table and waited for his coffee and orange juice to be brought to him. He picked up the morning's copy of the New York Herald and began reading. It was only as he reached the third page that he realised that Miguel still hadn't appeared with his coffee. Lowering the newspaper he was about to call again when he saw a familiar figure sitting silently opposite him.

"Harry," Bannon said with a start.

"I'm afraid Miguel won't be able to serve you this morning as he's...dead. In fact I think you'll find that they're all dead. That's the trouble in these Mickey Mouse countries; you just can't get the staff.," Grant said biting into an apple, his gaze fixed on Bannon. "Well, let's hear it."

"Hear what?"

"Whatever it is you're going to offer me not to kill you."

"Is there anything you want?" Bannon enquired calmly.

"Well, let's see," Grant said placing the silenced .45 automatic on the table in front of him. "I've already got the three hundred thousand dollars in cash that was in your safe through there." Grant nodded to the study across the hallway and took another bite.

"What about a job? I could clearly use a good man like you. All you have to do is to name your price." There was a trace of panic creeping into Bannon's voice as he began to perspire.

"Now Steve, we've tried that, remember? And you chose to send someone to kill me rather than paying me what I was owed."

"You're right," Bannon said quickly "That was a mistake, I admit that. But please, Harry, I'm sure we can work this out. You are an exceptional man, Harry. Clever, resourceful..."

"Bored now," Grant interrupted, snatching up the gun and firing a single muffled shot between Bannon's eyes. For a split second Bannon had an expression of both horror and surprise before he fell forward onto the table, dead. Grant took a final bite of his apple and, leaving the core on the table, picked up his bag containing Bannon's cash and casually strolled out into the Christmas morning sunshine.

As Grant took the long walk back to his Jeep he looked forward to catching the noon flight back to Thailand. By tomorrow he would be back on his little island paradise fishing once again in the Andaman Sea.

In the small churchyard in Biddenden the first flakes of snow fell on a single red rose. Charles Mabbitt placed it gently on his wife's grave. "Happy Christmas, my love," he said as two tears slowly rolled down his cheeks. As he stood alone in the stillness of the graveyard at the foot of Fiona's grave he made her a promise with such determined sincerity it would have chilled anyone listening. "If it is the last thing I do, I will make sure that Harry Grant is punished for what he has done."

Printed in Great Britain
by Amazon